THE DAY THE WHIMSY DIED

ALSO BY TIM A. MILLS

The Pushkin Paradox

Sidewise

Tomorrow Is Canceled

Hope Dies Last (Winter 2026)

The Virtuosi Chronicles

The Day the Whimsy Died

Joy to the Morgue (Autumn 2026)

THE DAY THE WHIMSY DIED

THE VIRTUOSI CHRONICLES
BOOK 1

TIM A. MILLS

THE DAY THE WHIMSY DIED

Book One of the Virtuosi Chronicles

First Edition

Published by **Swordistry** Columbus, Ohio

Library of Congress Control Number: 2026905092

ISBN: 978-1-947039-07-0 (Paperback)

ISBN: 978-1-947039-08-7 (Hardback)

ISBN: 978-1-947039-09-4 (Ebook)

Visit swordistry.com

For Julia, keeping me in tempo in song and blade.

CHAPTER 1
THE CALL

IT WAS the kind of spring day that made you wonder if winter had filed for an extension. Columbus weather usually couldn't make up its mind, but this spring had committed to gray with a twelve-week streak. A blue butterfly shot past my window in a straight line, like it was racing for the bathroom. Then another six followed him, equally fast and direct.

Butterflies didn't fly in straight lines. At least none I'd ever seen. A soft knock interrupted that thought before it could go anywhere useful.

A song existed in those unwavering butterflies. Or should have. Once upon a time, I'd have plucked out that melody before it flew away. Now I just watched them go. Three months since I'd written anything worth keeping.

Instead, I went to see who was knocking.

After wrestling the stuck door open, I found a kid on my doorstep who looked seventeen if he was lucky. Hair parted as if his mother had inspected it, shirt buttoned and ironed within an inch of its life. The kid had the expression of someone about to give a book report in front of the class, knowing he was going to screw up.

Poor sap. He could be doing whatever seventeen-year-olds do when they're not being voluntold into apprenticeships. Instead, he got the short straw. I could drag out his misery or be merciful. Given my recent creative drought, mercy felt like a foreign concept, but I was feeling generous.

"Yeah?" I asked.

"Morning, sir." The kid extended his hand, holding on to a rolled-up piece of parchment with a red ribbon tied around it.

"Message for you," the kid said.

I took it. "Thanks."

"It's from the Conservatory."

"No shit, kid," I said.

He stood there like he was waiting for a tip. "They said you weren't answering your phone."

"And yet that didn't stop them."

I closed the door, but the messenger reached out to stop me. "I was told to wait."

"For what?"

He smiled at me as if I were about to have him for lunch, but he was too late for that and too soon for dinner.

"I'm a Novizio."

I nodded. "Just say novice, kid. They're going to brainwash you with the rest enough. But in Ohio, they're just going to think you're weird."

The kid's lips thinned. "Okay, Virtuoso Kohl—"

I shook my head. "Dekker. If it ends up that I like you, it'll be Dekk. But never by title."

The kid swallowed hard. "I was ordered to remain, be sure that you understood the message, and stick with you like glue."

I laughed. "That Armando. What'd you do to get in trouble?"

"I transposed Mrs. Satie's piano down a whole step."

I cocked an eyebrow. His eyes narrowed, and a devious grin

crossed his mouth. "Until she looked to see what was wrong. Then I restored it."

"Uh-huh. Multiple times, I bet." The kid beamed at me. "You're all right."

I unrolled the parchment enough to confirm Armando's demands, and that I was to be polite to the kid. As with all Conservatory notes, the suggested tempo was noted: "report *moderato.*"

No doubt, it was another pointless task, or I rubbed somebody wrong. Odds were fifty-fifty. Perhaps Armando thought I taught the kid the B-flat Transposition spell.

I propped the door open. "Let me get my coat."

"And some shoes," the kid added.

As I headed to my couch, which doubled as a coatrack, I laughed to myself. Transposition spells were an old trick. One of the older kids must have put him up to it. I wouldn't. That would mean paying attention to students.

The kid had followed me into the apartment. "Have a name, kid?"

"Hoagland."

I grimaced. "Rough. Hoagy, right?"

"Yep."

I exhaled as I glanced in the mirror, realizing that I had seen better days. Hard to say if the war had made me rough around the edges or if I grew into it. The scar on my left cheek from my time in Germany was less prominent in my unshaved face. The Germans believed the scar would make me more handsome. I suspected it just proved I was dumb enough to stand in front of someone with a sharp saber for some ritual sword-fighting nonsense. But I was young then.

I slid on my boots, jeans half tucked into them. Not a style choice, a forty-two-year-old-man choice. In good conscience, I should have dressed better, but I wasn't feeling it. I grabbed a wrinkled, fading T-shirt and my faux velvet burgundy jacket, the kind of coat that made people think "aging rock star" or "Ren Faire reject," depending on their mood.

"What a mess," the kid said.

Damn. Now the kid thought I liked him. It was better that he found me grumpy and unapproachable. "Well, Hoagy, my friend, the great thing about being an adult is that you don't have to pick up your room."

"I meant the jacket."

Both things were true; however, I protested. "This is pure comfort clothing."

"It'll stick out."

I grumbled. "Well, kid, I've earned it."

"So not married, then," Hoagy said.

"You should've applied to the Academy for Smart-Asses. I hear they're always recruiting."

I slung my ossia over my back and pointed to the door.

"Is that some kinda weird guitar or lute or something?"

It wasn't a guitar, and it certainly wasn't a lute. At least not anymore, if anyone cared. It was the skeleton of one. The body had been stripped away, leaving only a beautiful dark mahogany, polished outline framing empty air. The neck was long, unfretted, leading up to a steeply angled pegboard.

"Lutelike," I said. "But an ossia."

The kid's eyes narrowed as he studied the ossia. "Weird lute, got it."

Hoagy and I headed downstairs and onto the street with my instrument in its case and strapped on my back, heading to the Conservatory.

We headed out of my building in Italian Village, which was neither Italian nor much of a village. But the rent was cheap in my little corner.

Royal Arts Fencing Academy—the Italian Village branch—sat three blocks north. Maestra Flanconade ran it, kept it open late for regulars who needed to work out frustrations with a blade instead of a bow, violin or otherwise. I'd been stopping by since the old days when I had a future. Most mornings I'd drill footwork before coffee. Not today.

The kid followed me down the street. "We're not going to drive?"

I frowned at the kid. "Why? Breathe some air."

"No phone. No car. A lute over your shoulder. You don't like modern things?"

My hand slid onto his back, and I shoved him forward. "I have a phone and a car. Sometimes I use them. But if you're going to live in the city, you should be in the city."

"I hope that's not part of the job."

"And, by the way, the ossia is very modern." We turned onto North Sixth Street and headed south. "Decided what your path is yet?" I asked.

"Not a bard," he said.

I laughed. "Kid, I'm not a bard. I'm a Trovatore."

The kid's expression informed me I was outdated. "Trovatore? Troubador? And you wanted me not to say Novizio. Sounds like a bard to me."

Let the kid have his moment. Bards were weekend warriors in puffy pants at ren faires. I was a Trovatore—a seeker, keeper of lore. No wandering minstrel I. Christ, I was starting to sound like one of Armando's speeches. The Conservatory did that to you if you weren't careful.

We passed the last playground before we made it into downtown. It was in a neglected park. A dozen kids played listlessly, their attitudes matching the gray sky. The dreariness informed the children of their color choices. Not a bright color in sight. The grass was brown with no hint that it wanted to find spring, either.

A late spring wasn't unheard of, but it felt different. I hadn't put my finger on it.

We walked through the Short North, which was a long

stretch of High Street lined with restaurants and bars masquerading as an arts district. It was too early for most of it to be open, so we walked in silence. By evening, there would be street musicians.

The kid didn't bother me with more questions the rest of the half-hour walk to the Cultural Arts Center, which was an Italianate-style brick building that was once an armory. Before that, the original structure had been a prison.

My personal prison—rather mine and the Novizio's—was through an unassuming door that nobody seemed to know or care about. Once inside, we descended the wooden stairs to a basement that extended under Bicentennial Park.

This was the entrance to the Columbus Conservatory, pretending to be an art center for tourists and normal people, Statics as we call them. A short walk down a dark hall lit by dim lights was a set of double doors.

A few feet ahead of the doors, as if standing guard, a statue of a woman dressed in the Grecian/Roman style of undress stood with her arms hoisted above her, holding a lyre on top of her laurel crown. The base was engraved VT QVEANT LAXIS.

"Know what it means?" I asked Hoagy.

"So that your servants may sing."

"Close enough. Old hymn to Saint John." The Conservatory loved this classical shit.

As we approached, the oak doors of the Columbus Conservatory opened without a knock.

Custode Monteverdi greeted us with a curt bow in his white robe trimmed in sparkling purple. Like all twelve of the regional conservatories, each had seven sanctuaries dedicated to specific purposes. Monteverdi ushered us to Sanctuarium Re. Each side of the arched entry hosted a marble statue of a woman with her hands at chest level, palms down, but fingertips up as if she were making a tent. Her pedestal read RESONARE FIBRIS.

"'To resonate through the heartstrings,'" Hoagy said.

"Well, at least they still make you study."

"An unreasonable amount."

Inside the sanctuary, the room defied a size that should seem possible under a park in a midwestern city. But the Conservatory had to find ways to be extravagant. Oil paintings of famous composers, glass cases with remnants of manuscripts, and ancient instruments replaced all religious accoutrements.

Most of the staff were in the Studi to work on their attunements or compositions in solitude. Armando Villard sat at a small table at the back of the sanctuary, looking as if he considered praying, fingers interlaced. The room was dark with a sliver of light from a faux stained-glass light pretending to be a skylight shining down on him, as if he was posing for a Rembrandt painting. He moved about as much as a Rembrandt painting.

Armando believed his portrait belonged on the wall. He was just the type.

I halted a dozen feet from him and didn't say a word. There wasn't any point. Armando would say what he felt to say whether or not I had an opinion.

"Hoagland," Armando began, "wait in the hall, please."

As soon as the door closed behind the kid, Armando grunted.

"There's been an issue," Armando said, his voice lingering in the air. I was never sure if it was his actual voice, the room acoustics, or some magical little treat he delivered for our benefit.

Armando insisted on stating the obvious. Perhaps in the job description for head of the Harmonic Council. Or, as he preferred: *Il Consiglio Armonico*, because everything sounded more important in Italian. The Conservatory—sorry, *il Conservatorio degli Stregoni*—was the musical Vatican, and they ordered the Council around. The Council ordered me around. I was still looking for someone I could order around.

All those fancy Latin inscriptions and Italian titles. The Conservatory loved its delusions, and if you're going to live one, might as well commit.

Armando was exactly what one thought an old Virtuoso should be, with his untamed gray hair and beady brown eyes looking to blame you for something. He was thin as a rail and dressed by the finest tailors. Armando had been a brilliant composer when he was young, a prodigy even, before the Conservatory discovered his "gifts" and perverted them.

Don't get me wrong, I appreciated that I got to be a Virtuoso and Trovatore carrying my harmonically enhanced ossia and spending my free time trying to remember how to write good music. Not that long ago, I could.

"Three twenty Sycamore," Armando said. "Do you know where that is?"

I gave a curt nod. "Edge of German Village. Brick street, lots of character, as they say."

Armando pursed his lips. "There's been an incident."

"Misuse?" I asked. "Or something worse?"

"Something worse, I'm afraid," he said. "But it requires you to be … very delicate. The DHR will be there. I'm hoping that you'll be there first and scope out the scene before they get their claws dug in."

The DHR was the Department of Harmonic Regulation. The DHR and the Conservatory were not best friends, closer to exes constantly doing shit to each other just to mess around.

"And they will be very interested in this one," Armando said. "In fact, they're going to see an opportunity."

"DHR always sees opportunities," I said.

"True." Armando sighed.

"So, what am I expecting to find? Do you know?" I asked.

"Yes. You're expected to find a dead body." He said it matter-of-factly. "And let's just say we know he didn't die naturally."

Not my first rodeo. There was something else. "Any idea of who did it?"

Armando shook his head. "No. But I believe there is more here than murder." He paused, his eyes locking on to mine. "Surely, you felt it."

"I'm not sure I know what you mean," I said without hesitation, although that was so that he didn't latch on to any pause in my response.

"It's pretty gray outside," Armando said.

"Yeah. Weather. What do you want from it?"

"How's your composition going?" Armando asked.

"In the toilet," I said.

"Yes. You're not the only one."

I shrugged. "As they say, misery loves company."

"I think misery has a lot of company right now."

Armando exhaled as if it were painful. It wasn't like him to appear so dejected and lifeless.

I didn't know what to say. Misery always loved company, and there was always plenty of it. I don't know why he was so morose. It's called Life. Sometimes it treats you that way.

"I need a tight lid on this," Armando said. "While you have issues that I and the Conservatory find frustrating, as you are my former student, I do know that I can trust your instinct and discretion."

With a shrug, I took a shot at him. "So you think that this death is related to your feelings? The misery or compositional dysfunction?"

Armando looked at me. In the dim light, his eyes appeared black with a pair of catchlights from the stained-glass windows that almost made him creepy.

"I know it," he said in a harsh whisper.

"I'll get right on it," I said.

Armando raised his hand. "Keep it professional with the

DHR. We do not want to incite them to push harder than they will."

"Understood," I said.

"Find out what you can and share as little as possible. We need to be ahead on this one."

"Got it."

I turned, but Armando stopped me. "Dekker, this one's gonna be tough on you too. Keep up the defenses."

I glanced over my shoulder and nodded.

"And take Hoagland with you."

"Why?"

"Part of the job. I dragged you around, didn't I?"

My heels echoed on the stone floor as I headed for the door.

This wasn't my first case. Wasn't that big a deal. I'd been running down suspects and dealing with magical issues for the better part of fifteen years. What did he think they were gonna throw at me I hadn't already dealt with? I knew the players and all the local composers. I had my ossia, and I felt good about it.

"It'll be different," Armando said as I reached the entrance of the sanctuary. "Steel yourself." I turned, and he half smiled. "Still fence?"

That was an odd thing to wonder. He knew I did. In fact, he knew I had been late to a few Council meetings because of my fencing. A guy's got to stay healthy and fit, and I'd rather do it with a sword than grunting at other people in a gym. Plucking an ossia or pounding piano keys would not keep you trim.

"Yeah, still fencing," I said. "When time allows."

"You'd better treat this one like your swordplay and have your defenses rolling all the time."

Defenses again. Odd. "I wouldn't have it any other way," I said.

"Report to me directly," Armando said, and shooed me away.

I was like the rest of the population and didn't want to hang out there.

People could be wary of those like me, the magically attuned Virtuosi and the Conservatory that lorded over us. Trained us, to be fair. Kept us in control. And of course, gave us work. In turn, we had the freedom to create as much as we desired.

All these hallowed halls we could use to our heart's content, but I preferred to compose at home. It made it easier when I wanted to take a nap. Or do something else.

These days, there was a lot of doing something else.

I didn't find Hoagy until I stepped back into daylight. He smiled at me. "Look what the Maestro got us."

Armando had ordered a car and driver sitting on Main Street for my arrival. I frowned at the kid.

"I guess everyone knows how you are."

"Guess so," I said, and hopped in the back as the driver held the door. At least I wouldn't have to drive around in circles looking for parking for twenty minutes and then walk anyway.

It might have been a forty-minute walk from the Conservatory, but whatever. Sycamore was mostly houses, but at the corner, the businesses intersected the homes. Number three-twenty couldn't decide and straddled the line.

Armando had told me to hurry, but I took my sweet time. It's the small moments of rebellion we cherish. Plus, I didn't want to appear to rush things. But it was a fine line. I didn't want to keep them waiting forever.

I steeled myself for whatever awaited me and the babysitting job.

The as yet unnamed dead body had to be musical or they wouldn't have sent me. Nor would the DHR have an interest. Guess the stiff was now a decomposer.

CHAPTER 2
THE SCENE

THE APARTMENT at three-twenty Sycamore was a narrow brick row house in German Village, the kind where you could hear your neighbor sneeze through the wall. The apartment was on the second floor, up a wooden staircase that groaned with each step. A middle-aged couple walked by, glancing up at the apartment.

What the hell was I talking about, middle-aged? I was closer to middle-aged than I preferred, but as usual, I had little choice in the matter.

There was barely room for it to open before a wooden staircase started upward. As I pushed the door, a woman in her mid-thirties, with dark hair pulled back, clear green eyes, nearly ran into me, apologized, and darted down the street. She looked like a librarian, not like someone who would have lived here. No offense to librarians.

The stairs groaned with each step, so I wasn't sneaking up on anyone. Although that wasn't the goal. At the top was a door on each side of me; the one with the yellow police tape made my choice obvious. Hoagy trailed behind at some distance.

I lifted the tape and entered.

A half dozen people stood in the room, five of them cops.

One of them was in plainclothes, wearing a blazer that looked like it used to be a couch. His slicked-back jet-black hair had retreated faster than I could have in prime fencing competition shape. An unbuttoned white shirt revealed his natural fur coat and a gold medallion of Saint Whoever woven into the hair on his chest. The medallion warded off people like me.

I hated to break it to him, but it didn't work. We just all agreed that we would make it appear to work so they wouldn't get as uneasy with us. When people got too uncomfortable, the pitchforks and torches came out.

Anyway, I'd known him for a long time. Detective Dash Handler was a good guy overall. Short, dark, and not much attitude. Good at his job.

He popped a sunflower seed into his mouth, which was a constant with him. Littering a crime-scene floor with shells was not ideal, but who was I to judge? This was his crime scene.

The house felt like someone had sucked all the personality from it, like a hotel room designed by someone who'd never felt joy and didn't want to get guests to start.

My place was no better. It was a permanent bachelor pad. I had a bed in my apartment, but it was more of a storage unit. I slept in the chair. It reclined. It was good enough. The table next to it was strong enough to hold a book or a bottle, whichever the night demanded. Like the kid said, a mess.

And the full upright piano sat ten feet away, in case I got a sudden burst of inspiration, which hadn't happened in, I don't know, weeks now. Or was it months?

I ate over the sink, so I never did the dishes. It was a dream.

Anyway, this place ... The cops buzzed around, looking at everything, turning it over. I guess looking for hidden hiding spots behind clocks on the walls, and everything else. But they had plenty of work cut out for them, given the chaos of the room.

A dining room table had been shoved against the wall,

blocking access to a door, presumably a pantry. Books covered the table in multiple stacks, and a dozen candles sat melted down an inch from their pewter stands, the beads of wax water falling into frozen pools on the table.

Sticky notes were on the books, the kitchen cabinets, everywhere. "Pick up reeds." "Practice measures 47-52." "Buy cat food." The mundane debris of life. I preferred to forget things without pesky reminders.

The chairs remained in the living room, one on its side, one on its back. Like with my place, the far wall next to a window had an old full upright piano. I bet the guy across the hall loved it.

The top of the piano hosted scattered music scores and more sticky notes. Naturally, the piano drew me to it like a fly to a cow pie, but I needed to do things in the proper order.

Dash greeted me, and we shook hands. He was one of the few who still shook hands. Even in fencing, a traditionally rooted sport, there had been a lapse in that department. Pandemics, culture wars, social media, who knows what caused it? The detective was one of those guys who had a firm handshake that became a competition. But right before you squeezed back too hard, he released.

He spat the sunflower shells to the side onto the shag carpeting. "This is different than usual," he said.

"I heard." I gave him a curt nod, my eyes still roving about the room. "Maestro Villard already gave me that sort of warning that's not a warning."

Dash clicked his tongue and shook his head. "That Armando guy."

"I know," I said.

Dash peered around me at the kid. The detective pointed at him.

"Tagalong," I said.

"Hoagland Porter," the kid said with a nod.

"It was take-your-apprentice-to-work day," I added.

"More than that," Dash said, tipping his head to the other street-clothed non-cop in the room.

The woman was in her sixties, built like a truck with arms and quads trying to go full Hulk on her and rip the seams. Her iron-gray hair was pulled tight into a ponytail. She approached me, causing Dash to step back.

Then it dawned on me. This was Councilor Lachlanna Foyle of the Harmonic Council. I had minimal interaction with her. Armando was the buffer. It took a long moment for me to figure it out. Her dark brown hair had gone from that to gray in ... weeks? She quit dyeing?

"Ma'am," I began, "I didn't expect to find a Council presence." Her eyes were like a machine inspecting me.

Councilor Foyle locked on to Hoagy. "Novizio?"

"Yes, ma'am. First day." He sounded too eager.

The Councilor frowned at me. "Wrong case to bring a nugget, Virtuoso Kohl."

"Armando insisted."

She shook her head. "Keep him in line. The Conservatory's reputation depends on discretion. Remember that."

Hoagy straightened like a board.

Armando warned me. Now she did. It wasn't like I didn't always work with the police. The kid would have been trained to be silent, too.

"Some deaths require Council oversight. I've examined the body." She frowned. "I'll let you do your thing. My skills are not there." She turned to Dash. "I assume you're satisfied?"

The detective cocked his head, which she took as the cue to exit. He threw up his hands. "Sorry, Dekk. I called her first."

"Right. Not much she can do for you."

"Her name is on some of the papers on the table," Dash said. "Just covering the bases."

Hoagy stepped forward. "She's a suspect?"

"You have to run all the leads," I said.

Dash inhaled as if he had taken a drag on an imaginary cigarette. "DHR's on the way. So get your look now before they show their claws. They've been all over the music scene lately, shutting down street performers and requiring new licenses for buskers. Chief thinks they're building up to something bigger."

"Yeah, got it," I said.

The detective put his hand on my chest as I walked by, halting me. "I'm first, Dekker. Whatever you see, I'm first."

I gave him a nod. "Dash, have I ever not made you first?"

"Perhaps." Dash half smiled and chewed on another seed. "The place is yours. Don't mind the boys."

I walked to the window next to the piano. The blinds were shut. I rotated the twisty stick and opened them. What the hell was the name of that stick? It was one of those things; you knew it had a name, but you never had to use it.

The apartment overlooked a courtyard, all paved except for four small triangles with grass that was pretty much dead. But it wasn't because we were in that part of town; it looked neglected. Each grassy area had one tree in it, leaves still pale green.

The courtyard pavement was all cracked. There was a swing set with half the swings hanging by one chain.

Four kids sat motionless on a wooden bench, bundled in winter coats like their parents forgot it was supposed to be spring, too. They stared straight ahead instead of playing, as if their puppy had just died and one of them would have to take the blame for it.

I felt that way, too. It was the way I felt about my music these days. Composition used to be like fencing. It was all about timing and finding the opening. Now I couldn't even lift my blade.

For that matter, I'd been losing a lot of bouts, too. I needed to think about something else.

"Dash," I began, "why does the DHR care about this murder?"

Dash spat another seed. "Suspected harmonic blah-blah, whatever. But it's something worse, so quit lurking about."

I pushed myself off the window frame. "What's worse?"

"Well." He scratched the back of his head. "The DHR investigator is his wife."

"Huh," I said. "No conflict of interest there."

Dash bobbed his head. "Yeah." He shook his head. "Buddy, she's a walking conflict of interest. Dealt with her before. So get looking."

Hoagy was eager to get started. At this point in his career, he had an inkling that he had some magical ability, but it was like a natural musician or athlete. The raw materials had to be shaped and molded into something. I wasn't the best suited for that job, but whatever.

As I started my exploration of the apartment, I explained it to the kid. In order to inspect something, you kind of have to get the feel of the room. Get the ambience out of the way so that you can tune into the rest.

All but Dash and one other CPD officer cleared the room. The cops weren't hostile to the Virtuosi, but they didn't understand them. In reality, they view people like me the same way fiction treats the police psychic. The higher-ups tolerated Dash's use of those like me because he was good at his job, even if he had this one quirk of liking that phony magic stuff.

The first thing I did was to inspect the sheet music on the piano. The paper was yellowed, but this time, it was because he had bought it that way. The papers had been sitting for a while. The lower left had a deep brown stain on it and the top left corner was mangled and had little holes in it as if it had been stapled to something. The sticky notes were chord progressions and other music nerd stuff.

The lines on the music staves were the only straight things.

Everything else was a bit off. Every note stem, every bar line was curved. I recognized the scribble intended to be a treble clef, but I didn't recognize what he had drawn. Notes sprinkled the thing haphazardly. At the top, the victim had scrawled the name of the piece: Sonata Allegra in G.

"Shouldn't it be 'allegro'?" Hoagy asked.

"Yeah." I ran my finger along the title. "Dash, you know what a sonata is?"

He spat out another seed. "Some kind of classical music thing?"

"Yeah, some kind of classical music thing." I muttered under my breath to Hoagy at my side. "People today don't know their Bachs from their baristas."

I looked at the key signature—seven flats, which suggested C-flat major. That was like writing a grocery list in ancient Sumerian. Technically possible, but who does that? And the time signature was 13/7, which was mathematical madness. Most music divides time into groups of two or four. This was like trying to waltz to a limerick. I pointed to it and winked at the kid.

"This isn't music," I told Dash. "Are you even sure this guy knows how to write?"

Dash threw up his hands. "Yeah. He's a graduate of Juilliard."

Ah, Juilliard, my nemesis. I had wanted to go there. My musical ability must have sucked even then because I didn't pass the tests. Instead, I attended the Conservatory. The Conservatory said it was on account of my innate magical abilities that made me a prime candidate to be trained as a Virtuoso. But I only aspired to be the next Rachmaninoff or something.

I should correct that. Rachmaninoff with an ossia. So I headed down the wrong path. But I could play the piano. And a lot of other things.

I lifted the cover of the piano in front of me. It was at least a hundred years old, I would bet. Mahogany, seen better days. The keys were still old enough to have been actual ivory, although they were chipped off and back to the original wood in many places.

I hit a couple of notes. The piano was out of tune, but oddly, universally out of tune. So, not that one note was okay, and one wasn't. They were all equally out of tune. It was such a minor amount—flat by the most trivial amount—that someone like Dash wouldn't recognize it, but I could feel it.

Hoagy looked like he had just eaten something sour. "Flat."

"Yes. But every note is flat. The same amount."

It shouldn't hurt your composition too much. Mozart never heard an A-440 in his life, but we still play his stuff with modern pitch.

"What would cause every note to do that?" Hoagy asked.

"Not sure. But …" I thought about it for a moment. "Verdi tuning? Close. Maybe."

"Why?"

I shrugged. "We can't read someone else's mind. But Verdi tuning was believed to be better on the vocal cords. Can be associated with spiritualism and healing."

"You think that's what it is?"

"Perhaps Verdi was just a little flat himself and pushed it on everyone else."

I grabbed the first sheet of Sonata Allegra in G, and stood there, hammering out the chicken scratches. I already knew that they made no sense; I could hear it in my head that they had no sense of anything.

The moment I played, there was a ruckus off to my right. A black cat charged and landed on top of the piano. As soon as it had reached the top of the piano, it jumped down, hitting the keyboard cover.

I yanked my fingers out just in time as the thing slammed

shut with the cat hissing at me. But I wasn't paying attention to the hissing; I expect cats to have a bad attitude.

My focus was on the fact that the cat had six legs and a tail that seemed chopped off and flattened as if it had been slammed in the door repeatedly by a toddler.

Hoagy's mouth dropped. "It has six legs."

"Keep this job and you're gonna see a lot of weird stuff, kid." I turned to Dash. "The cat has six legs."

Dash shrugged and spat out another seed. "Very observant, Dekker. We've been trying to catch her, but she stayed hidden until you played the piano."

He flipped open his notes. "Um. Mixolydian is her name. They call her Mixy." Dash bit another seed. "That's what the neighbor said. She's been here for a while now, the cat." He shrugged. "I guess she didn't like your playing."

"I didn't like my playing," I said. "This music is complete garbage. It makes no sense. The title makes no sense. The key makes no sense; the notes are even worse."

Hoagy was nodding in agreement.

The cat had fled but could still be heard behind the piano. I nudged the piano away from the wall a few inches to help her out, but she wasn't there. It sounded like she was inside the piano. Damn cats.

I straightened the music into a neat pile for some semblance of order and placed it on top of the piano. When I did so, I noticed a business card.

I picked it up. It had a nice vinyl record logo. I'm not much of a graphic artist, but it seemed good enough. The card said "Twelve Tone Spin Zone" and underneath that "Vinyl Records, Coffee, Live Sessions." Made sense. Vinyl, cassettes, all that analogue nostalgia was big business again. The card had an address in the Short North, the perfect place for a vintage vinyl store. I could pick up a couple of concert posters from 1975 while I was there.

"Interesting?" Dash asked.

I shrugged. "It was on top of the piano." I flipped it over. "Ask for Billie," I repeated after I'd read the card.

"Who's Billie?" Dash asked.

"Don't know. I'm not a psychic." I put the card back.

My eyes roamed around the room. The vic was important to the Conservatory and the DHR. A councilwoman was here and likely knew the murderee. And, upon further inspection, not a damn photo of the victim or his wife anywhere in sight. No wedding photos. No crappy phone photos blown up. Maybe that was a sign of the times, too, photos on your phone and online and not on the walls. There was also no hotel art or famous knockoffs hanging.

Dash rocked on his feet, his eyes narrowing at me. He tapped his wrist even though he didn't wear a watch. "DHR, Dekk."

Hoagy glanced at me. "So? Why does that matter?"

"The Treaty. Studied that yet?" Hoagy shook his head, so I gave him the short version. "After the war, a treaty was signed laying out jurisdiction, rules, other nonsense between the Virtuosi and the DHR."

"You mean World War II?"

I laughed. "No. The Eleven War. Doesn't matter."

But it did. I avoided closing my eyes or those images would return. My left hand still trembled when triggered.

"But the DHR is like cops?" the kid persisted.

"More like parallel authority. Similar to the relationship between the FBI and local cops, but dealing with music." I hesitated. "And anything they think is like magic."

"And the cops just go along with it?" Hoagy asked.

"We cooperate," Dash said, stepping closer. "Until we don't."

Between Armando, Councilor Foyle, and impending DHR I was antsy. Not the time to procrastinate. "Let's get to it, Dash. Who's the victim?"

"Let's go look."

The kitchen was pretty sparse, and all the appliances he could have stolen from my grandma's house. Table, too, but under the table was our guy.

There was some blood on the black-and-white-checkered linoleum. A violin string lay beside his head, which had been used to strangle the poor man, given there was a nice gash across his neck. No blood under the fingernails or bruising suggesting he fought much.

The violin with the missing string was a couple feet away, out of my reach. It must have been tossed there in the process. Old and uncared-for instrument.

But whoever killed him had some anger issues. A violin string was not a good choice. Thin. It would cut like a razor. I looked at my hands. Not shaking today, thank God. I made fists. The strength and determination for that wire would be something. Couldn't use steel gloves and hold the wire. But the string came right from the violin. Impulsive.

I stared at him for a long time and knelt to inspect him. Not my first dead body, but you never get used to seeing them. Or at least I don't. But in this case, I recognized him. I searched his face to confirm.

I glanced up at Dash. "Felix Cantabile? I can't believe it."

Dash clicked his tongue, flipped open his notebook, and flipped through the pages. "Yep. Full name: Felix Nicolo Cantabile. Goes by Felix. Knew him, eh?"

"Yeah," I said. "About twenty-something years ago."

I stared down at him. Fit. Colorful shirt with a black vest over it. Sleeves buttoned down. Black pants. Sandy-colored hair thinning in places, well taken care of and clean shaven. Open face. Felix looked about half a decade younger than he was.

"Looks as if he aged pretty well," I said. "Minus the gash in his throat."

Dash nodded. "Yeah, ruins the whole look."

My brain was retreating to twenty years ago. We'd just passed the anniversary. Now this. Felix and I had been roommates in music school. We got shoved together; neither of us was outgoing in terms of human connection, so it was perfect.

When we finally connected, we discovered we had a lot in common. He hadn't wanted to be a musician. His parents forced it on him because they were.

His mom was first-chair violin in the symphony, and his dad ran the whole place. So they were determined that young Felix was gonna follow in their footsteps. Even though he had rejected music as a kid, his parents felt that once he was in school, the interest would show up.

Felix took to it fast. I spent a lot of our free time teaching him music theory and helping him get proficient. A bit of piano and trumpet.

He wasn't gonna touch a violin. He didn't need his mom telling him how to play that thing. Looked like the violin still did him in. I wondered if that was Mom's violin under the table.

As it turned out, he had an aptitude for the trumpet and composition. I always told him he picked a trumpet because he couldn't use all ten fingers at the same time.

When we both applied to Juilliard, he got in and I didn't. Bastard. I got into the Conservatory. I guess it worked out at least in terms of who was bloody on the floor of a kitchen.

I hadn't seen him since he left. Still, I felt bad. I closed my eyes, and the images from that last night of the war at Harmony Hall burned into my brain. The flames. Felix dragging me out.

My eyes shot open, and I was determined to stay in this moment.

Dash was still flipping through his notes. "Guardian of Whimsy."

I stood and stared at him as if he had told me the Easter Bunny had just been elected pope. "What?"

Dash frowned. "I was told he's the Guardian of Whimsy. If

that isn't a stupid title, I don't know what is." He shook his head. "You people."

"Guardian of Whimsy," I muttered. Hadn't kept in touch. Hadn't known he'd become Guardian. But then I never keep in touch with anybody.

"Ah, you know it?" Dash asked.

"Yeah, I know it."

Damn that Armando. Always a pain in my ass both when I was a Novizio and now. Or damn the whole Il Consiglio Armonico. They had sent me into this blind. Why hadn't he told me about the Guardian status? I was also pissed that Armando, the head of the Harmonic Council, had sent me in unprepared. And Councilor Foyle made sense now.

I'd never met a Guardian before. Their identities remained hidden. So maybe I had met a bunch of them. They could all be my best friends. Oh yeah. I didn't have any. And it turned out the only Guardian I ever knew lay dead at my feet. I shook my head. Best not to wonder.

Hoagy had stepped around the table so that he couldn't see the body. "What's a Guardian of Whimsy?"

I shook my head. "Kid, you'll learn all about it. They are protectors, if you will, of the most important human virtues. And supposedly this"—I pointed to Felix—"doesn't happen to them."

"Shouldn't happen to any of us," Dash said.

"It'll happen to more of us if there is no Whimsy in the world, I suspect."

But something else nagged at me. The timeline seemed wrong. It was Friday morning. If Felix—Whimsy itself—died yesterday, why had my composition abilities started failing weeks ago? And why was Felix's piano universally flat? Not broken, just … diminished? Like everything in this apartment had lost a fraction of its joy. Either someone had drained Whimsy slowly, like bleeding a patient, or there was something about Guardian deaths I didn't understand. The thought made my stomach turn. So much for the Trovatore in me.

I took the ossia off my back, undid the case, and pulled it out. I did a bit of tuning to ensure that everything was good. Hoagy watched me, eager but not daring to get close to the body.

With that done, I squatted next to Felix and plucked the E string. The E string to normal people. It was something else to me. That note was a good representation of the violence that had occurred. But no. That wasn't right. I modulated to F. That felt right. Felix was always F. Fluid, creative, never quite fitting the mold his parents wanted.

I closed my eyes and felt the harmonic vibration move through the room as I played. The energy would insulate me from any memories of the past for the moment.

The strongest sense was the disharmonic ease that Dash and the CPD cop felt. I continued to find the notes. The cat, Mixy, was stressed. Hoagy was curious, whimsical perhaps. But that'd be gone pretty quick.

The three of them groaned at once. That was because the disharmony of the scene came out of the ossia, producing chaotic music that I needed to tighten. That was me attuning to the situation. I had to make sense of the magical harmonic auras in the room and focus on them. It took me a minute or two before I started zeroing in on specific chords and rhythms that I could listen to and sense what was happening.

"What are you doing?" Hoagy asked. "That's awful."

"Attuning," I muttered. "The Conservatory calls it harmonic synesthesia. Let me work."

I closed my eyes and played. F appeared first, Felix's note, strong and clear. Then G-sharp, sharp enough to cut. They clung to the air around his body like smoke that refused to dissipate. Near the window, a sense of something frantic and final. I opened my eyes.

"Cool. Will I be able to do that?"

"Probably not," I said. "Most Virtuosi feel magic. You may not want it anyway. It's like seeing the ghosts of other people's music."

I continued. F. G-sharp. Then C. It was confusing. Near Felix there were desperate thirty-second notes clustered in minor keys. I wrestled with the tune. Each string could give me a different view. Isolating them was the trick. Yes. Last night seemed right based on the harmonic decay near Felix. Comfortable, lush chords that morphed into melancholy. Whatever had happened resulted from one night.

There was also an unknown sense there from Felix, streaming to the window as if it were escaping. Like his essence was bleeding out into the courtyard below. So many messages. But even dead, Whimsy couldn't dissipate this fast.

What I sensed was from outside sources. In fact, they lingered and attempted to obscure things.

It was clear that he had been strangled. I could see that, but I could also feel it in the ossia. No sign of resistance or struggle, however. But the strangulation was masking something I couldn't put my finger on.

I pulled a notebook from the pocket inside the ossia case and scribbled down the notes of what I was playing.

I tried a different approach, shifting to a minor seventh progression. The harmonic resonance changed, and suddenly I could tune into the magical signature more clearly, like switching from AM to FM radio. The murderer had been someone Felix knew—no, trusted. The magical residue was calm, familiar, right up until the moment of betrayal.

It was the only composition I had done in a while; too bad it was not mine. But I'd have to analyze it later to see if I could make some sense out of it. Right now it was very misleading.

I stood, slid the empty case over my back, and continued to strum the ossia while walking back into the main room.

"Time?" I asked.

"Moments until DHR," Dash said.

"No. Time of death."

He flipped through his notes again. "Eight thirty to nine last night."

I walked back to the window overlooking the courtyard and opened it. With no screen, the spring air wandered in.

I didn't mind. Dash didn't seem to mind.

"Kid, got a phone?" I asked.

He was beside me in a flash with it in his hand.

I glanced at Dash. "Tell your guys not to touch anything. This one's a little weird. I need to sort it out."

"All right."

The detective didn't believe in what I did, but it was one of those things where you see so much evidence that it works that you have no choice but to accept it. And be grateful for the answers you get. A real time-saver for him.

The kid still held the phone out to me. "Call the Conservatory. Get Armando on the line."

I leaned against the windowsill, staring outside, strumming the ossia. The instrument tuned into something. I wasn't sure what it was; then suddenly, an enormously discordant chord came from the ossia as if I had just snapped all the strings at once.

Dash grunted in pain. I winced. Hoagy didn't finish dialing. That was strange.

I spun to the front door of the apartment and saw a statuesque woman standing in the doorway. Damn. DHR.

CHAPTER 3
SONNY DISPOSITION

THE WOMAN in the doorway was smartly dressed in black that somehow straddled the line between funeral appropriate and business meeting. Statuesque, too, although that wasn't fair to statues. They showed more emotion.

Dash almost tripped over himself getting to her.

The woman entered the room, her eyes interrogating the whole place.

She was all straight eighths. Not an ounce of swing in her. Like elevator music that had been promoted to middle management.

After her initial assessment, she turned to me without approaching. "Are you another detective?"

Detective Handler to the rescue. "This is Dekker Kohl, our musical consultant."

Dash's thin smile never reached his eyes as he stared at the tall woman. DHR reps understood "musical consultant" was a euphemism.

"Dekker, this is Sonny from DHR, but also Mr. Cantabile's ex-wife." The detective checked his notebook. "Head of Special Projects."

I tipped my head at her. "Pleased to meet you."

Felix got married. I never knew that. It was hard to pin her as his type, but who knows? Odd that he married someone from DHR.

She seemed familiar, but I hadn't run into her in any of my cases. From the look of her, she was not the hands-in-the-dirt, crime-scene type. She stood with her hands behind her back, shoulders back, chest out, jaw firm. No chance she intended to invade my personal space. Good.

Sonny's eyes moved over me as if I were a lab specimen she was cataloging. If I weren't careful, she was going to pin me to a board. "And you're here to magically read the scene?"

Hoagy stepped forward, but I didn't know whether it was to introduce himself or to defend the slam against us. I cut in front of him.

"Among other things." My eyes shot back toward the piano. "Did you know your husband was composing before he died?"

Something flickered across her face. Too quick to catch, but there. As if she had a momentary realization that the other people in the room weren't furniture. "Felix was always composing. Felix was … compulsive."

The way she pronounced "compulsive" made it sound like a disease she'd tried to cure.

I studied her face. "Sorry for your loss. I didn't realize he was married. Then divorced."

Sonny's mouth tightened. She tolerated me, but within seconds, she was gonna push me out the window like a Russian oligarch.

"Not ex-wife. Current. Just not …" She hesitated. "Together. Felix and I have been separated for some time." Her eyes locked on to mine. "And I am the DHR representative."

A second figure appeared in the doorway behind Sonny. Tall, angular man in a charcoal-gray suit that had been pressed with military precision. He had pale blue eyes that missed nothing and forgave less.

"Inspector Rimsky, Internal Affairs." Sonny maintained her gaze on me. "He's ... observing."

I cocked my head toward Hoagy, who had stepped from behind me. "I've got a shadow, too."

Rimsky put two fingers to his forehead in mock salute. "Standard procedure when DHR personnel are involved in active investigations." His voice carried a slight accent that made each word sound like a chess move.

"Involved how?" I asked.

"Mrs. Mordent's relationship to the deceased requires oversight." Rimsky's pale eyes fixed on Sonny's back.

This was going to be fun.

I started packing my ossia and slung the case over my back.

"Are you freelance?" Sonny asked.

"No, ma'am," I answered. "The Conservatory sent me."

Even twenty years later and a job with them, every time I heard the words "the Conservatory," I saw in my mind a bunch of thugs putting pressure on folks in the city, minding their own business.

Although in this case, they might muscle cash from you every time you played a song on the street or in your business. The Conservatory was the seat of all magic. Which equals thugs and forcing their will on others. But with a song in their hearts.

"And what were you packing up?" Sonny asked.

"A lute," Hoagy said. "He's a bard."

I glared at Hoagy. "My sidekick is misinformed. It is an ossia, and I am a Trovatore." Sonny's stare at me was devoid of human existence. "I left my puffy pants at home," I added.

Her attention shifted to Dash. "Does the jester need to be here?"

"We're not a stereotype. We are Virtuosi and lore keepers," I said.

Dash threw up his hands. "Conservatory said so, and he helps the Department on such matters."

"Does he?" Sonny inspected me from head to toe, undressing me, but not in a good way. Rather like she was gonna hose me down and leave me outside in the courtyard freezing. "I believe the Conservatory is unnecessary in these matters. DHR can handle it. I can send a report of my summation to your superior."

I shrugged. "Under orders."

Sonny glanced at the detective, who bit another seed in response.

Dash shook his head. "Look. Conservatory, DHR, I'm just the guy in the middle. You both have weight on different things. Let's just all get along and work together."

Sonny pressed her lips together. "In this working together, how much of a head start did you give the bard?"

"Trovatore," I muttered, fully intending to whack the kid on the head later. Then I gave Sonny a plastic smile like a salesman at a used car lot. "I've only been here long enough to unpack my ossia." I patted the instrument. "Gotta warm up, you know."

Sonny turned her head. "Roger!"

A skinny kid—I guess I shouldn't call him a kid, twenty-two if I guessed, but not that far removed from Hoagy—bounded in from the hall.

Sonny held out her hand.

"Yes, ma'am," Roger said.

Roger fumbled through the satchel over his shoulder, riffled through a bunch of papers, stuck them on a clipboard, and handed it to her.

Sonny inspected the clipboard, adjusting it because he hadn't aligned the papers. Then she flipped through to confirm that the kid knew what he was doing.

The kid must have passed. Good job, Roger.

Sonny glanced at me.

"You brought two. I brought one. Guess we know who's taking this seriously," I said.

Roger returned to the hall with the other cops.

She exhaled with a low groan. "I'm not sure why the Conservatory feels it necessary to send a music performer to assess a Harmonic Overload Incident."

Her voice had a flatness to it that could make a love song sound like a tax audit. She even made it sound as if the victim had accidentally OD'd on pop music. Hard to blame him if he had.

Dash grimaced. "Look, Sonny. The chief felt you might be too close to this one. Same reason your Rimsky is here."

Rimsky gave a curt nod.

"The chief doesn't make decisions for DHR," Sonny said.

Although clearly, that was not true.

Sonny stared at the clipboard and then at me. "I'm perfectly able to do my job regardless of what you two think."

She clenched her jaw and thrust the clipboard at me. "After you fill out the proper forms, we'll talk. Until then, I have a case to solve, and I expect you not to be in my way."

I stared at her, expressionless, like a statue. "When was the last time you saw Felix?" I asked.

"Paperwork." Sonny faced the detective. "How was he killed?"

"Strangled," Dash replied.

"With a G string," I added, since the detective wouldn't know the difference, but I could tell. My eyes shot to Sonny. "Yours?"

Decorum should have made me keep my tongue, but she was pulling it right out of me.

"I don't play the violin, Mr. Kohl," Sonny said flatly.

Okay. Let it rest. I was the only fish biting. The silence that followed was measured in whole notes at the slowest tempo still playable; even then, it might have been too fast.

"Inappropriate humor, particularly as I am a grieving widow, is exactly why this investigation should be handled by qualified professionals," she said, her breath about to freeze on contact if you were nearby. "Paperwork."

Sonny jabbed her finger at me. Grieving widow, my ass. Dash motioned for me to follow him and took the clipboard from her.

The detective, Hoagy, and I stepped into the hall.

I shook my head. "She's something."

"Don't give her a hard time, Dekker."

"Looks like she's a dealer in hard times."

"I warned you."

I nodded. "Doesn't seem to be grieving much."

"Could all be inside. Don't be too harsh on her." The detective shook his head, staring into the apartment. "This facade she puts up—this is the way she always is."

I sighed. "I feel sorry for your having to deal with her all the time."

Feeling a twinge of guilt about harassing the wife of a dead man, I took my time filling out the papers in triplicate, supplying my Conservatory ID, even with my correct name. Perhaps a forced silence was good.

Dash shook his head. "Not all the time. Special projects. I'm going to check on the damage and make sure she's not contaminating my crime scene."

Hoagy was staring right at me. "I don't get it. Who's in charge?"

"Whoever wins the argument," I said.

"Looks like you lost."

"Kid, the bout's just started." I glanced at my watch. "We'll give her two or three more minutes."

Hoagy leaned on the wall next to me. "Did she know her husband was a Guardian?"

"Nope. It's a secret thing. I didn't even know we had one in the city, and I'm one of the good guys."

Hoagy frowned. "You don't think Guardians should be in Columbus."

I pried myself from the wall. "Kid, I never thought about it." I thought for a moment. "Beats me. I would've thought they'd be at Isola Sonora. Let's go."

He grabbed my sleeve. "What happens when a Guardian dies?"

"The world goes to shit if it wasn't already," I said.

"That's not helpful."

"Neither is the real answer."

"Which is?"

"The Virtue is orphaned, and we live in a world without Whimsy now."

That was if the Conservatory hadn't worked out succession. And given the rush this morning, I was betting they got caught with their pants down.

Enough time had passed that Sonny could get over it, if it even bothered her. I handed the papers to the detective as I walked in. Sonny was moving through the crime scene like she was sight-reading sheet music written by someone with a grudge against melody.

"Dekker checks," the detective announced, although he had checked nothing.

Roger took the clipboard from the detective and dialed his phone while stepping into the hall.

The DHR statue glanced at me. "And why is it that you brought that thing?"

"The ossia?" I asked. "You never know when you might need one."

Sonny wasn't convinced. Rimsky appeared not to notice.

"It's much easier to carry on my back than my accordion. Damn thing bumps into everything."

She shook her head. "Mr. Kohl, it seems you earned your name from being so dreary and black in heart."

I shrugged. "No. I was born on Christmas Day to a single

mom. My dad had been dating her for some time until I popped out, leaving Mom with a little Kohl in her stocking."

That was true, even if she thought I was yanking her chain. Or mostly true. True enough.

"I'm sorry about your loss," I repeated.

Sonny walked through the room, inspecting it. "It isn't a problem, Mr. Kohl. We hadn't lived together for a couple of years."

I remained indifferent. "A couple of years?"

She stopped, and her eyes met mine. "Musicians are a hard group to live with, and I find great solace in silence."

Hoagy watched us like we were a marital couple in a spat.

She was a pain in the ass. I guess it made sense that she wasn't all broken up if they hadn't been together in a couple of years. And she was right. Musicians could be a pain to live with. Besides, we both had conflicts of interest in this case, which Armando had to have known. Bastard.

The detective remained with us, perhaps as the referee. Or in case she took a swing at me. She had three inches on me if you counted the heels.

Play in tune, Dekker. Fat chance.

The DHR had plenty of power, and they had lobbied to be sure that plenty of regulations existed to keep magic under their thumb. We wouldn't want any loose joy slipping about. Kids might dance on the tables and break out into song or something.

Despite the master/pupil former relationship and given my personality, Armando should have known better than to send me. He had to realize how I would be. Abrasive is in my DNA.

Sonny had made it to the piano and flipped through the stacked composition paper. "Interesting that these are organized, yet the rest of the place is in disarray."

"Yeah, I straightened them," I began, "when I looked at them."

Sonny glared at me. "Would you like to clean the whole place before I investigate?"

"No," I said. "I'll wait till you're done."

She glanced at the papers and appeared to be reading them, which was interesting. But then every kid on the planet was forced to play recorder or some dumb instrument when they were in school, trying to see if they had any aptitude for music or Virtuosi magic.

Sonny knew the difference at least via DHR propaganda if not experience. For most people, they never knew the magic was there. Felt something. Couldn't put their finger on it. It wasn't often we pulled out the big guns of spell-casting.

"What do you make of these?" she asked.

Interestingly, as she put them back in my hand, the cat showed up again as if she were ready to pounce in case I played the piano.

"Pesky animal. Mixy, get out of here." Sonny shooed the cat away, and the cat bolted. A six-legged cat didn't bother her.

Dash repeated his statement to me. "We've been trying to catch it for a while. Belonged to Mr. Cantabile."

Sonny cocked an eyebrow at the detective. "Felix got her for me. Our second anniversary." She turned away and returned her attention to the music. "I don't like cats."

Too cute and fuzzy for her taste, I suspected.

"Analysis, Mr. Kohl," Sonny said.

"I'm afraid I agree with the cat." I looked one more time to see if Mixy was around. I made a show of studying the manuscript again. "Gibberish. The key signature, the time, everything is just out of whack. C-flat major, but the title says G major. Perhaps Felix had lost his mind."

The detective's eyes bounced between Sonny and me.

The DHR rep hadn't thought of a response. Rimsky, neither.

"Hoagy," I began, "want to take a crack at it?"

He looked like a scared rabbit. "C-flat major has seven flats. I don't think it's very common."

"Not unless you like a good harp tune," I said.

"I never heard of 13/7 time signature. I've only seen the lower number be even."

Rimsky and Dash both had a look of confusion on their faces. Sonny didn't. I glanced at Dash. "Most time signatures are divisible by two: 2/4, 4/4, 6/8, et cetera. 13/7 is perhaps mathematically possible if you concoct some weird way to divide the measure and the moon is in Taurus."

Sonny set the music back on top of the piano.

My eyes met hers. "Either way, the victim was not composing music in a traditional sense."

Sonny picked up the business card. "Who's Billie?"

"No idea," I fired back at her. "Did your husband listen to records?"

Her hand paused. "He used to play me jazz records when we were dating. Said music was meant to be shared, not just performed." Her voice softened, almost like she'd forgotten I was there. "I haven't listened to music in … God, it must be years now." Then she caught herself, straightening. "Not that I know of," she said crisply.

I glanced around the room. No sign of a record player, and those old console stereos had died shortly before my dad left.

She took the card and brushed it off as evidence.

"Well, Miss Cantabile—" I halted because of the incoming attack of frosty eye daggers.

"I was never a Ms. or Mrs. Cantabile." Sonny inhaled sharply.

With that, we finally made it back into the kitchen. I watched her face as we entered, but one thing was for sure: she could mask whatever emotion thought about coming out. For a moment I saw a twinge at the side of her eye, but it evaporated in a flash. But even the best tacticians have tells. She grasped the ring finger of her left hand and then recomposed.

One tough cookie. In full investigator mode, Sonny squatted next to Felix, touching nothing.

"Bag this." She pointed at the violin string.

"Your G string," I said.

The detective had put on gloves and lifted the G string and put it in an evidence bag.

Sonny stood and straightened her dress. "I hope your musical ability is better than your comedy routine."

"No, they're equally dismal."

With a curt nod, she clenched her jaw. "I don't think we'll be needing you any longer. This is clearly a Harmonic Overload Incident."

"A Harmonic Overload put a violin string around his neck and attempted to reenact the French Revolution?" I asked.

Hoagy looked terrified by the way I confronted her, but he held his ground for the moment.

"Mr. Kohl," Sonny began, "I realize that as a part of the Conservatory, you have some small amount of power that could apply to Detective Handler here. But not to me." She paused before continuing. "In fact, I find the abilities of your kind abhorrent and not useful to an investigation. It isn't my place to explain to you exactly how a Harmonic Overload occurs. They are accidents, and accidents have all kinds of resolutions."

Roger returned. Sonny was aware of his presence, even though he was behind her.

"What is it?" she asked, without looking.

"I just got a report back on Mr. Kohl," Roger said.

Her glare may as well have handcuffed me to the table, and not in a good way. I squirmed inside. Rimsky stepped forward.

"Let's have it," she said.

"Mr. Kohl was roommates with Mr. Cantabile."

Now the first genuine smile showed on her face. It would have been pleasant if she weren't about to have me for dinner.

"Oh, really, now?" she said. "Looks like someone else has a conflict of interest in this case. The Conservatory is slipping."

I smiled back at her. That's what you have to do to bullies. Rimsky frowned and resumed his post, watching the animals fight from a distance. Hoagy hovered behind me.

"That was twenty years ago," I said. "And when I arrived, I didn't know." Now I felt on the hot seat, which made my mouth run more than it should have. "Only for about a year, and then he went off to Juilliard. I stuck with boring music school. The kind that annoys you the most."

Sonny sighed. "Don't worry, Mr. Kohl; most music schools don't bother me. Just the Conservatory."

Roger butted in again. "There's more, ma'am."

She glanced over her shoulder at Roger.

The kid handed her the clipboard, which had a new piece of paper attached to it.

She read it. Her eyebrows rose, and then she locked her stare on me. And she wasn't interested in my rugged good looks.

"I would say the Conservatory is getting very sloppy," she said. "Not only did they send you to investigate your roommate, but it also appears that both of you were Dynamicists."

I blinked at her. This day was gonna dredge up my entire past. I should have stayed in bed and pretended I was a composer. However, I noted to myself that she didn't know Felix had been a Dynamicist.

But whoever Roger spoke to was right.

Felix and I had both been Dynamicists during the Eleven War. But that was while we were in school, so it also made sense. Kids. Ideals. Things you lose when you grow up. Only left with a tremor and unwanted memories.

If I thought about it, Sonny would have been on the Compressionist side, trying to force all musicians into a box.

She still was. In fact, it was hard to look at her and not wonder why Felix would marry her. You can never predict who someone falls in love with. Opposites attract, as they say.

Now Sonny had spent her whole life squashing the thing that we both loved the most.

Sonny handed the clipboard back to Roger. She didn't tell him he did a good job, but she stared at Hoagy and said, "Some assistants do good work."

The paperwork was a diversion for Roger. Damn. Well played. Time to change the subject. "So, how did you meet Felix?" I asked.

"Not important to the investigation," Sonny said. "Given your Dynamicist past and your conflict of interest, I think that we're done here." She grunted at me. "You may report back to your superiors that this is a Harmonic Overload Incident."

This was the second time I was going to bring this up. "A Harmonic Overload garroted him? With a violin string?" Her gaze remained firm, so I continued. "Or musical voodoo."

Sonny straightened herself and continued. "The DHR stance is that it is a Harmonic Overload Incident until we say otherwise. This is exactly what happens when magic runs unchecked." She frowned. "But I understand. It's a condition with you. Felix had it, too." She shook her head. "He was obsessed with the idea that his creativity was meaningful. It consumed him and made him unstable. I tried so hard to help that man understand that his artistic impulses were just neuro-chemical patterns. Once you can accept that, you can find real peace." She smiled at me, this one pure plastic. "And you don't get frustrated by blank pages and quotas of nonsense that you create that nobody cares about."

"Perhaps you should have tried it," I said.

"I did," she said. "I spent a few years chasing the same delusions—music, songwriting. It nearly destroyed me." She said it like creativity was a disease she'd recovered from, like she was proud of being cured. She continued. "Perhaps you should be careful, Mr. Kohl. The artistic temperament can be"—she looked down at Felix—"dangerous to one's mental health."

"Sir," yelled one cop from the other room.

The detective looked. We all did.

The cop wore a crystal on a chain over his uniform as if he was warding against vampires. I hated to tell him that some old woman probably dug the crystal out of her backyard and it wouldn't keep away vampires or me. The man's other hand was clinging to his shoulder mic.

"Well?" Dash asked, shaking his hand at the man.

That appeared to be permission to say it in front of everyone. "Another body," he said. "In the alley next to the Cinnamon Hedgehog."

Dash shook his head. "Tell them to send somebody else."

"Yes, sir, I told them you were still at the scene," the cop replied. "But they felt it was related. They found a music critic in a dumpster."

CHAPTER 4
DUMPSTER DIVING

THE CINNAMON HEDGEHOG was the kind of jazz club you went to for the most authentic jazz and blues and a place you wouldn't tell your mother about. But to be honest, I suspect my mom might have met my dad at a joint like the Hedgehog.

Two CPD officers waited as we arrived. Dash was ahead of Hoagy and me; Sonny sauntered behind, arms crossed and brow furrowed. Hoagy was almost smiling, having enjoyed his first ride in a police car like he was five. Tomorrow I'd take him to a fire truck.

Rimsky had abandoned us when we left Felix's apartment. He had more pressing matters now that the new victim wasn't related to Sonny.

Two patrol cars had angled into the alley; the rest of the cars were double-parked on High Street. An EMS scrawled notes and talked to a couple of other cops while two others loaded up.

We stood in a street masquerading as an alley paved with uneven brick, wide enough to drive through but choked by overflowing blue dumpsters from the businesses on each side. It was so tight that no one would dare think of squeezing a car past.

Broken bottles littered the ground, and it wasn't uncommon

to find a passed-out drunk. Or, in this case, a dead guy. The smell of trash, liquor, and urine permeated the air.

Shoulder mics on the cops chirped with the calm female dispatcher, prompting quick responses from the officers on-scene.

"Who was the vic?" Dash asked.

"Jazzy Jacob," a beat cop replied.

Dash spat out another seed. "Shame. He was entertaining."

"How'd it happen?" I asked.

The cop looked at me, then Sonny. Dash put his hand on the man's shoulder. "He's all right. Conservatory." He tipped his head to Sonny. "DHR."

The cop nodded and addressed me. "A girl from the club found him." He glanced at his notes. "Angela. She's the morning prep girl. Arrived thirty minutes ago. Usually takes the trash out about this time."

Jazzy Jacob had been a music critic for a long time. It wasn't very far-fetched that someone didn't appreciate the latest review, but that left many suspects. But somehow the chief or somebody believed it was tied to Felix.

We walked to the dumpster.

Jazzy Jacob was a regular at the Hedgehog. When he started his career, he had worked for the *Dispatch*. These days he did what everyone else did and had a Substack and a YouTube channel. Probably a Patreon.

Hoagy looked up at me. "You know him?"

"Yeah, I know him—knew him."

Dash nodded. "Seem like the type to piss people off?"

"Isn't that implied in his job title?" I asked. "He could be merciless in his reviews, but seemed all right."

Jacob stayed away from my type, the magical sort. He was closer to Sonny's side on that one. Still, he didn't deserve to be a body in a dumpster. Not that I knew of. You never know about the lives people lead.

He lay on his back, half buried under trash, from people not paying attention when they threw the bags in. His shirt was open, with what appeared to be plum-colored lipstick, leaving a note behind on his chest that read "DISCORD KILLS."

I suppose that's true enough. Did the killer mean harmonic discord or disagreement? That could be an important distinction.

No bullet wounds, no stab wounds. I didn't see what killed him, but I didn't plan on climbing into the dumpster to find out. We knew Sonny wouldn't go dumpster diving, either. Dash wasn't the type. So the two beat cops climbed into the dumpster and started moving the trash bags.

The meat wagon was on the way to take him in and do an official autopsy, but Dash wanted to have an idea before then. His calloused hands clung to the side of the dumpster as he leaned over the edge, watching the cops.

Sonny came up with a conclusion, frowning. "Perhaps someone is taking all his scathing reviews and using them as a weapon against him."

I bobbed my head in agreement. See how well the Conservatory and DHR get along? "There's certainly enough of them," I said. "Ever read one of his reviews?"

"No," she began, "I make it a point not to listen to meaningless music." She delivered another Sonny smile right at me. "And the only thing worse than meaningless music is someone who spends their time telling others how meaningless the music is."

I shook my head. "Funny you would be married to a composer."

She grunted at me again. "I understand how you feel about it, but Felix was more than a composer. You're not the sum of your occupation."

"Yeah." I thought about it for a moment. "But I always knew

him as writing this bright, cheerful music, bouncy, very engaging, and it was his entire identity."

"You knew him twenty years ago," Sonny said. "And stayed in touch?"

Of course not, but I didn't plan to admit that.

I winked at her. "Did you drive the music out of him?" I asked.

"Nice try, Mr. Kohl. My relationship with him is not important. What is important is that Felix was murdered, and now at least the police think that there's a connection to a murdered critic."

Sonny glanced into the dumpster, careful not to touch it. "This one doesn't strike me as a Harmonic Overload."

"No, it wouldn't be," I said. Jacob was musically challenged. Failed drummer, I heard. Didn't matter. "You can't overload the natal key anyway."

Hoagy cocked an eyebrow at me. "A natal what?"

I exhaled to exaggerate my frustration, but it was a good call for the benefit of Dash and his crew. "Every person is born with a musical key signature tuned to them, sort of like a horoscope."

The big difference was that Felix was a Guardian.

Sonny gave a laugh, but it rang artificial and performative, probably for Dash more than for me. "Ah, the Conservatory and its nonsense."

I threw my hands up. "But those are the facts."

"Are they, Mr. Kohl?" she asked. "How did you know he was a Guardian? Did the Council tell you?"

"That's why they sent me here."

Sonny crossed her arms and cocked a brow at me. "And your roommate from college. I would think you would sense it."

"Well, I highly doubt that he was a Guardian when we were twenty-two," I said. "And I lost touch. People drift. That's life." I tried to fire eye daggers back at her. "You should be accustomed to that."

No response. I didn't expect one. Why didn't I know? I knew the answer, but I wanted it to annoy her. That was not in the handling-a-grieving-widow handbook.

She deflected with a distant gaze. "A colleague's daughter died chasing magical dreams. Jacob praised her and then berated her in a scathing review. She never recovered." Her voice went flat. "At least he got what critics deserve."

"That's not magical; it's tragic," I said. "Unless you believe all inspiration and creativity is magic."

"Wouldn't you like that? Talent without discipline is a loaded gun," she said, but she wasn't looking at me. "That's why we had to put controls on it."

The old argument. The same justification they'd used during the war. My jaw clenched and my eyes went to my hands. Not trembling yet. "The war wasn't about freedom versus control, Sonny. It was about existing and creating without government permission."

I looked away before I went too far. Sonny had to be four or five years younger than Felix and me. Too young to have fought in the war. DHR brainwashing, or did she just look younger than her years?

I pulled the ossia off my back and opened the case to distract myself before my mind wandered back in time.

Sonny shook her head. "You're gonna serenade the corpse?"

"Something like that," I said.

I started playing as usual. The instrument produced those awkward, weird notes that made people cringe, as if I were a first-year band student torturing the neighbors on the front porch.

I plucked out a D major.

Hoagy stepped close to me, managing to avoid looking at the body. "How do you know what note?"

"You have to find the root natal key." I repeated my chord, closing my eyes to focus on the harmonics. "Jacob's a D major naturally. Then you search for the lingering neighbor harmonics. They could be in harmony, or in the case of murder, usually not."

"And that tells you who did it?"

I glanced back at Sonny, shaking her head.

"No," I said, softer. "They don't believe, Hoagy. Once you attune to their root key, the harmonics, good or ill, lead you down a path. It's like anything else, you have to figure out what the clues mean."

"Then why do it?"

"Because they can't feel it or sense it." I tipped my head to the cops and Sonny while I continued to refine. "But the harmonic residue can lead us to something faster."

"Even if they're not magical."

"Usually."

But this one tuned much faster than Felix had. And I could sense the magical aura weaving its way around Jacob. Easier to read. I continued tuning.

And educating the kid. "The magical resonance at crime scenes fades fast, usually within hours. But Virtuosi magic isn't about creating something from nothing; it's about reading what's already there, interpreting the harmonic echoes that emotions and actions leave behind. Every strong feeling, every violent act, creates ripples in the magical field that someone trained can detect and decode."

Hoagy nodded, accepting. Soon, he would get firsthand experience in harmonic echoes. "And everyone that does it plays the lute?"

"Ossia," I corrected. "And no. Each Virtuoso has a preferred instrument or one that calls to them. I prefer the piano, but this is easier to lug around. I could do it on a harmonica if need be."

"Seems like a harmonica might make people stare at you less."

I frowned at him. "We're in the Arts District. You'll be fine."

Then I saw it, the ossia focusing in like tuning into a radio station through the static. Someone Hoagy's age would have no idea what searching through static would be like.

But I got it. Something else lingered in the sonic resonance. This death, too, was a cover-up. But it was easier to read.

"Irrhythmia," I announced, surprising myself.

"*Arrhythmia,*" Sonny corrected. "A fairly common heart condition. Nothing magical about it."

"This isn't a medical condition, Sonny. This is a spell. Someone with precise control over biological rhythms. The kind of magic that requires either significant training or ..." I paused as a flashback of Harmony Hall burning blocked my ability to see the harmonies in the alley. "Or a device designed to replicate it."

"Virtuosi do that kind of spell?" Hoagy asked.

"No. It's forbidden and leads you down a dark path." I shook my head. "It's Ombrosi magic."

Dash, still gazing into the dumpster, grumbled. "Who do you know that's one of those?"

"Ombrosi? No one. I've never met one."

"That you know of," Sonny said. "Like Guardians."

"True."

"Ah, that!" Dash pointed emphatically inside the dumpster.

A cop lifted a pair of gloves and bagged them. Dash showed it to me.

It was a pair of brown leather gloves. Large. The kind you buy at Macy's for actual winter instead of fashion. Sturdy and warm, but laceration on the palms that looked like they cut through the material. Traces of blood, too. That tied the two murders together.

I resumed attuning, strumming the last chord, and looked at Sonny. Then I wanted to hit one of those special chords that would just twist her inside out and make her uncomfortable.

One perk of being able to attune, although the Conservatory frowns on it. Too Ombrosi-like. Kills all the fun.

But I decided I should be a nice guy. Save that for later if she kept being a pain in my ass.

I needed to set the record straight before it was forgotten. "Not arrhythmia, *irrhythmia*. Someone forced his heart into perfect time. The human heart isn't supposed to be that precise. It needs to swing a little, adapt to life's tempo changes."

"I'm sure it happens without your type," Sonny said.

"I'm sure it doesn't. It means that someone had cast a spell on him. The perfect rhythm eventually gets the breathing all in the same tempo. The victim hyperventilates, blood pressure spikes, vessels can't take the pressure—then wham!"—I hit a major chord on the ossia—"dead on the ground." I leaned closer to her and plucked a little arpeggio. "Stroke or heart attack. Dead from perfect time."

Sonny rolled her eyes. "Sure he did."

"We'll see what the coroner says," I riposted.

Sonny shook her head. "Sounds like nonsense to me."

Lucky for her, a black Suburban pulled up as if requested at that moment so she wouldn't have to hear me anymore. The coroner's investigator walked up the alley to us and peeked over the dumpster.

"Whew! That's something," he said. He turned to Dash. "You boys done?"

Dash looked at me. "We done?"

"Yeah." I nodded. "I got it."

The coroner's man beamed at me. "Mumbo jumbo, eh?"

"Mostly mumbo," I said. "But I like a little mambo, too."

He nodded, snapping on blue latex gloves, and strolled around the dumpster to get the lay of the land. The investigator stopped and bent over. He showed us a lipstick tube.

"Midnight Crimson," he said, reading the tube. He glanced at Jacob. "One thing solved."

"Is Midnight Crimson unusual?" I asked.

"Boutique stuff," Dash said. "My wife likes it. Stupid expensive."

"Hard to get?"

"I'm sure you have no one to buy it for," Sonny said. "But if it's boutique as the detective says, you can get it at Mancini's."

Mancini's was a small store a block or two up the road that aspired to be Sephora, but couldn't pull it off, so it opted for midquality, discount brand names, and weird stuff so the kids on campus could buy something, too.

Meanwhile, the investigator had ruffled through Jacob's pockets. "No phone. No wallet, just a money clip."

The clip was loaded. It was one of those wallet alternatives like you find advertised on endless YouTube sponsorships right after VPN and *Ground News* plugs.

Then he showed us a notebook. "Some pages torn out, otherwise random notes."

He bagged the book and handed it off to an assistant.

"Any preliminary cause?" Dash asked.

My answer wasn't good enough. Typical. "Bruising on the neck may suggest strangulation. Don't hold me to it."

Dash looked at me. Sonny was smiling. "Arrhythmia," she said.

"*Irrhythmia.* I stand by it."

That was the end of it. He would take pictures, do all the dead-body stuff, and then cart him off.

The party broke up pretty fast. Sonny was the first to leave on account of my shining personality. Dash and the boys helped the coroner.

But it wasn't finished for me. I had to discover more, because Armando and the Council were going to want to have more than lipstick and a little irrhythmia here and there. Were the murders connected, and why?

Since Jacob had died next to the club, that's where I would

start. But not now, because the club wasn't open yet, which was typical for this type of joint. This kind of entertainment was a nighttime-only event.

It was convenient; it kept the hours short for all the employees and made it easy for the cops to have a schedule when they wanted to pick up drunks and make a few extra bucks.

Sonny left with her last word directed at me. "It's more proof that an artistic temperament is dangerous. This is simple murder for reviews."

But Jacob wasn't artistic. He was the antiartistic type. And he had pissed off many people. I would have to suffer with the internet and figure out who he had pissed off most recently. In Sonny's view, musicians were unstable enough to murder. Virtuosi, too, in her book.

Since we were downtown, Hoagy and I were going to hoof it despite his protests. We headed down High Street.

"I suppose a lot of people don't like music critics," he said.

"Somebody has to be the gatekeeper." I steered him into a Mediterranean café. "Even if TikTok would rather do the job."

The question that roamed in my mind was who died first, Felix or Jacob? The signatures didn't tell me the time of death precisely, and I hadn't tried to get it due to the distractions.

I could have asked the coroner's man while he was standing there at the dumpster to take a swing at it, but there wasn't one at Felix's by the time we left. So I was going to be out of luck until a report was filed.

But it made me wonder: if it was the same person as Armando suspected, then that person had to get from the Hedgehog all the way to Felix's. Or vice versa.

It took us ten minutes after we got in the car, and we didn't have to look for parking spots. The killer would have to find a parking spot or take forty minutes to walk.

I'd have to work out the timeline. What was the connection

between a dead Guardian and a dead critic? But right now I had a business card in my pocket and questions that wouldn't wait. Time to see what Billie knew.

CHAPTER 5
THE SPIN ZONE

PEARL STREET WAS narrow and brick-paved, the unwashed backside of trendy High Street. The Twelve-Tone Spin Zone didn't have a sign. You had to know it. The Spin Zone had its own character, like cheap rent, stale perfume, and old vinyl.

I led Hoagy down concrete steps in desperate need of repair and through a wooden door. A bell jangled. Inside, a bright magenta neon sign announced where we were as if you could find this place by accident.

Hand-painted letters under the neon offered new and used vinyl, or you could get cash to unload yours on them. There might have been a dozen people in there flipping through the stacks. A balding man with thick glasses leaned on a column, reading a small tablet.

If you came in looking for that missing piece of vinyl, it would take you hours to locate. The Spin Zone drew customers who still believed in liner notes and album art, and the coffee was stronger than the Wi-Fi. Although there was no sign of the promised coffee on the business card. Nor the live sessions unless they meant the vinyl kind. Or post-Buckeye-game partying outside.

I walked past the record bins lining both walls while

breathing in forty years of musical dreams gone stale. Vinyl and cardboard had been slow-dancing in the dust long enough to create their own perfume. Part chemical sweetness from decomposing album covers, part the ghost of cigarettes.

The customers flipped through the records, cassettes, and CDs. It was like walking into a mausoleum for dead formats, where the corpses were still trying to make music.

Paraphernalia was tacked all over the walls. Two black fans were mounted on opposite ends to announce that there was no air-conditioning, but they could still move air. No charge.

To the right was the checkout counter with two teenagers sitting on stools, slumped, looking bored. The girl had six piercings in one ear, five on the other, and a nose ring. The boy was lagging with only five visible piercings. When no one offered to help me, I knocked on the counter. Their name tags, written in silver marker, read "Sage" and "Riot." I didn't comment in order to avoid being called a Boomer, which I wasn't. I was broke, lived through 9/11, the Eleven War, the Great Recession, and a pandemic. Boomers got money and retirement.

"I wonder if you could help me out," I said.

Hoagy wandered off, investigating the stacks or avoiding the Boomer.

Sage, the girl, must have noted the ossia case on my back, which would look like a small guitar to her. "Wrong kind of music store, mister. No instruments."

"Good. I was planning to keep mine." Sage didn't have a response, so I didn't push it. She might not be able to handle someone like me. "I'm looking for Billie."

Sage didn't bother to look at me, as she was too busy messing with the artwork on her nails. "Billie? Just Billie?"

"That's what I said. Billie in?"

Sage frowned and shook her head. "Not today."

"Got it. What time tomorrow?"

"No idea, mister. I don't keep schedules."

I nodded. "Have you ever met Jazzy Jacob?"

"Yeah, man," Riot said, proving he was alive.

"Yeah?" I raised my eyebrows. "When was the last time you saw him?"

The girl exhaled and shook her head. "Now you think he's a calendar?"

I'd bet these two kids were doing jobs they didn't like. Hell, the name tags were likely gags. It wasn't nice, but I felt compelled to jar them a little.

"Apparently, neither of you is," I said. "Look, Jacob's dead. Murdered. Found him in a dumpster. You want to help solve it or keep playing twenty questions about your work schedule?"

The girl's piercing-laden face went pale. "Dead? Like, actually dead?"

"The deadest," I replied. "So, when did you last see him?"

"Three days ago," Riot said.

Another customer approached the counter with a stack of records.

The girl stood from her stool and put her hands on her hips, still managing to slouch, though. "You here to buy a record or just poke us with questions?"

I planned to poke. "Who is Billie?"

"You don't know?" Sage looked at the boy. It was the first time they seemed to care what the other one thought.

"I'm investigating," I said.

"So you a cop?" the boy asked.

"No, a Trovatore."

The teenagers stared at me blankly.

"He means bard," Hoagy said from a row of vinyl over.

They laughed in unison.

Riot shook his head. "You're being a pest. Shove off."

"Thanks for the advice."

I looked around the store. The man leaning on the pole

approached and held up his tablet with the browser pointed to Jacob's Substack.

"Jacob was here last week. Right before his review of Reed Holloway's new album." He tipped his head at the tablet. "Read it yourself. Think he did a video, too."

Of course he took off before I got further than the title. I leaned against the record bins just to remind the kids that they didn't run the world yet. They just thought they did. The algorithm told them so.

Hoagy had his phone in his hand. "I need to borrow that."

I opened a browser and skimmed the article while the kids glared, including Hoagy.

To my surprise, the review was bland. I always heard Jazzy Jacob was a talented writer, full of colorful language and a sense of poetry. Interlaced with gibes and biting comments, which was probably why he was discarded with the garbage.

The critic felt Holloway was as bland as his writing was. I assumed he wasn't trying to match the style, but he did.

"Not one of his best," a dishwater blonde, mid-thirties, said as she excused herself so she could look in the bin I was guarding. Another reason not to carry a phone. Too many busybodies. I'd keep my issues and tastes inside my head under lock and key.

"Yeah?"

"His last couple were real snoozefests," she said. "You should look at the one on the singer Honey Lane, Reed Holloway, or trombonist Boomer Blake."

"You follow Jacob's reviews pretty closely," I observed.

She shrugged. "My husband is a fan of the local music scene. Somebody's got to figure out who's worth seeing when they're not marquee names."

"That's the second time I've heard the name Reed Holloway in the past five minutes. Important?"

She tilted her head. "Are you investigating the reviews or the musicians?"

"Both now."

She frowned. "Holloway's a bit nuts."

"Sure," I said. "Were Jacob's reviews always like this?"

"Nah. Recent change. Steady stream of them. 'Bout two or three weeks," she said.

"You a Patreon of Jacob?"

"No. I don't Patreon anyone."

I peered over the paper at Hoagy. "What'd ya find?"

He shook his head as he inspected a frayed album. "Duran Duran? This shit's old."

"Me, too," I said. "Let's beat it."

CHAPTER 6
THE CINNAMON HEDGEHOG

COLUMBUS HAD ABOUT five jazz clubs in walking distance of the Short North. The Cinnamon Hedgehog was next to the alley, where we found Jazzy Jacob's body. Like every other music venue in the city, the club had a fresh coat of DHR inspection stickers on the door. More than I'd ever seen before. The bureaucratic paper trail that usually meant someone was building a case. The Hedgehog was skinny and smashed up against another building. There were no windows looking into the place, which might make one think that it was suitable for something else.

I had sent Hoagy back to the Conservatory to report back to Armando with specific instructions of what to say and not to say. Then he was to go home. A bar wasn't for him.

The nondescript rust-colored door opened inward with the tinkle of a bell. The Hedgehog was two stories, narrow as an alley. Old wooden floors stained and moving under your feet. The passage between tall bar-height tables was tight enough you had to turn sideways if someone was sitting down.

About three-quarters back, the actual bar started—the kind with the big round wooden lip so you didn't swipe your drink off, or maybe so you could lay your head down to rest once you got too drunk. Mirrors and tons of liquor lined the back wall, all underlit so the bottles glowed. Today the light was flickering, and the bar was empty. Not yet opening time, but the door was unlocked because staff was arriving. More importantly to me, that included the players.

The brick wall on the left held a neon sign of the logo, an Art Deco hedgehog sitting on piano keys. In case you didn't know where you were.

At the back, a small stage one step up from the main floor, big enough for a drum set, an upright piano, a bass player, and three or four horns if they didn't mind how each other smelled. Don't put anyone in front of the trombone player if he wanted to keep his head. Right next to the stage, behind a ragged curtain, dark stairs headed up to the second floor. A swinging door to the kitchen was straight ahead.

The stairs were skinny and sketchy, leading up to where the band practiced and the crowd of poetry lovers gathered in the evenings to wax philosophical and torture others with their own verses. The upstairs went over the coffee shop next door and provided more space meant for hangout rooms and changing areas the musicians needed.

I walked down the narrow paneled hall and stopped at the last room on the left. The door was open. I leaned against the doorjamb and knocked.

A small wire patio table with two chairs sat in the center of the room. In one of them sat Locrian Morgenstern, better known as Cree, a sax player who was a regular feature of the Hedgehog and a somewhat regular feature of my life.

She was all right if you could handle the relentless optimism. I tolerated it. She probably believed in leprechauns and fairy dust. She was just the type. On the other hand, I didn't know for sure they didn't exist.

But Cree was stable and predictable. Right where she was every night, the Hedgehog had been open for years.

We had a long history together. I liked her, and she liked me, just not at the same time. We tried dating a few times. Once in high school and once in college. She got restless. We tried again about eight years ago for a weekend before I got called away on a case. Then we flirted with it again a year ago. Same result: great friendship, lingering tension, terrible timing. Overall, she was a year younger than me, was there on that last fateful day at Harmony Hall, and tolerated me.

She was a redhead—the curly kind—where it looks like the hair is going to explode outward if you don't get it under control. She normally dressed in ridiculous color schemes. She preferred greens, reds, oranges, and copper—everything that I would never wear in my life. But today, she was pretty dressed down in a bronze blouse, with a bronze jacket over top.

Cree was slight, shorter than me by a head. Sonny had interrogated me about wearing poofy pants. Well, Cree literally had poofy pants as if she forgot decades had passed since her clothes were what the cool kids wore. The pants might have pleats on them, too. Normally, she wore suspenders under her jacket, a blast from the Technicolor past.

Cree's eyes were always lit. Her small mouth was cocked in one direction and often opened with her tongue tucked in the corner.

She didn't notice me right away because she was engaged in a heavy conversation with a guy I didn't recognize. He was also slight and angular. Sleeves rolled up past the elbows. Wore a skinny tie as if that was still in fashion. And he sported a pompadour. He had thick horn-rimmed glasses. The man had one arm resting on the table and the other smashed against his cheek. He stared at her as if every word from her mouth was a revelation.

Cree was smiling back at him, blinking. And I recognized that look. I'd been on the other end of it.

I knocked again. Her head turned, and she beamed at me.

That was one of the good things about her. There were many, but that was one of my favorites.

"As I live and breathe, Dekker Kohl," she said.

She jumped up from the table, ran to me, and wrapped her arms around me, nearly pulling me from the doorway. After releasing me, she kept one arm around me and petted my lapel with the other hand as if she was waiting for me to purr. She knew I wouldn't.

The man at the table stiffened, and his eyes narrowed.

Cree hooked her arm in mine and pulled me toward him.

"You two probably haven't met," she said.

"Don't believe so," I said.

The man stood, scooting the chair back, scraping it across the floor, and stuck both hands in his pockets. He was her height if you didn't count the pompadour.

"Riff Parker," he said.

"Dekker Kohl." I gave a nod. "Good to know ya. Playing here now?"

He nodded enough to be counted but not enough to mean it, and his eyes shot to Cree. "Yeah, man. Just got in town a couple weeks ago. Cree here got me a job."

I winked at her. "Yeah, she's good like that."

A couple of weeks ago. Coincidence? Probably. Cree had been bringing musicians to town for years. That was her way of keeping the scene alive. Or entertaining. Still, the timing nagged at me.

I looked at his hands, long spatulate fingers. He must have the full eleven-key hand span. "Pianist?"

That's a stereotype, but I just took a stab at it. I mean, she had liked me once, and she mostly knew me for my piano playing, not my ossia playing. But when you're investigating things magically, you take what you can carry.

"Yep," he said. "You?"

Cree leaned into Riff. "Also a piano player. From the Conservatory."

Riff looked at me with the usual look—the one where you want to protect yourself but you wouldn't know how. "How's that for a job?"

I frowned. "Pays the bills."

Cree still had a smile plastered to her face. "Dekk wrote me a song."

I nodded.

Riff looked concerned. "Oh yeah?"

"It was a long time ago." I shrugged. "I'm like the dinosaurs and just waiting for an asteroid to hit."

Cree smiled again. "Dekk, play it for him. Come on."

Perhaps one reason the Conservatory took me was that I was not a session player. I enjoyed writing and experiencing the music, but I did not want to sit on that stage downstairs entertaining the masses. Or the sixty who could come in. But she was insistent.

And as usual, I gave in to what she wanted. Just to the left, an abused player piano sat against the wall. It didn't even have a cover for the keys anymore. And the hint of fake leather on the stool was only a suggestion that there used to be something there.

On top was an old glass ashtray, which she used to collect junk like earrings missing a match, buttons, and her keys. Among the lost things, she still had the spare key to my apartment on her key ring, hanging over the edge of the ashtray. Appropriate. Lingering on the edge. Never got around to asking for it back.

Next to the piano was an old futon couch combo laid out flat, ready for a bed. I didn't want to think about what was going on with Riff. I'd been Riff once.

But I did as I was told, and I sat at the piano. I tried to play our song, the one I wrote for her, at the same time Felix and I were roommates.

I hadn't thought of that till now. That brief time in our lives before.

My fingers found the keys, but the melody felt complex. Why had I been so aggressive with the chord changes? Now I would write something more efficient if I could even remember how to write. Cree was pleased with my attempt to remember the song and didn't mind the missing notes. She hadn't heard it in years, after all.

Riff clenched his jaw. Yeah, she did it to him on purpose.

She'd be better with him, more stable, not from the Conservatory. But that didn't stop a deep part of me in my gut from wanting to punch him in the face. Good thing I needed my fingers to play the piece.

She leaned into Riff, trying to get him to move to the music. Playing both of us, I guess. But it wasn't malicious. She still moved like she was ready to fence someone. All coiled up, energy ready for quick decisions. Twenty-something years of almost, but never quite. And she was still the most interesting thing in any room.

Cree was the one who got me on the fencing team back then because of her overwhelming joy at stabbing people with sport swords.

She was working up Riff physically, but her eyes were working at me. This was the game we'd always played—push and pull, advance and retreat. Riff would learn that soon enough, or he wouldn't. Most of them didn't last long enough to understand that Cree collected people who made her feel alive, and I was permanently in that collection. Not threatening. Just permanent.

Same old Cree, trying to get inside my guard. We'd grabbed coffee a few times in the past year, traded texts—rather, I saw texts when I realized I had a phone. We stayed in orbit without colliding. That was the way of things.

I stopped the song. It wasn't quite done. I wasn't sure I was going to remember the rest, but I'd had enough. That's not what I was there for.

"I need some help, Cree." I stood from the piano.

Her eyes met mine and she saw how serious I was. She turned to Riff, put a hand on his chest, and said, "Okay, I'll catch up with you soon."

Cree kissed him on the cheek and lightly shoved him toward the door.

Riff paused in the doorframe and held out his hands. "I won't be trouble," he began, "Maybe I can help. Outsider perspective and all."

Cree winked at him. "Dekk and I go way back. High school even."

Riff looked back at me with something sharper than jealousy. "You know, she talks about you a lot. About the old days, when music meant something." His fingers flexed unconsciously. "Must be nice having that history. That ... connection."

The pianist exuded genuine pain, not just possessiveness. This wasn't some casual fling for him.

He lingered another moment, like he wanted to say more, then shook his head and disappeared down the hall. I heard his footsteps on the stairs, then the faint sound of the piano downstairs—angry, discordant. Working something out.

Cree winced. "He'll get over it."

"Will he?"

"He'll have to." She pulled the door shut.

After Riff left, Cree's performance mask slipped. She sat at the piano and played a few bars of something I didn't recognize. She wasn't a piano player, but she knew enough to one-handed play something besides "Heart and Soul." Her tune was melancholy, searching, nothing like her usual exuberant style.

"I haven't been creative in weeks. A couple months?" She avoided looking at me. "Every melody I start just dies halfway through. Like the music forgets how to be happy."

Before her thoughts took her too far away, she changed the subject. "I was just thinking about the English lit guy. Remember him?"

"Dr. Phrygian."

She snapped her fingers and pointed at me. "Right, Dr. Faustus Phrygian. He was a piece of work."

I nodded with a chuckle. "With that damn full-size rubber chicken in his jacket pocket."

Cree laughed, too.

She got up from the piano and moved back to the table, pouring herself a whiskey. I wish she hadn't, but it wasn't uncommon in a place like this. She needed to fit in. I sat in Riff's spot.

"He's your new one," I said.

She frowned at me. "It's not like we were ever going to be anything."

"We were once. We could be again."

Cree smiled at me. "Well, in the meantime, I'll take Riff for a spin."

I frowned. "Good sax, bad sax. You'll take any sax you can get."

She shook her head. "You know who liked your sense of humor more than me?"

"Nobody living."

"Not true," she said. "Angela."

Angela had been her roommate. They were like glue. And unlike Felix and me, they remained besties all the way to the present. "How is the old girl?"

"She's great. Promoted last week. Want to give her a call?"

"No, thanks. Schedule's booked solid."

"She thought you were magical."

"Funny." I shook my head. "I remember her scribbling in Felix's journal just to piss him off."

She laughed. "Never worked." Cree paused, her face becoming more serious. "I'm assuming you didn't come here to give me a hard time."

"Nope." I leaned back. "That's a bonus. I'm on a case."

She frowned at me, but she didn't mean it. "So I'm just an interview. Or am I a suspect?"

"Want to be a suspect?"

Cree shrugged. She took a sip, smiling over the glass. "I'm not the type that is ever suspicious of anything, right?"

Back then, she had suspected everyone of everything. I met her in band. Her way of hitting on me? Getting me to join the fencing team. Odd way to show affection—stabbing me with a sword—but whatever.

Turns out, you'd be surprised how many band kids fenced, or how many fencers played an instrument. Both need rhythm and timing. The difference is in fencing, you're trying to find an opening to finish, and in music you're trying to create one to keep going. Cree tried to keep both going. She wanted to play with her food as much as possible before she ate it.

I needed to stick to the topic. "You know Jazzy Jacob?"

"Yep. Nice guy." Her eyes grew wide. "Did something happen to him?"

"Yep," I replied. "Murdered. Thrown in the dumpster right outside here. Big lipstick scrawled across his chest that said 'DISCORD KILLS.'"

Her face tightened, and the joy drained from it. No reason Whimsy needed to die. I could kill it on my own. Cree went through a range of thoughts, her lips trembling and eyes flitting about. Processing. Then she settled back into avoidance.

"You don't suspect me of doing it?" she asked.

I smiled back at her. "No, hon. That lipstick was plum. No. Crimson Midnight? Something like that. I don't know. I've never seen lipstick on you that wasn't bronze." She gave me an uncomfortable smile back. Most people can't maintain their sense of humor when discussing dead people they knew. They prefer to feel things. "Anyway, when'd you see Jacob last?"

"Couple nights ago." Cree looked away. "He wrote a review of Reed Holloway, who was here that night. I got the night off just to sit in the audience."

"With Riff, I presume."

She clenched her jaw. "Is that an official Conservatory question?"

"Nah, that one's your business. Did Reed Holloway talk to Jacob?"

"I don't know, Dekk. I don't keep track of the social doings of band members." Some life returned to her. "It's really hard, you know. They're a weird group. So I can't possibly keep up with it."

"Yeah." I glanced over at the futon. "You might have been busy."

She smacked me on the shoulder, but it was a playful move.

"Do you know whether Holloway had a reaction to that review?"

She took another sip and poured some more. "No, but I imagine he did, wouldn't you? And he's a little cuckoo."

"Maybe. But I haven't been able to write music for a while now."

Cree set the glass down. "Really?" Her eyes narrowed, and she leaned forward. "How long has that been?"

"I don't know," I said. "Feels like forever."

She leaned back and nodded slowly. "Interesting."

"Frustrating."

"You're not the only one I know that's been having problems. Creating things." Cree bobbed her head in answer to her internal dialogue. "That was part of the whole problem with

Reed's performance. Jacob thought it was kind of flat." She paused. "Not flat in a musical way, just no life."

"Yeah, I saw that. When did you first notice it?" I leaned forward. "The pattern, I mean."

Cree thought about it. "Maybe three weeks ago? Reed was the first one that really stood out."

"Three weeks." What was the connection? The Guardian of Whimsy was murdered yesterday. Why three weeks? "Anyone else you haven't mentioned?"

"Jacob was on a real tear for a couple of weeks there. He ripped into Ruby Blue. Her voice sounded too shrill." Cree took another sip. "And he commented in another column about Honey Lane, saying that for someone so dressed to please the crowd and so sultry, she ought to smoke another carton of cigarettes to get close to what she was aiming at."

"Not nice."

"Yeah, not nice." Cree chuckled. "Not completely untrue. Honey was a mess that night. I don't remember ever seeing her that bad. I was playing with her. Riff, too, and we just couldn't keep up. She was changing the tempo. Going flat. No honey in that voice." She leaned closer to me. "I swear to God, every song she picked was in a minor key, even the ones that weren't."

"Yeah? Well, we all have our moments."

Cree sighed. "You know, as I said, there's been a lot of them." After a moment of silence, she continued. "Slide Donovan was in here last week. She played trombone like the slide wouldn't go up all the way, missing half the notes. It was even noticeable to people who didn't know the music."

"She's as straight as they come." I ran the picture of her through my head. "And not the type to be drinking anything."

"Then there was Ivory Fontaine a couple nights later." She grimaced at me. "I know you don't like him."

"I like him fine."

Jasper Fontaine, aka Ivory Fontaine, was that old-school kind of piano player. Always wore a suit jacket and a tie that was always loose. He smoked with an ashtray right on the piano and wore a fedora tipped back. Jasper—who hated that name—usually had a whiskey sitting on the piano. The man was a walking stereotype. And I didn't know why anyone thought his gravelly, nasty voice was worth listening to.

"You might have wanted to see him that night." Cree shook her head. "He was sitting up straight, polished, and his voice almost purring. But he was singing a different song than he was playing."

"Huh." I tried to imagine it. "That's a lot of people having trouble all at once." I pulled out my notebook. "These are all regular performers here?"

"Most of them, yeah. You know Honey and Ruby. Why?"

"Jacob reviewed any of the others? Besides Reed and Honey?"

Cree frowned. "He did a piece on Slide about a month ago. Before things went south. It was actually pretty complimentary. You know Slide."

"And Ivory?"

"Jacob wouldn't touch Ivory. Said reviewing him would be like reviewing a museum exhibit—historically interesting but not exactly news."

Cree traced her finger around the rim of her glass. "I'm surprised that the Conservatory sent you over here. Jacob wasn't magical, was he?"

"No, no, no. He wasn't." I scratched my head and frowned. "I originally went over to see Felix."

She didn't respond right away.

"Been a long time."

"Back then was when you were cute and adorable." She laughed. "Although Felix didn't think so when you kicked him out of the dorm."

I smiled back. "Yeah, well, sometimes a guy's gotta play."

"Uh-huh." She nodded with a smile.

"Well, Felix is dead."

"Oh." She looked concerned for a moment; then she leaned forward and grabbed my hand. She was very gentle, her hands soft, like she put lotion on them constantly. "I'm sorry."

"It's all right." I shook my head. "I hadn't seen him since he ran off to Juilliard."

"You were salty about that one," she said.

"Turns out, after Juilliard, he came back." I rubbed my chin. "He showed me up and went to Juilliard. Then he came back, and he showed me up again."

"What does that mean?"

I sighed. I wouldn't have taken the job. "He became the Guardian of Whimsy."

"The what?" Cree asked.

"The Guardian of Whimsy."

"What does a Guardian of Whimsy do?" she asked.

"It's a Conservatory thing."

Cree shook her head. "Oh yes, your secret little club, and I don't know the handshake to get in and have the discussion."

"All right," I said. "All the Virtues have a Guardian. There are multiple guardians. Whimsy's one of them."

"You knew he was this Guardian of Whimsy?"

"No, I didn't know until I was told." I glanced at the door. "While looking at his dead body."

"Felix and Jacob in one night?"

"Yep. That's the case." Our eyes met. Something in her made my eyes water for a moment before determination beat it back. "Jacob here last night?"

"Yeah."

I knew that, but you have to softball them to check on the truth. Truth. Another one of the damn Guardians. "Know when?"

"Oddly, Dekk, I don't clock people in and out for your convenience. But we were setting up for the second show, so nineish?"

"How long?"

"I don't know. I don't keep track of music critics."

"Was he there when the second show started?"

"No idea, Dekk. We were full. Did he kill Felix?"

"And then himself? No."

Cree remained silent for a long moment. I didn't know whether it was for her to think about Felix or me. "What happens when the Guardian of Whimsy dies?"

I stared at her. "I suppose composers can't write. Singers are flat. And trombone slides don't move. Not important." I should have knocked on wood.

Cree's face danced through a range of feelings. I stood. I kissed her on the cheek; then I drew my thumb across it. "And apparently some girls are monotone."

Cree glanced down at her jacket and her blouse. "Not related," she said. "Riff doesn't like my usual style."

"Maybe Riff's monotone."

"You can hope," she said, shoving me.

"Yeah? You know what the Russians say?"

"Drink your tea and don't sit by the window?"

She shoved me again, this time toward the door. "Hope dies last."

The copper in her curls caught the light as she shoved me again. I'd seen that copper shimmer in firelight before, twenty years ago. The last night of the Eleven War. The three of us standing outside Harmony Hall.

"You ever think about that night?" I asked.

Her smile faded. "Which night?"

"You know which one."

"I try not to." She turned away. "We all try not to."

"Yeah. Me, too."

CHAPTER 7
SECOND INTENTION

CREE'S WORDS kept circling back. Three weeks ago. Reed was the first one that stood out.

Three weeks.

The piano was universally flat. The chaos in that apartment. I'd looked, but I hadn't seen. Which meant I needed to look again.

The problem: Felix's apartment was still a crime scene. Dash would be pissed if I contaminated his crime scene. Couldn't be any worse than all the sunflower seeds littering the place.

I had agreed in principle to stay away. I always did. Lying to cops is easy. Lying to yourself about why you're doing it is harder.

It was after ten. Late enough that neighbors were asleep, early enough that drunks hadn't stumbled home yet. The brick street was empty, lit by streetlamps that cast more shadow than light.

I approached from the alley side, ossia case slung across my back. If anyone asked, I'd claim I was visiting a neighbor. Or walking home from busking in the Short North.

The wooden stairs groaned with each step, announcing my trespass to anyone listening. No one was.

The yellow tape was still up. I ducked under it. The door wasn't locked. Why would it be? Crime scene was processed, apartment secured. Just yellow tape keeping out the honest people.

I wasn't feeling honest.

Besides, I knew how to pick a lock harmonically.

Inside, the apartment felt different in the darkness. During my first visit, others filled the space. Dash's sunflower seeds. Sonny's ice-queen presence. Mixolydian hissing from the piano.

Now: silence. Empty. Haunted by what had happened here.

The apartment felt like our old camp dorm room, the one we'd shared by mistake at band camp right before our freshman year. Same creative chaos. Same sense that the disorder was a system only Felix understood.

He'd taught me his musical puzzle games in that room. Twenty years later, I was standing in his last puzzle, trying to solve it.

The piano sat against the wall, fallboard closed, keys hidden. Sheet music still scattered on top. Sonata Allegra in G still in the neat pile I'd made.

I walked to the dining room table pushed against the wall. Books stacked high. Candles melted down. Sticky notes. Same as before. I moved the books aside. Music theory. Harmonic analysis, orchestration, counterpoint. Standard stuff for a composer.

Except.

I pulled out my ossia and played a soft D and felt the room's resonance without interference from others or lingering resonance from the body.

The cat jumped into my lap. "Go away." I gave it a nudge, but the cat wrapped four of the six paws around my hand and playfully bit. "Not the time."

I plucked the note again, and the cat shook her head as if I had hit a sour note. Interesting. Watching the cat, I danced around the D. D-sharp. C. Nope. D. Then chord tones: D major, D minor. No reaction until a D minor flat 5.

The harmonics of the chord hung in the air, prompting Mixy to shake her head as if it were painful. Something tugged at the back of my mind. So long ago. Felix and I used to ... what was it? Some game we played with intervals. Dissonant chords. He hated them. Said they made his teeth hurt.

The cat shook her head again at the chord. Maybe cats just hated that interval, too. Or maybe she'd spent enough time around Felix to pick up his aversions.

Mixy jumped off me and started toward the piano. Halfway there, she stopped and meowed at me.

"All right, dammit. I'll see if I can find something to feed you."

The cat took a couple more steps to the piano and meowed again. I was about to deliver some witty commentary that the cat wouldn't understand when I noticed that she wasn't bitching about food.

She clawed at the bottom side of the piano, trying to get back inside. The wood wasn't of one uniform piece. There was a fine line showing that it had been patched at some point and made to blend in. After I'd messed with it for a minute, the panel pushed in, spring-loaded.

"That's how you did it," I said.

I reached inside and found a leather journal, the kind that looks like you're creating a prop for your D&D campaign. The pages were trying too hard to look ancient, and the binding was hand-sewn.

Felix still kept a journal. Mostly empty, but with a few notes. Journaling was on his should-do list. Felix's cramped handwriting rushed to get the words out as fast as possible.

I flipped to the last entry. Dated three weeks ago. Right when the creative malaise started.

*"I don't know why she's suddenly back in my life as if
nothing ever happened. Why? The talk is meaningless.
The interest feels artificial. Did she know something?"*

What an idiot. What a brave, stupid, idealistic idiot. I reached for Mixy and rubbed her head. "Good cat." I kept reading. Earlier entries painted the picture:

*"Sonny came by today. First time in six months. Said she
wanted to 'talk.' Drank tea together. Left when I told her
I didn't feel well. Not upset. Promised to return."*

The journal continued. Scrawled names of Honey Lane, Ruby Blue, Boomer Blake, Cree, and others. He knew them all. Councilor Foyle stuck out. He felt interrogated by her but gave no details. Checkmarks were next to Ruby and Honey. Cree and Felix were onto the same thing.

I flipped back through the journal. Most pages were blank. Then I found it.

One page, dated three months ago, had nothing but a hand-drawn staff of music. No words. Just notes: An A whole note, then an E whole note. Then a melody in quarter notes: D | E-flat | C | B-flat | E-flat | D.

My chest tightened. I knew this. Not the melody—the method. It was from Professor Copland's Music Theory II class, which only the true music nerds took during camp while most were marching in the hot sun on the football field. My mind longed for those days.

I remembered the first time. Felix had passed me sheet

music during a lecture on figured bass. Just notes, no words. I'd counted chromatic steps from D without thinking: F = D, F-sharp = E, C = K, C = …

"Dekker."

He'd grinned when I whispered it. "Musical cryptography. Renaissance spies used to hide messages in plainchant. We can do better—twelve chromatic tones instead of seven diatonic notes. Count from whatever root we pick."

"What's the point?"

"Private communication. Plus, it drives Copland insane when we're not paying attention."

We'd spent that semester encoding stupid jokes in the margins. *Your hair looks dumb. Meet me at Goodale Park. Copland's toupee is crooked.*

The cipher was simple: pick a root note, count chromatic steps from there. In the key of G: G = A, G-sharp = B, A = C, A-sharp = D … all twelve semitones covering most of the alphabet. Repeat the pattern an octave up for the rest. Numbers used the same system—G = 0, G-sharp = 1, A = 2 … up to E = 9.

We did it across the spectrum. Random keys. Usually no titles. Often in 13/7. Maybe not always. But a lot. It was about experimentation. After all, Bach had his coded signature: B-flat | A | C | B natural. Some real German nerd shit.

Twenty-plus years. I'd forgotten. But Felix hadn't. But now I remembered. We created that cipher on July 13.

Footsteps on the stairs.

I froze.

The footsteps stopped outside the door. A key rattled in the lock.

Shit.

I moved quickly, quietly, toward the kitchen, taking the ossia with me. No back exit from this apartment. Only the front door, where someone was currently entering.

The door opened. Light from the hallway spilled in.

"—sure this is necessary?" A woman's voice. Not Sonny. Younger.

"Completely sure." A man. Deep voice. DHR tone. "She said someone was snooping around. We need to lay down the … deception spell, I think they called it."

I pressed against the kitchen wall, barely breathing. My ossia case would be visible if they turned on the lights.

"How does this work?" the woman asked.

"It's like a music box. Wind it up, and it dilutes the magical whatever."

"Do you believe that?"

"I believe cold, hard cash, so who cares?"

They were cleaning the scene. Removing evidence. Not the kind Dash would find. The kind I would. Or those like me.

I needed to leave. Now. But they were between me and the door.

I played three notes on the ossia with my hand clamped down on the sound board—barely audible, but lingering. The curtains near the window fluttered. Loudly.

"What was that?" The woman turned toward the window.

"Cat, probably. They said there was one. Doesn't like people. Check the bedroom."

While they moved deeper into the apartment, I slipped toward the door. Moved quick, quiet, decades of fencing foot-work keeping me silent.

I was through the door, under the tape, down the stairs before they realized anyone had been there.

Outside, I didn't stop until I was three blocks away. Killing Whimsy had a lot of participants.

CHAPTER 8
THE EXCHANGE

THE NEXT MORNING, I stepped out for coffee at one of downtown's endless redbrick buildings on Fourth with oversize windows, exposed ductwork, and concrete floors. When it was busy the acoustics could drive you mad. But it was a straight shot from my apartment, so before coffee, convenience overcame sound quality.

Cree got me thinking. Columbus had always felt insular, cut off from the coasts. Flyover country. The kind of city that didn't make national news unless something burned down, or the Buckeyes blew a national championship. But lately it felt heavier than usual as if someone had transposed the whole town down a half step. Everything in minor keys, melancholy undertones I couldn't quite name.

After hearing about all the problems at the Hedgehog, I was disappointed in myself. I'd been composing less, feeling that creative drag, and hadn't recognized it as a symptom of something bigger. Reading the patterns was supposed to be my job. Well, part of it. The other parts were lore keeper, investigator, and researcher. But I'd missed the signs even while they were happening to me.

But today I planned on doing something unusual and against my better nature. I left my ossia at home. Walking into DHR headquarters with an ossia seemed like asking for trouble. Instead, I had a small wooden piccolo in my pocket, just in case. The two pieces of the instrument were easier to tote around and gave off fewer bard vibes.

I'd barely finished two sips of coffee when Hoagy plopped down in the seat across from me.

"How'd you find me?" I asked.

"Conservatory said they had a good guess."

That should have been a sign for the paranoia radar to go off in my head, but I hadn't had my coffee yet. "You didn't ask for a transfer?"

"Not yet." He smiled with more courage than he'd shown the day before. Maybe seeing a couple of corpses builds character. "I considered the repair shop since I'm good with my hands and archivist, which seems kinda boring."

"Uh-huh. Well, I've got a boring job today, too. I'm headed to the DHR."

"They're the bad guys."

"We are to them."

"Great. We driving?"

I sipped my coffee. "How far away is the DHR?"

"Walking distance?"

"True."

The Conservatory hid underground beneath Italianate arches and ornate stonework. DHR sat downtown in a brutalist concrete tower, all gray angles and small windows, like someone built a filing cabinet forty stories tall.

After entering the building, I walked through the security scan. I had to pull out the piccolo. So it wasn't going to be a mystery that I brought a musical instrument. The security guards laughed at me. But that's okay. They didn't know. Hoagy made a quick comment about switching instruments, which I ignored.

The Department of Harmonic Regulation was the kind of place where they'd file a report in triplicate before letting you sneeze in B-flat. I walked past a motivational poster that read "Harmonic Stability Through Regulated Expression." With effort, I tried not to let my cynicism show. The last thing I needed was some bureaucrat flagging me as harmonically unfit for duty.

I approached the information counter—gray marble, perfectly square—with Hoagy trailing behind me, eager for whatever came next. Four employees staffed it, two men and two women, all severe-looking in their muted colors and identical short haircuts. Square, too, in their own way.

The receptionist looked up at me with a smile so regulated I wasn't sure she remembered what genuine happiness felt like.

"How may I help you today?" Her voice had that training-manual brightness, curiosity processed through a Proper Harmonic Resonance in the Workplace seminar until it lost all its syncopation.

I leaned against the counter. "I'd like to see one of your DHR representatives."

"Who?" the man beside her asked.

"Actually, I don't remember her last name." I thought hard about it. Dash had told me. "First name's Sonny. Tall, blond, looks like she stepped out of a Renaissance fountain." I gestured with my hand to show her height with the heels.

The man grunted. "Sonny Mordent, one moment."

The receptionist resumed clacking away at her keyboard with her excessively long nails.

The man picked up a phone from the desk behind him. He was describing me to whoever was on the other end.

The man glanced at me. "Do you have an appointment?"

I beamed back at him. "No. I just popped in. Sonny and I are working on the same case. So I'd like to ask her a couple of questions. And maybe give her some information."

The attendant returned to the phone.

After a minute, he sighed. "I'll need you to fill out form DHR-14B in triplicate."

"What does that form do?" I asked.

"DHR-14B is a formal request for an audience with regulatory personnel. Three-to-five-day response time. It has a fee of forty-seven fifty."

"Better call Sonny back." I pointed to the phone. "She won't want to wait three to five days. And neither do I."

All four attendants were staring at me now. Gesturing toward the phone, I asked, "Want me to show you how to push the buttons?"

He picked up the phone to dial. The man frowned, spent a couple of minutes bobbing his head. "Yes, ma'am." He turned to face me. "Ms. Mordent will see you now."

"Thank you."

"Forty-seven fifty."

I paid him the forty-seven fifty with minimal grumbling, then scribbled my way through the form while mentally composing an invoice for Armando: form DHR-14B processing the forty-seven fifty. Note: Dekker Kohl is not your personal secretary, your errand boy, or your mother. If the Conservatory wants to play bureaucratic footsie with the DHR, they can pay for their own dancing shoes.

"Seventh floor, 745," the man said.

I gave him a curt nod and headed toward the elevator bank, all dull silver that didn't even try to reflect anything. The kid and I stood in the elevator with a dozen people, no one saying a word. Everyone stared straight ahead, not willing to be brave enough to breathe.

We arrived on the seventh floor, saw a sign pointing the direction, and headed down to the office of Sonny Mordent.

"Let me do the talking," I said. "Just listen. Make notes. Whatever. But no ideas."

Inside, there was a waiting room. I hoped she wasn't like a doctor.

A woman sat at a desk behind a sliding glass window. I announced myself and was told to sit down. After forty-five minutes, the receptionist led us down the hall to an office with slat walls with black backing. The door was made to look like it was a hidden door, although it wasn't that well hidden.

The receptionist opened the door, gestured for us to enter, and announced me. Sonny sat with her back to the door, shoulders shaking slightly. An old photograph of her and Felix sat on her desk, showing happier times. She wiped her eyes and slipped the photo into her drawer when she heard my footsteps, the timing just a little too perfect. But then that's the only way to score a perfect touch—perfect timing.

White today. Mourning period over, at least publicly. Two days seemed fast, but DHR probably had regulations about appropriate grief timelines.

Sonny turned away and stared out the skinny window with her hands on her hips, observing the city. There wasn't much to see from the seventh floor, but whatever.

"You should set an appointment, Mr. Kohl." Sonny's voice was flat.

I shrugged. "I like to be a free spirit."

Sonny turned and faced me. "The rest of the world doesn't like that."

She pointed to the black, silver-trimmed chair across from her glass table desk for me to sit.

I did so. Hoagy stood close to the door, hoping for a quick exit, I'd guess.

She sat with parade-ground posture: spine straight, knees together, hands folded with thumbs interlocked. The chair had a backrest, but she'd never use it.

Shoulders were back. Her chin was high. And she waited.

Leaning back in my chair, I slouched and looked around the room. "Nice office." I didn't mean it.

I spun the chair back and leaned forward, crossing my arms on the glass top. "Look," I began, "I think we got off on the wrong foot. The Conservatory sent me to get ahead of you yesterday. DHR and the Conservatory have some issues."

"Yes." Sonny's face may as well have been carved in granite. "The Conservatory runs rampant and needs to be, let's say, cautious with their abilities."

I nodded. "I don't disagree, and you'll find that even though I work for the Conservatory, it is just a job."

Sonny didn't react.

I pushed forward. "Okay, look, I don't care about the DHR." I shook my head. "Nor do I care about the long history between the two organizations."

Sonny's brow furrowed. "Did you fight in the war, Mr. Kohl?"

Well, that was gonna go right to the heart of it, wasn't it? I pushed my left hand into the table, willing it to stay. "I guess you could say I was part of it." I needed to be careful in how I approached the subject. "But I didn't fight directly. It shouldn't come as a surprise to you as a music student that I would not be happy with the attempt to regulate those like me."

Sonny grimaced. "That's okay, Mr. Kohl. I don't have any issues with musicians, obviously, since I married one. I don't even particularly have an issue with the magical ones." She tipped her head at me conspiratorially. "Again, I married one." She resumed her proper posture. "The issue is that when it is allowed to go out of control, it causes problems, and it doesn't just cause problems for you. It causes problems for everybody. That was, after all, the whole reason for the war."

She didn't quite have her story straight. The Compression-ists wanted more control than what she let on. But then, when the war broke out as Felix, Cree, and I were about to graduate, Sonny still had a couple of years to go. So her memory of it could be just as bad as mine, or Felix's. Or Cree's.

"It's entirely possible," I began, "that we both had the wrong idea of the war."

Another plastic smile. "The DHR had its view it needed to maintain, just as the Conservatory was going to push its agenda."

I crossed my arms and leaned back. "I didn't come here to reminisce about the war. There'll be time for that later. The world seems to want one now."

"You have something that can help me?" she asked.

"Yes. Seems that Jazzy Jacob's reviews caused some problems."

"I'm aware of that." Sonny's eyes narrowed; then her eyebrows rose as an idea formed. "You don't mean to suggest that Felix killed himself after killing this Jazzy Jacob, do you?"

"No." I hesitated. Wow. Leave the detective work to the professionals. "I don't think he would do that."

"He did write a bad review of my husband."

Sonny stood and walked over to a charcoal table against the wall. The table had a small tray with a water glass, a box of tissues, some hand lotion, and a stack of papers. She returned with a stapled stack of papers and threw them in front of me. It was Jazzy Jacob's Substack column, the one that criticized Felix Cantabile.

I nodded.

She straightened the dress and sat back down, knees locked again, hands on the table. Sonny sighed, then turned and faced the exterior windows.

Her voice softened. "I realize it is difficult for you to understand," she began, "that a man like Felix would marry someone like me."

I remained silent.

"I used to be musical myself." She sounded as if she were defending herself. "I never quite had the talent Felix had."

She had mentioned that before. Why was she trying to convince me? Or herself?

Sonny continued. "At some point, I realized that music would not be my thing. And that I needed to stick to something more practical." For the first time, she leaned back in her chair, putting her arms on the armrests. "So I ended up in school for business administration. I imagine I was there a bit after you two graduated. But I had never met Felix or even heard of him at the time. Then I got hired at DHR."

She spun back to me. "Like you, Mr. Kohl, I didn't choose DHR because I believed in their mission. In fact, I was already dating Felix when I got this job." Sonny laughed to herself. "Felix wasn't happy about it. But being a musician, I'm sure you understand that he also couldn't earn enough for the both of us. So somebody had to do something."

"Yeah, it's a rough way to go," I said.

"I didn't mind his playing in the clubs late at night. Felix was doing what he loved. I also didn't care that DHR was trying to keep musicians in check." Sonny leaned back again, relaxed. "But shortly after we broke up"—she said it like they were boyfriend and girlfriend that had a spat rather than a marriage falling apart—"I realized ..." Her gaze shifted to some imaginary place. "No, I learned some things that made it very clear that DHR, while like any government institution, may seem to run amok, its core mission has the right idea." She nodded, although the gesture seemed an internal reflection. "And I think that at some point, you may realize, perhaps even during this case, the truth." Her lips curved into a thin smile. This time at me. The smile appeared genuine. "Also, I believe you'll find that creativity under constraint is far better than creativity run amok."

Sonny wasn't wrong. Deadlines. Budgets. All those things

forced creative souls into cubbyholes that they had to fight their way out of. But they usually ended up with a better product, even though we all wanted to freewheel it.

"I made some progress," I said. "Consider this a peace offering."

Sonny's eyes lit up. "What did you discover?"

"First, I stopped by the Twelve-Tone Spin Zone to ask about Billie from the business card. There was no Billie. The two kids working the place were not sure Billie would even be in this week. So I think it's safe to say that Billie probably didn't kill Felix or Jacob."

Sonny pursed her lips. "Unless Billie took time off to cover his crimes. Perhaps that is who we're looking for."

"Possible." I frowned. "But that isn't what I felt when I read the room." Sonny opted not to comment on how I read the room. "I visited the jazz club and talked to some people there." She waited for the story to progress, with no signs of impatience. "No offense, Sonny. May I call you Sonny?"

"Sure," she said. "Everybody does, Mr. Kohl."

"Dekker." I nodded. "Like I said. No offense, but those types are gonna talk to me before they'll talk to you."

"None taken, Mr. Kohl. I understand. They see me as the enemy."

"Don't worry," I replied. "They see the cops the same way."

"What did you discover?"

"Well, I haven't gotten us anywhere yet." I shifted in my seat. "But I discovered that there are numerous creatives who are struggling right now."

"Like a mass drain on creativity." Sonny might as well have been discussing an autopsy. "I know your theories and the Conservatory theories on what happens when Whimsy dies."

"Not my theories." I held up my hands. "You don't believe in Whimsy?"

"I used to be whimsical," Sonny muttered. "When I was with

Felix. His music was so light and bouncy and exciting. And he was so out there in personality that for a while, yes, I felt it. It's like a drug."

I saw her attempt to extend four more vertebrae. Maybe for her birthday, I'd get her a stick to lash to her back.

Sonny closed her eyes. "But like I told you, eventually we must all find reality and accept the fairy tales that don't exist from when we were children." She opened her eyes and looked at me, gently, not accusing. "We must accept that the whimsical strains of your instrument are not the product of magic but of trained mathematics." Then she added, "I am aware that the creatives are in a slump. And I will tell you we have been trying to treat some of them."

"What do you mean by treat?" My eyebrows rose.

Sonny stood. "How about if I just show you?"

We stood. She glanced at Hoagy. "I'm not sure your assistant will want to see what the Conservatory indoctrination does to people. Or more specifically, the removal of it."

I glanced back at the kid. He seemed uncertain. "How bad can it be? Three bodies instead of two on his first day?"

"A wonder they give you an assistant," she said, heading to the door.

"True."

We exited her office. Sonny informed the receptionist that we were going to go to the studio, which was just another part of the building a floor up.

The studio was in the center of the building, so there were no windows. Sonny led me into a control room facing a sound room with a lot of acoustic treatment. We stood behind a piece of glass, looking into the room.

Behind the glass, a young woman, perhaps thirty, sat in a wooden chair and played a violin. Her performance was divine; her delicate fingers danced across the strings. I almost wept. Sonny's face softened, too. Hoagy watched us.

"Who's she?" I asked.

"Vittoria Dolcenote." Sonny explained, "This room is magically isolated. And you see she is very creative."

"Whose piece is she playing?"

Sonny smiled. "She's making it up." Her eyes were still smiling as she turned to me. "I know you don't believe me, Mr. Kohl. So let's go."

Sonny opened the door to the studio. Miss Dolcenote stopped playing. She stood and tipped her head forward.

"Vittoria," Sonny said, her voice bright. "This is Mr. Kohl. He is a musical expert." Sonny nodded to me. "He has some questions about your music."

"Yes, yes." Vittoria bobbed her head.

"Your playing is beautiful," I said. "Where did you learn it?"

"I was making it up," she said.

"Where did you go to school?"

"I didn't. I learned to play very young from my mom and then from there, I studied on my own, but I didn't completely become proficient at it until I got here."

My eyes narrowed at Sonny.

"She came six weeks ago," Sonny said.

"Yes," Vittoria agreed. "Has it been six weeks? I have been so creative. I have never been like this in my life. It is fantastic."

"That's great. Are you writing it down?"

She shook her head. "No, no, no, no. I will remember. It is so fantastic."

Sonny wasn't kidding about the room. I could feel it. It was like someone had draped a heavy blanket over me, muffling everything. I glanced at Hoagy. He wouldn't be able to express what he felt, but I could tell that he did.

"Can I examine her?" I asked Sonny. "Read her signature?"

Sonny laughed. "Of course, Mr. Kohl. Transparency is important."

I assembled my piccolo and attempted to attune to Vittoria.

She put her hands over her ears, as did the others. I was trying an F major riff, but it sounded out of tune. Then I modulated to E-flat. Same thing. Perhaps it even sounded identical to the F.

My head was throbbing. The room wasn't just suppressing magic. Something else pushed back against my attunement. Like trying to read harmonics through static. Or through something that was feeding on them.

I stepped out of the room.

Sonny smiled at Vittoria. "Dear, let's leave the violin here. I think it's time that you had lunch. Have you done that?"

"No, Miss Mordent, I haven't."

"Okay, then lunch it is."

Vittoria packed her violin with great care, left it on the chair, and then followed us out the door. Once back in the control room, Sonny placed her hand on the violinist's shoulder. "There's some blank sheet music over there." She pointed to the table behind the control panel. "I think Mr. Kohl would like you to write down a bit of the melody you were playing."

"Oh yes, of course," Vittoria said.

She walked to the table, grabbed a pencil, drew clefs all the way down the page, and then stopped.

"What's wrong?" Sonny asked, closing the studio door.

Vittoria turned, and her eyes lowered. "I'm sorry, ma'am. I don't remember what exactly I played."

Sonny smiled again. "That's okay. You can work on it after lunch. Mr. Kohl will be around."

"Oh, thank you, sir, thank you."

The fog in my brain was lifting, so I played a quick three notes. F major. Clean. And then I felt it. Vittoria felt harmonically balanced. Almost autotuned without the T-Pain distortion.

"Wait," I said. "Vittoria, can you play something for me?"
"Like what?"
I glanced at Sonny, who had crossed her arms and frowned.
"You choose," I said.

Hoagy darted into the studio and grabbed the violin case.

Vittoria pulled out the instrument and played Wieniawski's *Scherzo-Tarantelle*. So she was talented, but she lost her creation. I commended her playing and thanked her while she packed up.

Vittoria left the room and headed toward lunch, wherever that was.

Wait. I played F major again, clearer now that I was out of that room. Vittoria's signature felt … wrong. Not T-Pain auto-tuned with that digital shimmer. More like Milli Vanilli lip-syncing someone else's performance. She wasn't creating the music. She was channeling it.

But channeling what? The room supposedly suppressed all magical influence. If removing the Conservatory's "interference" freed her natural creativity like Sonny claimed, Vittoria should still be able to create outside the room—just without magical enhancement. Instead, she couldn't remember a single note. That wasn't freedom. That was dependence on something she could only access in that dampened room.

Where was her "creativity" coming from?

"You see, Mr. Kohl," Sonny began, "in the isolation room, where magic cannot exist, she was creative and wonderful, as you said, but out here, she's not."

"Okay," I said, "what is the point?"

"The point is that the harmonic resonance of the Conservatory is stifling her. Too much reliance on magic weakens you."

"That doesn't make any sense," I said. "If the Conservatory was stifling her, removing its influence should free her own creativity. She should still be able to play outside the room—just without the magical boost. But she can't remember anything. She's not free. She's dependent on whatever's in that room."

"Unless it was always planned to be that way," she said. "And now, Mr. Kohl, my husband is dead." She inhaled deeply. "I don't really care about that critic. But my husband—who

I think you'd agree had genuine talent—has been silenced permanently. And that would be the real problem."

Sonny's explanation was tidy. Too tidy. The dampening field suppressed magic—but that should have freed Vittoria's natural abilities, not created dependence on the room itself. Unless she wasn't accessing her own creativity at all. Unless the room wasn't removing something harmful but providing something external.

But providing what? And from where?

Whimsy fleeing from the world made the DHR propaganda seem more real. But this felt like something else. Something they wanted me to misunderstand.

I frowned. "So you don't think that there's a connection between his death and the people who have been losing their creativity?"

"No," she said. "He is a victim of it. How many people have lost their creativity?"

"So far that I know of, eight. I'm sure there are more. Those are just the ones I discovered yesterday."

"Mm-hmm. And I can tell you a couple of others." She hesitated. "There's Eric Mueller. He's a drummer. He also has this problem. We just started him on audio therapy. Much how we did with Vittoria." Sonny saw I wasn't planning to interrupt, so she continued. "There's Joan Hernandez, who is a songwriter, suffering from what she calls creative anxiety. She's currently in counseling with one of our specialists before she can go into the safe zone and begin resuming her arts. So, Mr. Kohl, ponder what your conservatory does." She smiled again. "In the meantime, you said you were here to help me?"

"Yes."

"What are the names of the people who were having creative blocks that Mr. Jazzy Jacob criticized? I'd like to get them help."

I rattled off the list. She'd get the names anyway. Jazzy Jacob's reviews were public, and DHR had files on every working musician in the city. At least this way I'd know who they were targeting for "treatment." She wrote them down on a blank sheet of music paper, folded it up, and held it between her fingers.

"Wait," I said. "I forgot one. Roland Tomasi. He took the review pretty hard."

She unfolded the paper and added the name. But Roland Tomasi didn't exist. One sliver of creativity remained in me, anyway.

"Thank you, Mr. Kohl. Is there anything else I can do for you?"

I nodded. "Yes. These rooms are fascinating. How'd you build them? I'm guessing you didn't hire Virtuosi architects."

She smiled at me. "No. I wouldn't trust the Conservatory to build something meant to suppress their own magic. Instead, we got a youth music teacher from before your war who wasn't tied into either side."

"Yeah? Who was that?"

"Dr. Phrygian. A brilliant man. He designed all the protocols and understands the danger from you all."

Phrygian. Unbelievable. I stared back into the empty studio. Something lingered in there. Almost forming into something, but a shadow instead.

I stared at the studio's dampening equipment. It looked eerily similar to what the Compressionists had used during the war. Same harmonic suppressors. Same gray efficiency.

"You know," I said carefully, "I've seen rooms like this before. Twenty years ago. They called them 'reeducation centers' back then."

Sonny's expression didn't change. "The war ended with a compromise, Mr. Kohl. Sometimes the right ideas come from the wrong people."

"Or vice versa." I thought about Professor Copland hooked up to those machines, electrodes on his temples. The same four-bar phrase played over and over. Variation is chaos. Improvisation is dangerous.

"You weren't there," I said quietly. "You didn't see what they did to musicians in rooms like these."

"I saw the aftermath," Sonny replied, her voice sharp. "I saw what uncontrolled magic did to my family. To Felix. To everyone touched by it." She turned toward the glass. "Sometimes the cure requires uncomfortable medicine. Now, if you don't mind, I've got a meeting." Sonny led us out. "It would be my suggestion to you that you not bring up our conversation at the Conservatory."

"Of course not." My eyes met hers. "I came here without their knowing."

Sonny placed her hand on my arm. "I'll let you know when we start treatment on the names you gave me. You can see the outcome of your work. Perhaps there is hope for you."

I didn't tell her what had happened to Hope. The Russians were wrong. Hope doesn't die last. Sometimes it's first.

CHAPTER 9
THE BALCONY

WE'D LEFT the DHR building ten minutes before, but Phrygian's name kept circling my head. Hoagy stared at me like a dog waiting to be fed as we waited at the crosswalk.

"You haven't said a word," he muttered.

I nodded. "Right. Processing."

"About the woman with the violin? That was terrible."

"Yes, but no." I had been silent since we left Sonny's office, but not on account of the torture they were doing to the players. "I've got to go back."

After security, we were back at the information counter. "I'd like to see Dr. Phrygian."

The same man grumbled at me. "No appointment for that one, either?"

"Sorry."

"He's not much for phones," Hoagy added.

After a few calls, the man shrugged. "No one seems to know where he is."

"Did he come to work today?" I asked.

The man stared blankly at me. "You want me to call and see if anyone's seen him?"

I smiled. "How about I show you how to use that computer

on your desk to see if he logged in today? Clocked in? Whatever you do here."

"We are not permitted—"

"Fine," I began, "give Sonny Mordent a ring again. She seems like someone who wants you to bother her all the time."

One of the other receptionists looked at her companion, then me. "Dr. Phrygian is here today. He never leaves once he's here, so I'd check the cafeteria."

I thanked her and dragged the kid along.

"Why do we care about this guy?" Hoagy asked.

"One, he invented that room upstairs. Two, I used to know him, and it doesn't sit right with me."

The cafeteria was a carbon copy of hundreds of others in office buildings and hospitals. They'd recently renovated it to hide the 1980s, but you could still see it underneath. The smell of paint and soy burgers was strong.

My target sat in the far corner at a four-person table alone, eating a croissant and drinking coffee. I hadn't seen him in decades, but his features were still there. His sandy hair wasn't as full anymore. He appeared thinner than I remembered, though maybe that was just his ill-fitting jacket, shirt, and tie competing to see which had the best shade of pea green. He always had a sort of Spanish features that made him interesting. He still sported an oversize mustache hiding his upper lip, all white now. His chin had retreated some, and the once powerful man was withdrawn and stooped. He had a book open on the table while he used a fork to stab at the croissant.

"Hoagy, go have a Coke and a smile for a minute. I need to talk to the old man alone."

"Jeez." Hoagy wandered off to the food line.

The kid wasn't happy, but he didn't need my entire backstory. He was shadowing me until he picked a career path.

Once at the table, I gestured to the chair across from Phrygian. "May I?"

He looked up at me, brow furrowed. "Please." He didn't mean it, but I sat.

"You won't remember me, but I was your student many years ago."

Phrygian nodded. "I had decades of them. Long before you. So, no, I don't remember."

I extended my hand. "Dekker Kohl."

He shook my hand. "Still don't remember you." He sipped his coffee, hiding his expression.

Hoagy sat at a table with a drink and a giant chocolate chip cookie. He was probably blowing bubbles in his drink. His expression and Phrygian's agreed I was annoying.

"I was just upstairs with Sonny Mordent in one of your dampening chambers. Or are they compression chambers?"

Phrygian pointed his fork at me. "You may see me as an old man that you remember, but I'm not stupid. I was never a Compressionist. Nor did I participate in that silly war. You're barking up the wrong tree, Mr. Kohl. Compression would compress the sound to amplify it. My chambers dampen the external influence from the Virtuosi."

All right. Good response. "You call them something else?"

He sighed. "Resonance Isolation Studios. Although most of the staff calls them Null Rooms."

"The staff seems more honest."

"You're one of them, right?"

I leaned back in my chair and smiled. "Virtuosi? Yes."

"Well, you didn't learn that in my class."

"I did not."

Phrygian had finished his croissant. He placed the napkin on the plate and the fork on top. "If I have answered all your questions, I have work to do."

"Building more chambers?"

He pretended to sip the coffee, but the cup was empty. "DHR

won't want me discussing its plans with you. I'm sure you understand that."

We both stood. "I understand. But what I don't understand is how someone so inspirational to all of us would work for DHR, the very opposite of creative expression and art."

"Try losing a child to an uncontrolled magical accident. Here, I help people. Good day, Mr. Kohl."

This was not the man I remembered. "Did a Virtuoso cause her death?"

Phrygian squeezed his eyes shut. "They filled her head with crap, and then that critic broke her. After that ..." He didn't finish. Didn't need to.

"What critic?"

"Jacob something."

My stomach dropped. "Jazzy Jacob?"

Phrygian's silence was answer enough. I let it go for now, but the pieces were starting to connect.

I told Hoagy I needed some time to think, which was best done alone. The kid grumbled but accepted it. Besides, he still had a giant cookie to finish.

I walked home on autopilot, mind still stuck on Phrygian's cold eyes. When I arrived home, I made myself a sandwich and ate it over the sink. I tickled a couple of keys on the piano, considering writing something, then plopped down in my recliner. I wasn't sure that I had accomplished anything.

I pulled out my ossia and polished the wood. Until Cree had mentioned Dr. Phrygian, I hadn't thought about him for years. Then Sonny. Then the shell of the man I just met in the cafeteria.

In high school, six or seven years before the war, Phrygian had been an English lit teacher. He was also the head of the drama department with an outsize influence on music. Dr. Phrygian was an interesting character. The hair was longer then and more like a mop on his head. And his eyes had sparkled with enthusiasm.

He always wore a blazer with a full-size rubber chicken in the right pocket and rolled-up papers in the left. On Fridays, he wore a ratty green T-shirt with bullet holes from his Peace Corps days. We never knew if he was serious, but looking back, he was definitely messing with us.

Phrygian was a great guy. Most of the students hated him because he was tough, and he wouldn't take any shit from anybody. He made us do all kinds of theatrical things in English lit, acting out scenes, making up our own little skits and going up onstage in the auditorium to perform them.

I still remember the day that I heard him swear for the first time, delivering a tirade when some of the so-called cool kids mocked a boy who struggled to do his performance because of a speech impediment.

These days, a teacher like that would be fired on the spot with all that language flying at us, but then most of what he did in class would be unacceptable today.

One memory stuck with me all these years. We were reading *Romeo and Juliet*, as everyone must. Reading the play was such drudgery. Dr. Phrygian felt we should understand it and everything because the story was about a couple of teenagers in love.

Maybe, but it was hard to get past the language. The sword fights were interesting. But only two of us in the class enjoyed swordplay. Cree and I usually sat next to each other, cribbing each other's notes. We were sure that Dr. Phrygian knew, and he didn't care.

He was always very aware of the relationships going on in the room. If you got detention, which I got more than a few times, he sat you next to the person who would most annoy you. Or next to the girl you were crushing on, like this blonde, green-eyed girl, Heidi Wellington.

At sixteen, she was everything. Cree and I hadn't even gone

out on a date yet. I wasn't interested in her at that time. But in later years, I learned she had been interested in me then. That was the way it went. By the time I realized I was interested in Cree, she was already dating the drum major of the marching band and hanging out with the cool kids—well, as cool as a band kid could be.

We were reading *Romeo and Juliet,* and we were right at the part where Romeo has to give his speech to her on the balcony. Naturally, Dr. Phrygian had Heidi Wellington stand on top of her desk to play Juliet.

My face went blank.

Dr. Phrygian knew who to pick to do this. I would play Romeo against my will. I had my paperback book of the script. He made me kneel in front of her, staring up at her. Doing the whole Romeo nonsense. Because he believed the way for us to empathize with these teenagers was to experience it ourselves. To truly cement the feelings, I had to substitute the name.

> *But soft, what light through yonder window breaks?*
> *It is the East, and Heidi is the sun.*
> *Arise, fair sun, and kill the envious moon,*
> *Who is already sick and pale with grief …*

Reading poetry aloud was embarrassing at that age, but delivering that speech to Heidi was one of the most humiliating experiences of my life. But Phrygian was right. I understood Romeo's longing because I'd felt it. The words weren't dead anymore.

Even though all the students hated him, including Cree, I felt a connection with him. A kindred spirit. Though I wanted to kill him that day.

Shakespeare stopped becoming about the dead words and hard language and became about a genuine connection and longing. Phrygian also taught us that music mattered and authenticity was important.

Years later, in music school, when I was questioning whether I'd made the right choice, I bumped into him in a restaurant. He was waiting for a to-go order, sitting there, still in one of his jackets, still toting around the rubber chicken.

He remembered me.

Phrygian understood my creative impulses and was the only teacher supportive of artistic pursuits. Not even for a second did he push the idea that I needed to be a doctor, lawyer, architect, civil engineer, or whatever. Musician, composer, whatever one dreamed of, he supported everyone in the creative arts.

I fell asleep with memories swirling together—Phrygian, Felix, Cree—all younger, all smiling, all gone in different ways. All back to haunt me.

I woke up an hour later with a crick in my neck and Phrygian's words still echoing, "Try losing a child to an uncontrolled magical accident." If Phrygian blamed the Conservatory for his daughter's death, maybe that's where I'd find answers. And Jacob. The Archives would have records. Accident reports. Something that explained what turned an inspiring teacher into a man building magical dead rooms.

CHAPTER 10
THE ARCHIVES

THE WALK from my apartment to the Conservatory had done nothing to cool my temper. Sonny's horrid machine, the changes in Dr. Phrygian that were traitorous to the man I remembered.

Custode Monteverdi greeted me as I entered the Columbus Conservatory. "Good afternoon, Virtuoso Kohl. Your Novizio is in the library."

Damn that Armando. "Thanks."

Hoagy looked eager to see me, which I assumed was because I would alleviate the boredom, not from real excitement.

"I waited here, assuming you needed to go to the Archives."

I shook my head. "You know this isn't the Archives, right, kid?"

"Yeah, of course."

Yeah, he didn't. It was written all over his face. I led him away, and we headed down the long hall toward the actual Archives.

"Talk to Armando?" I asked.

"Yes. He told me some interesting things about you, the dead guy, the war, and that you fence. You can teach me that, right?"

"No." The kid looked dejected, so I modified my statement. "The thing about fencing and magic is that you have to train. Even the most naturally gifted have to study, plan, and learn to see and feel all the angles. You don't know what you want to do at the Conservatory yet. So let's focus on that. I fenced before I heard of the Conservatory."

I needed to get a better grip on what I was after. Felix was a Guardian. I was a Trovatore, a lore keeper. And I realized I hadn't lived up to my end of the bargain. I might have nodded off during those parts.

"Hoagy, the Archives are very important to those like me. So now's your chance to see what we really do." My eyes met the kid's. "Most of the job is boring, nonmagical stuff. No fortune and glory, kid."

"So you want to show me how to read dusty old books."

"Yep. Big part of the job. Writing articles and contributing, too."

We were already deep underground when the corridor opened into the grand hall, where large meetings happened. I never came. It was another we-think-we're-the-church thing.

The staircase to the right led down another level. Low ceilings, velvet ropes, and a dozen seats facing the crypt. Eleven prominent composers were buried there. Each had their own unique view of music.

A few people lingered in the crypt at all hours, all Conservatory members. I greeted them with whispered well-wishes, and Hoagy bobbed his head at them. Then I faced the main crypt.

I mumbled a few words and hand-conducted the conclusion of an imaginary symphony. Crossing yourself, but for magical musicians. As long as they weren't making me confess my musical sins to a choir, I was good.

At the side of the crypt was a service door that read "No Admittance." The sign was for lower-level members, Initiates, and for the rare researchers that got permission from the Council. But what it really did was lead to the Archives.

Since Hoagy was assigned to shadow me or spy on me, I assumed that it would be okay to take him in.

Behind that door was the kind of place where the walls, floor, and ceiling were white stone. Stone walls flanked the center aisle with arches every couple of feet. Dark, crystalline globes about a foot in diameter floated around the Archives, illuminating the place. They brightened and dimmed when you were near in some annoying color pretending to be daylight.

"How did you do that?" Hoagy whispered.

"It's magic."

"I know that." He rolled his eyes at me. "I mean, I thought you had to have an instrument."

"Instruments help focus the magic. It makes attunement easier. Experienced Virtuosi can do it without, but magic has a cost, kid." I stopped. "What instrument do you play?"

"Trombone."

I nodded. "That one's going to be fun to attune with. Hope you're never in close quarters."

"You don't like trombones?"

"I like them fine. The point is you practice, right? You perform sometimes? Can you do it endlessly?"

He frowned at me. "Of course not. People get tired."

"Right. You get tired, the notes might slip a little in pitch or timing. Multiply that by, I don't know, a dozen or two dozen. Could be dangerous."

His eyes wandered around, looking at nothing as he contemplated the whole thing. "How do you recover?"

"Breaks. But I'll tell you a secret I learned from Maestro Jin-Soo Park. Silence will help you recover faster. Music needs rests. You do, too." He seemed to understand. "Let's practice the silence part for a few minutes."

I didn't lie to the kid, but it was good for both of us to have some quiet.

Rows of bookshelves stretched behind the arches. Every manuscript ever found, hundreds of music theory tomes, a few crackpots trying to reinvent the wheel, and detailed accounts of the Eleven War. I'd avoided those. Figured if I wasn't mentioned, I wasn't missing much.

At the back was a glass room with fewer bookcases inside. No Static would ever be allowed in there. Inside was the repository of Musical Methodology for the Magical Arts. That one the Conservatory held most sacred. They called it the 3MA, because even the Conservatory drew the line at making people say "Repository of Musical Methodology for the Magical Arts" every time they needed a book.

A Static sat at a table near the glass room, flipping open a giant tome. Pretty. Intriguing. Long fingers. Nails unpolished. She found the page she wanted, put a pair of pince-nez glasses on, and read while dragging a finger down the page. Not impossible to find a Static here, but uncommon. She wore a silver badge with a photo, indicating a special level of permission. Someone close to Council level had vetted her.

She stopped and glanced at me. Our eyes met for a moment —intelligent, curious eyes behind those old-fashioned glasses. She tilted her head as if trying to place me, then returned to her reading.

I ducked between the bookshelves, but curiosity got the better of me. I circled around to see what had her so absorbed. From my new angle, I couldn't make out what she was reading as her hands slipped over the pages.

"What are we doing?" Hoagy whispered.

"Kid, go read a book."

She must have heard Hoagy, because she glanced up again. This time, instead of ducking away, I nodded politely. She responded by closing the tome, not hurriedly, but deliberately. She gathered her things, but left a stack of papers on the table—deliberately, from the way she glanced at them once before leaving.

As she passed my section on her way out, she paused just long enough to whisper, "Your son seems bright." Her voice belonged in jazz clubs after midnight.

My face remained rigid despite the urge to confront her. I was the old guy with a tagalong. Not the cool musician type anymore, if I ever was.

With a thin smile, she added, "Some research is better done in less … official locations."

"You've been following me," I said. "Playground. Spin Zone. Here."

"Paranoia is not healthy. You should see someone about that."

"Not the DHR."

"True."

Then she was gone, leaving me with the distinct impression that I'd just encountered someone who knew exactly why I was there.

No time to deal with her. I found Guardian records in Section G, Subsection VII. I sent Hoagy to find anything referencing Phrygian. My shadow joined me at the table.

"That woman you like left something behind," Hoagy said.

"I don't like her, I was trying to figure out who she was."

"Could have asked."

"Remember the part about silence?"

He dropped a stack of papers on top of the book in front of me. It was a printed stack of articles from the internet. The first was the article Jazzy Jacob wrote about Felix. Two months ago, Felix did a community event at Franklin Conservatory.

That conservatory was not like ours. It was a couple miles

east of downtown, mostly known as a botanical garden. But there were event spaces that weren't full of weeds. The only magic was the wonder the Statics felt walking through. I'd bet now the leaves were drooping as much as the people.

Anyway, Felix did an event for grade-schoolers, and Jacob was there to berate him for not being the best teacher on the planet. Something to file away in my brain for later.

The stack also had an article from three weeks ago called "The Silencing," which was a rundown about musicians not being like they used to be in the good old days. He concluded that it was getting worse on a massive scale. It was hard for him to find a good performer.

He ran down some of the same names I had ratted out to Sonny. Good. At least there was another source for her to have gotten the information.

As I flipped through the articles, I realized that while Jacob's articles were not complimentary, he had been documenting the decline, the failed creativity, etc. He didn't call it that, but it was a record. That made me wonder if he knew.

I could read the articles anytime. The important stuff was only in the Archives.

Hoagy had his own book. He exhaled and stared at me.

"What?"

"You wrote a whole article defending the ossia is not a lute thing?"

He slid the book to me. It was a more recent addition, and it did, indeed, have my article "On the Ossia: A Trovatore's Perspective." Proper byline. The whole nine yards. I didn't realize they had printed it.

"Accuracy in reporting," I said, trying not to smile. The kid frowned. "It's not a lute. Not a guitar. Not an oud. It's an ossia. An instrument with a distinct purpose and history. Construction methodology. Tonal characteristics. The confusion stems from surface-level visual similarities and lazy scholarship."

Hoagy's eyebrows climbed. "Dude, it's basically a lute, though, right?"

"No." I could hear my voice getting sharper. "The ossia has unique magically attuned construction, different string tension, and serves an entirely different harmonic function in Trovatore magic. Calling it a lute is like calling a trumpet a trombone just because they're both brass."

He flipped the pages in front of him. "Bro, it's four thousand words about why it's not a lute."

"Three thousand eight hundred," I muttered. "And it's a legitimate musicological concern."

"It's a lute."

"It's an ossia, and we're done with this conversation. You're looking for Dr. Phrygian."

We returned to the business at hand.

Four hundred years of records, all meticulously organized. Someone had been keeping score. Seven Guardians had died violently in all that time. The last one bought it in 1847. Either Guardians lived charmed lives, or someone worked overtime keeping them breathing.

Guardian of Joy — Elena Brightwater.
Murdered by her own brother in a fit of jealous rage.
City of Venice fell into three months of perpetual rain.
Successor appointed immediately, but Joy took twenty
 years to restore.

I slid the book to Hoagy and dug into the next record. That should keep him from discovering any other articles I wrote.

"Holy crap," Hoagy whispered, pointing at an entry. "Guardian of Knowledge was murdered in 476."

I leaned over to read the passage he'd found:

> *Guardian of Knowledge — Marcus [...] Corvinus.*
> *Murdered in 476 in Alexandria*
> *Perpetrator never identified.*
> *Succession failed. Knowledge dissipated.*
> *Result: The Dark Ages. Literacy collapsed across Europe*
>   *for three centuries. Virtue naturally regenerated circa*
>   *AD 800 through monastic preservation efforts and*
>   *immigration of Middle Eastern scholars who had not*
>   *experienced the "Dark Ages."*

"Wait." Hoagy's face had gone pale. "The actual Dark Ages happened because someone killed the Guardian of Knowledge?"

"According to this." I studied the sparse entry. "Three hundred years without a Guardian. Libraries burned. Scholarship nearly vanished. And they never caught whoever did it."

"That's terrifying."

"That's what happens when there's no succession plan and no emergency measures." I tapped the page. "Felix had been requesting succession planning for months. The Council kept saying no."

Hoagy stared at the entry. "So what you're saying is we're about to have three hundred years without Whimsy unless we figure something out in five days."

"More or less."

"Wait." Hoagy frowned, his finger still on the date. "AD 476? But the Conservatory wasn't founded until 1623, right? How were there Guardians before the Conservatory existed?"

"Good question." I flipped back through the records. "Guardians have existed for at least two thousand years, maybe longer. The Conservatory was founded *because* of disasters like this one."

"So Guardians used to just ... exist? Without any organization?"

"They still do. The Conservatory doesn't create Guardians—Virtues choose their own protectors. What the Conservatory does is provide structure. Training. Succession planning. Community support." I gestured at the ancient records. "Before 1623, Guardians were scattered. Isolated. When one died, it was chaos. The Dark Ages. The Great Silence of 1347."

"So the Conservatory exists to prevent—"

"Exactly. To make sure what happened to Knowledge doesn't happen again. To ensure that there's always a succession plan, always a backup." I met his eyes. "Which makes it even worse that they ignored Felix's requests. The whole point of this organization is preventing orphaned Virtues, and they let it happen anyway. Turns out bureaucracy has its own body count."

Hoagy was quiet for a moment, processing. "So, what happened to Guardians before the Conservatory? Who trained them?"

"Oral tradition. Master-apprentice relationships. Random chance. Some Guardians went their whole lives without knowing what they were. Others figured it out and did their best." I closed the ancient tome. "The Renaissance made organization possible. Music theory became formalized. Notation standardized. Virtuosi could finally communicate across distances, share knowledge. In 1623, a group of Guardians and master Virtuosi founded the Conservatory to ensure this knowledge wouldn't be lost again."

"And the DHR?"

"Oh, very late addition. Since the Eleven War. But there have been organizations like them. The mirror. Magic always draws detractors. They wanted regulation. We wanted preservation."

I shook my head. "Same old argument, different century. Inquisition. DHR." I threw up my hands and returned to the entries.

Each violent death in the records followed the same pattern: immediate environmental effects, a successor named within days, gradual restoration over months or years. But after 1623, a successor had always been ready—always trained, always prepared. The Conservatory's whole purpose was ensuring that readiness.

Until Felix.

That's when I found the anomaly, a handwritten note that I recognized as Armando's scrawl because he liked to loop his ascenders excessively high.

> *14 October Guardian Cantabile reports unusual fatigue.*
> *Recommend successor selection process begin early.*
> *Council vote: 4-3 against.*
> *Reasoning: Guardian appears physically healthy, with no*
>   *evidence of declining power.*
> *Request dismissed as anxiety. Further, he has only been*
>   *Guardian for nine years.*

Another note from two months ago:

> *Guardian Cantabile again requests succession planning.*
> *Reports strange dreams, sensation of "leaking."*
> *Council vote: 6-1 against.*
> *Fleurette notes: "Guardian appears more creative.*
> *Compositions show increased technical proficiency."*

An entry from three weeks ago made my blood run cold:

> *Guardian Cantabile collapsed during morning practice.*
> *Council agrees to begin successor evaluation process.*
> *First candidate interviews are scheduled for next month.*

They'd planned to look for a replacement next month.

I pulled up the succession protocols, scanning for the critical information. The process took six months minimum, requiring the current Guardian to consciously pass their power to a successor while both were alive. That plan was in the toilet.

My heart stopped at the final entry:

> *In cases where succession is not completed prior to*
> *a Guardian death, the virtue becomes "orphaned" and*
> *historical precedent suggests orphaned virtues dissi-*
> *pate entirely within seven days unless emergency*
> *measures are taken.*
> *See: The Great Silence of 1347 (Guardian of Harmony*
> *murdered, virtue lost for seventeen years until natu-*
> *rally regenerated).*

Seventeen years without Harmony. I did the math. The bubonic plague. The Hundred Years' War. The Little Ice Age. Fun stuff.

Wait. Seven days. That's how long an orphaned Virtue lasted before it dissipated. Felix died Thursday. Which meant I had five days to figure out what emergency measures looked like, or the world was about to learn what life without Whimsy felt like. It would go beyond Virtuosi and players and hit the Statics.

What would that world be like? Gray. And depressing. And full of PowerPoint presentations. More likely, they would continue to doom-scroll and not notice because the AI told them they were geniuses and doing a brilliant job.

I was still processing this when I found the medical files. Felix had been seeing Conservatory physicians for months. Fatigue, weight loss, what they'd called "spiritual drainage." But there was another file marked "External Consultation."

Hoagy pointed to a document.

The external consultation said:

> *Sonny Mordent, Department of Harmonic Regulation,*
> *has been consulted regarding Guardian Felix's condition.*
> *Ms. Mordent's expertise in magical medical conditions*
> *may provide insights our staff cannot. Dr. Viktor Melodius*
> *objected to her involvement.*

Sonny hadn't told me that. But why would she? We would agree on one thing, however: Dr. Melodius was a quack.

I grabbed everything I could carry and headed for the exit. Hoagy left his book on the table and raced to keep up.

Footsteps echoed from the main corridor. Multiple sets moving purposefully.

I killed the floating orbs in our section with a wave of my hand and grabbed Hoagy, pulling us both between two tall bookcases in Section F. We pressed against the cold stone wall. The remaining orbs deeper in the Archives still glowed, but we were in shadow now.

"How did you do that without music?" Hoagy whispered.

"There's a sensor inside. Not magic."

He frowned.

"It's a library, kid. You want everyone whistling Dixie in here?"

Three figures in Conservatory purple and gold robes swept past the aisle opening, heading deeper into the Archives. They thought they were alone.

"Kohl was the wrong one to send," one said. I couldn't place the voice. Above my pay grade.

"He's wandering off script." That voice I recognized. Lachlanna Foyle.

"The critic angle?"

"Following his nose like always. We knew what we were getting."

"And the Novizio complication?"

"Armando's mistake, not ours. But it might work in our favor."

"If we can control it. The next one's scheduled for—"

"Not here."

The first speaker continued. "We'll deal with it. Right now Inspector Rimsky is topside demanding answers and information both on Kohl and the Guardian."

"None of them follows orders," Foyle said. "Rimsky is supposed to be ensuring that the DHR woman is focused on the job and not her relationship. Perhaps feed Rimsky a bit to confuse things. Make him think she killed Felix."

"Yeah. Send him on a wild-goose chase," said another one.

They moved deeper into the Archives, voices fading.

I stayed frozen until I couldn't hear them anymore. Then I grabbed Hoagy's arm and headed for the exit, moving fast but quiet.

"Who were—"

"Not here," I whispered.

We made it to the crypt level before I let myself think about what I'd just heard. A Guardian was already dead. More were targeted. And somehow, impossibly, I was part of their plan. Or an impediment? And they intended to frame Sonny. Hard to feel bad for her, but still …

The question was whether they'd recruited me or just wound me up and pointed me in the right direction.

Either way, I was dancing to someone else's tune. I hate when that happens.

CHAPTER 11
REED HOLLOWAY

I HAD a list of composers and musicians thanks to Cree, backed up by the mystery lady's stack of articles documenting Jazzy Jacob's critical hits. The same names I'd already ratted out to Sonny. At the North Market, Dash gave me addresses for the price of lunch, making me promise not to tell anyone. That wasn't for me. That was to make sure Hoagy kept his trap shut.

Who was the kid going to tell? The president of the chess club or the first-chair trombone? Never mind. School was out, or he wouldn't be following me.

Dash didn't want to give the addresses to me, but the Conservatory helped him out plenty, and if I went back to Armando and said I needed these addresses for the case, the Harmonic Council would have applied pressure to the Department.

The only hitch was that they had yet to find Honey Lane at her listed address.

Reed Holloway, the most recent of the musicians criticized by Jazzy Jacob, lived the farthest away.

"It's your dream come true, Hoagy."

"What's that?"

"We're going to drive somewhere."

Dollars to donuts he wished we didn't. We walked to the storage unit where I kept it. Columbus street parking cost more than my rent, and I'd never remember to use their damn app. I pulled the dusty cover off like a magician revealing his best trick.

The 1972 Opel GT gleamed in Strato Blue Metallic underneath. European lines, pop-up headlights that twisted open instead of folding up, and a body style that made people think mini Corvette.

With a wave, I gestured for him to climb in.

"Is it safe?"

I understood. He was young and didn't appreciate a classic. The kid stared at the patched sheet metal where the original floorboards had rusted through. You could still see my rough welds where I'd covered the holes. The carpets were long gone.

"Perfectly safe," I said.

The kid stared at me as I pulled the choke, pumped the gas, and got the old beast to roar to life. The horror on his face was priceless.

"Want to make sure you have GPS tracking on your phone?" I asked. "You know, in case your mom needs to recover the body?"

His eyes bulged, and he remained silent, maintaining a death grip on the door while we hit the road.

The trip took about an hour, eventually ending on winding roads through Licking County. The scenery would have been beautiful if the trees weren't still struggling to find spring. The canopy had the leaves of spring but the death of winter.

We arrived at 1313 County Road 315. I stopped in the middle of the empty road. Ahead of us, a handmade sign advertised cabins for rent. The yellow curve warning sign beside it had bullet holes. Rural Ohio hospitality.

To our right was a drive with a padlocked gate. After parking the car along the fence line, we stepped over the barrier and headed down the gravel drive.

It took five minutes to walk to the house, including slowing down as we approached.

The small ranch house was deteriorating. A barn sat a hundred feet away to the right. It had seen better centuries. The barn was black with faded yellow lettering suggesting that we chew Mail Pouch Tobacco. The whole structure leaned slightly left, ready to give up.

The house was quiet. I knocked on the door. After a couple of minutes, I pounded again, but no one answered. The overgrown driveway was empty.

It seemed Mr. Holloway had better things to do than mope over a review. With no answer, I poked around a little, because that's what people do. If Holloway wasn't home, at least I could get a sense of the man. Musicians left traces of themselves everywhere.

I headed over to the dilapidated barn. The door was cracked open, so I poked my head in.

Inside, an obnoxious orange car sat with all four tires flat, and the body rusted out.

"Maybe you should make an offer on the car," Hoagy said.

"I'll let your mom buy you a car, kid."

The barn used to be a horse barn, and all the stalls still had hay scattered about. One stall had a table and two chairs. Composition paper lay on the table, and an old horseshoe lay on the paper as a paperweight.

I stepped in and peered at the paper.

Funeral March for a Music Critic, it read.

That wasn't a good sign.

"He writes music in the barn?" Hoagy asked, shaking his head.

"Composers write wherever the idea takes them. Probably sketching ideas."

I reached into my pocket and retrieved the piccolo. The instrument might help me attune to what was happening here. But not yet. Moving to the barn's far end, we headed out the back door.

A giant muddy field stretched from the barn to within a couple hundred feet of a tree line. Between here and there, numerous cardboard cutouts stood in the muck.

I approached the first one. Ellington. Then Tchaikovsky, Coltrane, Khachaturian, Berlioz. Geraci. Classical next to jazz, all with dings in them.

"Recognize them?" I asked.

"Composers."

A loud crack split the air. Berlioz's cardboard face exploded beside me.

I spun around. A man in red-and-black-checkered flannel stood at the tree line, maybe two hundred feet back. He had a rifle aimed in our direction. He fired again. Bernstein wobbled to my right.

"Down!" I grabbed Hoagy and ducked behind Tchaikovsky. Hoagy used me as a shield.

"Hey," I yelled. "I'm not here to hurt you. I'm here to help."

"Don't need your help." The man reloaded his weapon.

He kept firing. The cardboard composers were falling in front of me.

"You Holloway?" I stepped closer, hands in the air.

"Was," he said. "Now I'm nobody thanks to that piece-of-shit Jazzy Jacob."

The man was overweight but losing it, wearing jeans three sizes too big. His thinning brown hair blew in the breeze, his brow locked in a permanent furrow.

"I understand." I nodded and took another step. "You kill him?"

Holloway fired three more times. "No, somebody beat me to it."

"How about we talk about it?" I asked.

"Nothing to talk about." Holloway reloaded. "Jacob said my last album sounded like a washing machine having an existential crisis."

Sounded like something I would say, I thought. "That's what critics do." I risked another step forward.

Hoagy was content to stay put.

"Thirty years of music," Holloway said, his voice cracking, "and he reduces me to appliance anxiety."

I raised my hands higher and leaned closer. "Please, can we talk?"

Holloway fired again. "What's there to talk about?"

I didn't budge. Now I would have to do something. Holloway fired again, and I squatted behind another target.

This one, Rachmaninoff.

I raised the piccolo and played a quick melody. Nothing fancy, just a simple wind-calling ostinato in D major. The surrounding air swirled, responding. I felt the pull, the way magic grabbed you when the resonance was right. The magical current caught me like a favorable tide, propelling me forward with supernatural speed. The wind swept through the field. Holloway stumbled back, off balance, and I slammed into him hard. We both went down. The piccolo dropped beside us.

I came up on top of him, both of us struggling with his rifle. Finally, I gained enough control and put the barrel of the rifle against his neck, applying enough pressure to make him feel as if he was in trouble.

The tremor in my hand was back, masked only by my aggression. "I just want to talk," I said.

"Ain't no talking to be done." Holloway sneered. "My life's ruined."

"Everybody has to deal with critics," I said. "Why'd you kill him?"

"I didn't kill nobody. I saw it on TV like everyone else."

Holloway quit the struggle against me. "But I ain't sorry he's gone."

"I don't suppose anybody is." I stood, removed the rifle from his hands, and helped him up.

Hoagy emerged from behind Rachmaninoff, staring at me like I'd grown a second head. "You just …"

I took a deep breath and centered. Spells that intense worked, but they often took the wind out of you. Hoagy picked up the piccolo and handed it back to me.

My little trick didn't faze Holloway.

"You wouldn't understand," he said. "You got to be a musician to get it."

I frowned. "I am a musician."

Holloway wandered in circles, conducting an invisible, erratic orchestra. "Weeks and weeks of nothing. Can't get nothing down. One piece, just one piece I've been working on."

"I saw it," I said.

"Ain't no good."

I exhaled and grimaced. "Not good timing, anyway. Regardless, can't always be perfect on the first draft."

"That's the twelfth," he responded.

Holloway stopped in front of me. His hands trembled. "You know what it was, right?"

"What was?"

"He's the one who killed Felix Cantabile."

I stopped. "Who?"

"Jazzy Jacob."

I shook my head. "Not possible."

"Yeah?" Holloway sighed. "Jacob killed him and then took off and then killed himself."

"Yeah?" I said. "Then he wrote 'DISCORD KILLS' across his chest, and jumped in a dumpster to die. Happens all the time."

Holloway laughed. "Coulda happened. Doesn't matter. He had help."

"Why would Jazzy Jacob wanna kill Felix?" I asked.

Holloway looked over my shoulder at Hoagy. "The kid's okay."

"Because Jazzy Jacob was feeding information to the DHR."

I hesitated. Holloway was crazy. Probably drunk. Disgruntled, to be sure. Could I believe him? "How do you know that?"

"Saw it with my own two eyes," Holloway said.

I nodded. "I see. You saw him talking to Sonny Mordent?"

Holloway shook his head. "No. Who? Cree, the sax player. She was talking to him, and then she headed to the DHR." He stared at me and smiled. "Know her, do you? I saw Cree go into the DHR because I followed her one day right after getting whatever info she got from Jacob."

"Why did you follow her?"

"Nothin' creepylike." Holloway shook his head. "I can be a bit paranoid. So after I saw her and Jacob, I just followed my nose."

"What day was that?"

Holloway shrugged. "Four, five days ago? Time blurs out here. I followed her. She walked to the DHR. She came out later."

"So that means she gave information to …?"

"I don't know who she gave information to. But she also talked to a DHR—an agent, a man—followed her for a block. She confronted him. Seemed friendly enough. Then guess what happened? Felix died. Then Jacob died to clean up the mess."

"Who was the man who followed Cree?"

Holloway shook his head. "I don't hang out there. How would I know? Tall. Gray suit. Light eyes. Looked annoyed. Walked like a cop."

Rimsky, I thought.

"And before that?" I pressed. "Before she went to DHR?"

Holloway scratched his head. "She met someone. Short lady. Dark hair. They talked for maybe five minutes outside a coffee shop. The dark-haired one gave Cree something—looked like a business card or a key. Then Cree headed straight to DHR."

"You recognize the woman?"

"Never seen her before. But she moved like she knew she was being watched. Kept to shadows. Professional."

"So this paranoia of yours has you just following people around?"

"Suspicious people. What else I got to do? Can't create. And I don't want to end up in one of those rooms." He shook his head and stared at the ground. "We fought for the freedom to create. That went tits up." He frowned and rubbed his chin. "They're part of it. Cruel joke. All I got out of it was nightmares and no soul."

Walking up to him, I opened the rifle, cleared the chamber, and handed it back empty. The shells went into my pocket. "Thanks for the help. Try not to shoot us while we leave."

As we walked back to the car, Hoagy pulled out his phone. "That security camera back at the barn—did you see it?"

I hadn't.

"Wasn't recording. I checked the model number. Store-bought dummy camera. Holloway's paranoid but cheap." He pocketed the phone. "Thought you should know."

I looked at the kid with new appreciation. "You just happened to know security camera models?"

"YouTube. You can learn anything if you're bored enough."

Maybe the kid wasn't just deadweight after all. Time for the next stop on the list.

CHAPTER 12

RUBY BLUE

RUBY BLUE LIVED in an old factory that had been carved up into a communal living space in the Arts District, the kind of place that screamed "struggling artist" in industrial fonts. After finding her apartment number, Hoagy and I climbed three flights of concrete stairs.

The ceiling was a dozen feet high, but the walls of the apartments were standard size. Keeping secrets here would be impossible. But they were all artists, so drama was to be expected.

"Who is she?" Hoagy asked.

"Singer. Hits all the bars and festivals around here."

"Blue is an unusual last name."

"Yeah, Hoagy. Because it's not her name. Ruby Azul, second-gen Brazilian. She anglicized it when she hit the stage."

Hoagy frowned. "She should accept who she is."

"Sure," I said. "Until she got tired of every drunk yelling, 'Sing us a song, Ruby Asshole.'"

His face went through several expressions before landing on mortified. "Oh."

"Yeah. Stage names are practical."

Ruby answered the door in a faded silk robe that used to be emerald. Her blonde hair with blue tips hung limp and unwashed. I'd heard her make grown men weep at the Cinnamon Hedgehog. Now she looked like someone had drained all the music out of her and left the husk behind. Dark circles, hollow cheeks, shoulders slumped like cut puppet strings.

"Ugh. You're not the pizza guy," Ruby grumbled, her voice hoarse.

First test: "Dekker Kohl, Conservatory. I'm investigating—"

"The creativity thing?" She laughed bitterly. "Join the club. Come in, but don't expect entertainment. I don't make donations."

"No worries. We're not a church."

So she knew about the Conservatory, which wasn't always true. Most people never had a reason to learn about it. Most never knew magic existed until some weird shit happened. Then humans, as a whole, could make up an explanation to move on with life without dealing with it.

Ruby stared at Hoagy. "Hope your kid's not sensitive. He may find real life in here, and it's not all PG-13."

"He knows where the door is if it gets too much."

The apartment was in chaos. Sheet music scattered everywhere, a piano bench overturned in front of a Yamaha consumer piano that might have cost a couple hundred bucks, and three different microphones set up as if she'd been desperately trying to find her voice again.

Three bare bulbs lit the place. No windows. The standard office drop ceiling made it feel like a cubicle farm for broken artists.

"When did it start?" I asked.

"Two weeks ago. Right after that bastard Jacob's review."

Interesting. Less time than the others.

The singer snatched up her phone and scrolled for a long minute. "'Ruby Blue's voice has all the warmth of a dental drill and half the precision.'" She tossed the phone several feet away to the couch and shook her head. "But he wasn't wrong. Something died in my voice that night. I thought it was just nerves, but ..."

She ran through a C major scale. Every note hit its mark. Perfect pitch, perfect technique. Completely dead. It was like listening to a metronome pretend to be music. She tried a jazz ballad next. The melody was there, but the soul wasn't. All the technical parts working, none of the magic.

"It's like singing through glass," Ruby whispered. "I can hit every note, but there's nothing there. That motherfucker."

"He's dead," I said.

She stared at me. At first she didn't believe me, but after she inspected me and the kid, her expression changed to horror, quickly masked. "Good riddance."

I pulled out my piccolo. "Mind if I try something?"

Ruby threw her hands in the air. "Knock yourself out. Hope you don't want accompaniment."

I played a simple tune, feeling for the room's magical resonance. What I found was wrong. The place felt hollow, like a theater after everyone's gone home. The air was thin, colors muted. Even sound died fast, swallowed by something that had nothing to do with soundproofing. Someone had drained this place.

My eyes met hers. "Ruby, have you been to see anyone about this? A doctor? The DHR?"

Ruby's eyes widened. "How did you know? They said they could help. Took me to this room where I could sing again, but only in there. Useful, eh? They said it proved my problem was 'magical dependence.' Quacks."

"How old are you?" I asked.

"Really?"

I smirked at her. "Old enough to remember Harmony Hall?"

She shook her head with a smile. "I'd rather not. Thank you."

I held up the piccolo. "One more quick check?"

"Knock yourself out."

I walked the perimeter of the room. Everything was as before, but as I approached Ruby, it changed. It was like a depression surrounding her. A physical dampening pushing down on her, trying to smother what was left.

"Did they come get you and take you to DHR?" I asked.

Ruby's eyes shifted. "Not exactly. Look, they said they could help. And they have. When I'm in that room, I can sing again. Really sing, you know? Not this ..." She gestured at herself. "Whatever this is."

"How often do you go?"

"Three times a week. Sometimes more." She wouldn't meet my eyes. "They're studying me. I know that. But if it means I get to feel like myself again, even for an hour ..."

"Ruby." I kept my voice gentle. "What are they asking you to do?"

Her jaw set. "Nothing. Just sing. Report how I'm feeling. And ..." She hesitated. "They want me to recruit others. Other musicians who are struggling. They said I could help them. Freakin' marketing people."

Hoagy's face went white. "You're working for them."

"I'm surviving," Ruby shot back. "You don't know what it's like to lose the only thing that makes you you. If I have to sit in their weird room and fill out questionnaires to get it back, I will."

I played another pattern on the piccolo, good at testing creative response.

The reading confirmed it. Ruby's creative signature was fragmenting. Each trip to DHR's isolation room was making her dependent on it. Like an addict needing progressively larger doses.

"Ruby, they're not helping you. They're training you to need them."

"Sure. So you say."

"How did you know how to find them? It's not a place to randomly wander into."

"A friend told me about them, so I went down to see if they could help. They couldn't." She grunted, then continued. "It would take several sessions they said. Bollocks."

"Who's the friend?"

"My friend. Former friend." She shook her head. "They stopped going because of some creepy, weird shit going on when they do their compression thing."

"Like?"

"Like … leaking."

"I missed the name," I said. "The friend was that drummer guy?"

She put her hands on her hips. "You think I'm an idiot?" Her robe shifted. Hoagy discovered something interesting about the drop ceiling. Kid had good instincts, at least. Ruby continued. "He is not a drummer. I like men with a little more finesse."

I nodded. "So he's your boyfriend."

Ruby stared at Hoagy. "Ever get tired of it?"

Before the kid could answer, I cut in. "I'm sorry, but I'm trying to solve a murder."

"Yeah? Well, I know my not-boyfriend ain't dead. And who cares if a music critic is?" She pointed at me. "You can twist your words up all you want. I'm not spillin' it."

"Musician?" I asked. "Conservatory?"

"Some things in life should remain a mystery."

"Tall guy? Short? Give me something."

"Tall. Uses all ten fingers." She mimed a piano playing on her body. "That's all you're getting."

That narrowed it down, but it was something.

Ruby grabbed a jacket and zipped it up over her robe. Sliding flip-flops on, she said, "Damn pizza man. I guess I'll have to get food on my own." She pointed out the door.

We went ahead of her. She paused at the door. "Hey, Dekker? If you're seriously investigating this, there's a lady you should talk to. She's been asking questions about musicians losing their creativity. Organizing something, I think."

"Got a name?"

"I'm sure she does. Left me her card. You're impossible." Ruby stepped back into the apartment and rummaged through papers on her counter. "Had it somewhere … ah, here."

The card was simple: a treble clef symbol and a phone number. No name. No address.

"When did she contact you?"

"Week ago. Said she was documenting what's happening to us." Ruby shrugged. "Seemed legit. More helpful than DHR's bullshit."

I pocketed the card. "Thanks."

We headed out. On the way, we passed the children's playground near Ruby's apartment.

At the back of the playground, a brunette woman stood, hair pulled back, arms crossed, watching. She should have been watching the kids, but instead she tracked my path. She wore a jacket with the collar pulled up, attempting to obscure her face. Then again, maybe she wanted me to see her. No doubt it was the mystery lady from the Archives. Maybe she was on the payroll as my shadow, too. I could trade the kid in for her.

A dozen children sat on the swings. Not swinging. Not moving. Just sitting there with their feet on the ground, staring at nothing. No shouting, no laughing, no running. One mother pushed her toddler back and forth as if she were winding a clock. The kid didn't smile. Even the pigeons had given up chaos. They walked in a straight line, pecking at crumbs like assembly-line workers. The playground looked colorful and dead at the same time.

Seven days, the Archives said. But maybe that was optimistic. Maybe Whimsy was already "leaking" away, one playground at a time.

"She seems nice," Hoagy said.

"She's following us."

Hoagy looked back toward the building. "Where? I don't see her. But we should try to help her. She seems depressed and needs some support."

"Ruby?" I chuckled. "Kid, you're gonna get yourself in trouble if you try to fix everyone."

"I know, but ..." He kicked at the sidewalk. "She's really struggling. And if the DHR is doing this to people, that's not okay."

Did the kid want to fix me, too? Lost cause.

"Ruby will get fixed when we get to the bottom of all this," I said.

"But how are all these people related to Felix? They certainly didn't kill him."

"So sure, are you?"

"Think so."

"Harmonics. All these things are related, and we're trying to piece music back together. Problem is, the sheet music didn't have numbers on it."

Hoagy nodded. "Like that Sonata Allegra in G?"

"Something like that."

CHAPTER 13

THE RAID

AFTER LEAVING Ruby Blue's converted factory, we walked the streets in the late afternoon with nowhere to go and all day to get there. The shadows were starting to stretch. The air had taken an unseasonable turn toward cold, causing Hoagy to hunch his shoulders and shove his hands in his pockets. Unlike me, he wasn't wearing a jacket.

I was contemplating our next move when we passed the Hedgehog and stopped dead. The door was open. Too early for business, too late for cleaning.

I stepped into the doorway and felt my blood turn to ice water. I motioned for Hoagy to hold back.

Rimsky stood in the middle of the room with his back to me, but this wasn't the casual surveillance I'd seen before. This was a full-scale raid. The DHR had gone from surveillance to shock and awe. Subtle as a car crash.

He had some DHR goons with him, and they were treating the Hedgehog like a crime scene. Or pretending to be pirates. They upended tables, cleared every shelf, inspected every photo on the walls, and grunted at their literal captive audience. They weren't looking for evidence. They were sending a message. Every overturned table, every dumped shelf screamed the same thing: we can do this anywhere, anytime, and you can't stop us.

Two men and two women each sat at their own table, isolated from the others as a DHR goon interrogated them.

The inspector led his own interrogation. And it happened to be of Cree and Riff. He allowed them to sit together. Cree was defiant. Riff appeared to be calculating something.

Two of the DHR guys wheeled a cart from the back. Now it had Cree's saxophone along with other instruments. I knew it was hers because of the rose-gold tint. But even if that were not true, the look on her face told me.

"You'll get it back," Rimsky said to Cree. "If you cooperate, it will be before you need to perform again. We know musicians have been gathering here, discussing the … situation."

Cree glared at Rimsky. "Musicians gather here to play music when you goons aren't interfering. There's no secret cabal to create a musical revolution." She looked at Riff. "The stupid ideas these people get."

Rimsky's lips thinned. "I heard that the audience likes you. I understand. You're quite the performer." He stepped to her table, placed his hands on it, and leaned closer to her. "We're investigating the connection between this establishment and recent irregularities in the musical community."

Hoagy leaned into me, trying to get a better look. "Aren't they the cause of the irregularities?"

"Them and Whimsy dying," I muttered.

Things were escalating fast. Once Whimsy gasped its final breath, there would be no one to stop the DHR from controlling everything. It wouldn't be only the artists giving up; the whole world would surrender to acceptance of whatever they did. No one would need Whimsy.

"What about my flute?" One woman shot to her feet before a goon's heavy hand shoved her back down.

"In good time," Rimsky answered.

The two men with a cart headed for the door, so I pulled Hoagy outside ahead of them. We ducked around the corner into the alley. The cart rattled behind us.

"Let's go," one man said.

I pressed Hoagy against the brick wall on the far side of the dumpster where Jacob had been found. We were out of their sight line, but barely. The cart wheeled past us and stopped.

"Inspector Rimsky said we had to return this stuff," the other said.

"Bureaucracy, you know. It got lost."

They laughed and stopped in front of the dumpster. These weren't investigators. They were thugs with badges, and the distinction mattered less every day.

The first one spoke again. "Nobody wants any of this stuff, so we'll just dump it here."

"Not the sax," the other said. "I can pawn that thing for some serious cash."

"It's not real gold."

"Don't care. I like it."

The two men hoisted the cart and dumped it. The sound of those instruments hitting metal was like watching someone throw a symphony into a meat grinder. Every crash was somebody's dream dying. The men walked away. I peered around the corner to confirm that the two men had Cree's sax and were walking away from the Hedgehog. Rose gold, custom work, probably worth three months of her rent. To them, it was beer money. That's the thing about thugs in uniforms, they never see the difference between property and dreams.

Hoagy and I returned to the front door of the club. Things were getting heated. Rimsky was pointing at Cree like a bad fencer that doesn't know what the target is. His words were quiet, but he seemed controlled.

"I thought he was DHR Internal Affairs," Hoagy whispered.

"Seems he got promoted to everybody's affairs."

When Rimsky reached and finally grabbed Cree by the collar, she stood and wound up to take a swing at him. Riff stepped between them, stopping the hit and breaking Rimsky's grip. The pianist held Cree back with all his might, and I could see that it was a struggle.

My eyes surveyed the room. The goons appeared committed to their task. No signs of discomfort keeping musicians and staff in compliance. Rimsky paced the floor, continuing to ramble about where they were hiding the musicians secretly planning something to counter the increased inspections and regulations.

With a nod, I crept back. Hoagy was already leaning on the wall, so I joined him.

"Hoagy, we're going to have to do something."

"Good."

"It could be dangerous," I said.

"We have to help them."

My eyes roved up and down the street. Empty. Even at the intersection with High Street. I muttered something about how unusual it was.

Hoagy held up his phone to me. There were warning to stay away from this block and the Hedgehog due to a possible gas leak.

"Clever," I said.

"It says ordered by the police."

"That's for the Statics. Most don't know about the DHR."

The kid frowned at me. "You shouldn't call them Statics. They're people."

I noted the increased comfort he had with me. Speaking up was a good asset to have later.

"Shit. This is just like the war all over again. Thanks, Felix."

The DHR raid triggered something I'd kept buried. Not just memories—muscle memory. My left hand shook.

Twenty years ago, the Compressionists had come for Professor Copland's workshop. They'd taken twelve of us that night. Only eight made it out. Felix had been the one who warned us, arriving breathless: "They're coming. Thirty seconds."

We'd scattered like notes in a broken chord. Some made it out windows. Others weren't fast enough. Now history was repeating in a different key. Different uniforms. Same oppression.

"Did he cause this?" Hoagy asked.

I shook my head. "No." I changed the subject. "How's your trombone playing?"

"I passed the prescreening for a summer program."

"Cool. Where?"

The kid's face contorted like I just punched him in the gut. "I have no hope with the Curtis Institute of Music. I might try IU. My dad forbade me to consider Michigan."

I chuckled. "Of course. I assume you're avoiding telling me Juilliard."

"I was told it was a sore spot."

"Kid, I'm too old to care. I've got a good life, but if you have the chance at any of them, take it. Beats this gig if you have talent." Back to the task at hand. "Have you been taught any spells for that trombone of yours?"

"We started working on it. Seems like parlor tricks to me."

I knew what he meant. It wasn't enough to have innate ability. Like everything, it required practice and refinement. And just like regular music practice, it required scales, theory, and other things kids thought boring. Virtuosi drills were on another level.

I glanced at the kid. "Parlor tricks are about to save your friends. You in?"

The kid's jaw set. Whatever doubts he had, he swallowed them. "Yeah. I'm in."

We ducked down the alley where we found Jacob to get to the back entrance to the Hedgehog. The door would be locked, but that was no issue for me. No guards at the door. I instructed Hoagy how to do an F major ostinato, humming the pattern to him.

"Sustain it. Keep it steady and whatever you do, don't pay attention to what's going on in the room."

"I don't have a trombone."

"There's one sitting on the stage next to the piano. The goons didn't see it."

"You want me to play somebody else's trombone?"

"Yes. To help them."

He was clearly uncomfortable with the idea, so I went into teacher mode and explained his ostinato would function like a ventriloquist, making sounds, footsteps, whatever came up in his mind, around the room. I gave him a couple of pointers on how to stay focused and how to breathe to keep it steady. Not from a note perspective but sustaining the energy for the magic.

Piccolo out, I picked the lock with a five-note motif, and we snuck in. The backstage smelled of old velvet and spilled beer. Every footstep sounded like thunder in my ears, but the voices from the main room covered us.

It was easy to get to the crushed-velvet curtain behind the stage and convenient that there was a three-foot gap between it and the brick wall. The air gap was to help the acoustics, but like a lot of things, it had become storage. Once at the far end, we stopped.

"Stay to the side of the piano. Wait until you hear me play a C eight—"

"You can play that high?"

"Hoagy, I'm a Virtuoso in many ways."

As Hoagy crept behind the curtain to take position, I worked my way back, wound through the kitchen to the stairs headed up to the second floor. I glanced to make sure no one was there.

I exhaled sharply. It was only going to get worse if I delayed. I let out a shrill note. Everyone in the room jolted like an alarm had just gone off. Eyes bounced everywhere, looking for the source.

From behind the piano, Hoagy began his spell. Not perfect, but it was doing the trick. In fact, the kid adapted pretty well and figured out how to divert their attention to the opposite side of the room from where I was.

I crept around the perimeter of the bar and ducked behind it. As I peered over the bar to get the lay of the land, Hoagy lost control of his spell. He went too hard on it and didn't know how to sustain without exhausting himself.

"Arrest him," Rimsky said, pointing at Hoagy.

Dammit. I dropped down behind the bar.

"What for? He's a kid," Riff said.

Rimsky answered, "Interfering with an official investigation."

The piccolo wasn't going to help in this situation. Too airy. Not enough sonic heft. No offense to piccoloists.

There was a scuffle. Behind the rows of bottles against the wall was a mirror. Between bottles, I could work out that Riff had been detained by two men as he protested and sat nearby behind Rimsky. Now Cree faced him alone.

Hoagy was forced to drop the trombone and sit next to Riff.

Rimsky should have stuck with Riff. But interrogators never know when to quit. They think pressure breaks people. Sometimes it just pisses them off. Meanwhile, I came up with a new plan, and I hoped Riff was going to understand it.

I reached up and snagged a wineglass from the small sink, moving like a cat burglar in a crystal shop. The tap whispered as I added water—too much, then just right. I filled two more glasses, adjusting their water levels. Hoped my guess was right.

Three glasses, three pitches. I ran my moistened fingers around the rims until the crystal sang: B-flat, D-flat, F. The minor triad rose pure and haunting in B-flat minor. Perfect for what I had in mind. The crystal tone mixed with my whistled harmony, and every DHR agent in the room was blinking back tears like someone had been cutting onions with a chain saw. Can't do that with a piccolo!

I stood and walked around the bar, careful not to disrupt the water. The spell was already decaying. My pitch wavered as I whistled the harmony, and the glasses' resonance was fading. I needed a stronger conductor, fast. Rimsky seemed the most aware that something was wrong but not able to put a finger on it. Riff looked at me while I whistled.

Whistling isn't as strong as an attuned instrument, but it still worked. I'd exhaust the spell faster. The crystal sang pure and cold, like winter air made audible. Riff's eyes were watering, but he could still move. Adrenaline, or maybe he was just tougher than the goons. When he showed recognition, I tipped my head at Cree, and he got the idea.

They headed out the front door as quiet as possible. The others played follow the leader. Cree would make sure they scattered.

I made it to the piano and switched before the spell could collapse. My fingers found the keys, and I launched into jazz improvisation in B-flat minor, keeping the harmony alive. The piano was stronger than wineglasses and whistling, but I was already tired. My pitch had been wavering like a violin played on a moving train.

The extended chords and sonic characteristics of the piano were always great conduits, but you couldn't just haul a piano around with you everywhere. And a Keytar was not enough, as fun as they were.

I struck a sharp augmented chord, and Hoagy was free. He headed for the trombone.

"Get them all out," I said, diving back into the improvisation to keep the guards and Rimsky under control. Every few seconds I punctuated the harmony with a crunching disharmonic hit because sometimes I can be an asshole.

My arms were seized and pulled behind me. I was dragged to my feet, the piano bench clattering, and thrown to the floor.

Rimsky stood over me. He'd grabbed me while the spell was still active. That shouldn't have been possible. The wineglasses had every other goon in the room blinking back tears, but Rimsky had moved through it like walking through smoke.

Rimsky. Bastard. He did that before the spell broke. I'd have to work that out, but at the moment I closed my eyes. My mind submerged into some deep place where I couldn't hear the room, only my internal silence as Maestro Park had taught me. I was no good to anyone until then …

Tacitare. The necessary silence between spells. Maestro Park's lesson: tempo isn't speed, it's the measure of space between actions. I sank into that internal quiet, waiting for my reservoir to refill.

The room was a mass of noise. Chairs being knocked over. A good old bar fight was going on, and I was slobbering on the floor, regaining my strength. My vision was unfocused. But Cree and Riff had come back. They were attacking the goons with everything they had.

Rimsky appeared to be watching. Yeah, right. Don't get your hands dirty.

That was the last I saw as my mind retreated further into tacitare. Now it was just muffled rhythms, irregular, the result of regular humans doing things.

I lost track of time in tacitare. Could have been two minutes, could have been fifteen. When my eyes opened, the fight was winding down. The world came back in pieces: dented polished floor, overturned chairs, Hoagy staring at me with wide eyes.

"I screwed up," he said. His voice was small, tight. "I'm sorry."

"You lasted longer than most apprentices would. Don't beat yourself up."

He did, too. But it was too much if he had tried without backup.

I nodded and sat erect. My shoulders ached where Rimsky had wrenched me from the piano, but that was nothing compared to the bone-deep exhaustion of back-to-back intense spells. Across the room, Riff sat in a chair next to Cree, both breathing hard. Behind them, two DHR goons were zip-tied to each other, looking dazed. Rimsky sat zip-tied to a chair.

"Nice work," I said to Hoagy, gesturing at the goons.

The kid flushed. "Riff did most of it. I just … helped."

I had to hand it to the pianist. When it mattered, he'd stepped up. Maybe I'd been mistaken about him being just another pretty boy with fast fingers.

Cree seemed groggy. The magic always left Statics with gaps in memory and a feeling like they'd just woken up. But she'd been around Virtuosi enough to recognize what happened even if she couldn't remember the details.

The goons had it worse. They looked like they'd been drugged.

Riff had broken free when the spell hit the goons. His adrenaline must have been through the roof after standing up to Rimsky. Cree had already bolted for the door, so she'd missed seeing him fight. Probably for the best. He seemed like the type who'd downplay it later.

"You okay?" I asked Cree.

"Yeah. Thanks, Dekk."

"Don't thank me yet." I stood, wobbly for a moment, then back to my usual self. "Two of those goons walked off with your sax. They're planning to pawn it."

Riff's jaw tightened. "Like hell they are."

I watched them bolt out the door. The goons had a head start, but I'd put money on Cree. A woman chasing her stolen sax moves faster than gravity.

"What about him?" Hoagy asked, pointing at Rimsky.

"What happened to the other DHR guys?" I asked.

Hoagy said DHR goons had scattered when their boss got zip-tied by a pissed-off pianist and a teenage trombonist. Perhaps trying to explain to their supervisors how they'd lost control of a raid to two civilians and a kid.

I glanced at Rimsky. "Release him."

Rimsky rubbed his wrists as Hoagy snipped the zip ties with scissors from behind the bar; then he stood to his full height in front of me.

"This will not go well for you," he said.

"Really? Why? I thought you were Internal Affairs or something, making sure Sonny isn't overwrought with grief and can't do her job." My stare met his. "Or is that not your job?"

"It will be reported to the Conservatory."

"Reported to the Conservatory?" I let the silence hang. "Go ahead. Tell them you got taken down by a guy playing wineglasses and a high school kid."

Rimsky's jaw worked. His eyes promised retribution, but his body language admitted defeat. He straightened his jacket and walked out, every step measured, like a conductor who'd just lost his orchestra.

CHAPTER 14

SLIDE DONOVAN

THE RAID LEFT ME DRAINED, but there wasn't time to rest. The Hedgehog was shut down pending investigation, which meant Rimsky had won even while losing. I had maybe a day before Rimsky made good on his threat to report me to the Conservatory. Which meant I needed to work fast.

After the raid, I wanted to get back on track, so I asked around where I could find Slide Donovan in the coffee shops. Finally, one woman suggested that Slide often sat with her trombone in Goodale Park near the fountain.

"Maybe you should slow down," Hoagy said.

"No time. Look over there."

Across several tables, patrons sat with coffee cups and bagels. They weren't drinking. Or talking. Their thumbs scrolled on their phones; they weren't even looking at the screens.

Hoagy's face fell. "Not just artists anymore."

"Right. Which is why we need to move fast. But you look like you need caffeine, and I could use a minute to think." The raid had taken more out of me than I wanted to admit. "Coffee?"

"Good idea," the kid said. "I could use some coffee."

"You allowed to do that?"

Hoagy frowned at me. "I'll get you some, too. It's good for the heart for old guys."

Minutes later he returned with a coffee for me and some frozen monstrosity of coffee for him. We sat for a moment.

Coffee shops should be full of chatter and keyboards tapping, laughing. None of it. Hoagy looked at me. "Not just artists anymore," he repeated.

"Right. So drink your coffee snow cone, and let's get going. We're going to need as much time as we can get if we want to at least start the process of a new Guardian before Whimsy is gone."

Hoagy sucked on his straw. "You want to find the replacement? Shouldn't the Council?"

"I think they ignored the whole situation." I shook my head. "We won't find a replacement, but if someone jumps out at me, I'm not keeping quiet about it."

"Like who? Ruby?"

I laughed. "What happens when you mix Whimsy and paranoia?" The kid's eyes were wide. "A merry-go-round that keeps checking the exits."

"Once she gets her voice back. Maybe a new purpose—"

"Kid, Ruby Blue isn't going to save the world."

With a frown, we headed out. I could always disappoint somebody without effort.

The park was a short distance away. Benches lined the pathway around the pond. On one size was an empty gazebo, and in the pond on the other size was a wedding cake like bronze fountain with two elephants at the top spraying water from their trunks. Appropriate for the world in this state, one elephant sprayed full force and its partner dribbled.

I inquired of an elderly couple sitting on a bench waiting to feed pigeons that seemed unlikely to show. They gave me directions sufficient to figure it out.

The trombonist's place was just off Warren, a street I walked every day. Hoagy and I walked down the gravel alley behind the apartments and found a low wooden fence surrounding a yard only ten feet wide. A cracked sidewalk led to two concrete steps and a back door with a window covered in grime. The knob was stiff, but it was unlocked.

"Slide," I called.

We went upstairs, making sure we made enough noise not to be a surprise.

The trombonist was lanky, clothes always baggy because of it. But she would make a great épée fencer. Except that Slide was hunched over, disguising her height or pretending to be an old woman. Her curly blonde hair had been pinned back and looked like it was considering real hard the switch to gray.

I'd heard Slide play many times at the Hedgehog. Her trombone could make you laugh, cry, or fall in love depending on her mood.

She was surrounded by equipment that looked more scientific than musical. Three different metronomes ticked at slightly different speeds. Salt lines marked the floor. A recording setup captured everything.

"Dekker Kohl." She didn't seem surprised. "Wondered when you'd show up."

"What is all this?"

"Fighting back." She gestured at the metronomes. "Polyrhythms to disrupt whatever's causing the drain. Salt lines from an old folk magic book. Bullshit, I suspect, but I'm desperate. And recordings." She pointed to dozens of tapes. "Every day I record myself playing. Compare the waveforms. Document the decay."

Hoagy stepped closer to examine the setup. "Cool. You're treating it like a scientific phenomenon."

"Because it is." Slide pulled out a notebook covered in graphs. "Look. Here's my creative signature three weeks ago.

Here's yesterday. The degradation follows a logarithmic curve. Whatever's draining us is getting stronger."

I studied her graphs. "Have you shared this with anyone?"

"DHR tried to recruit me. Offered treatment. I told them to shove it." She laughed bitterly. "I may be losing my ability, but I'm not losing my data. Someone needs to document what they're doing to us."

"Good." I played a diagnostic riff. Her signature was damaged but fighting. Unlike Ruby, who was surrendering, or Reed, who was giving up, Slide was treating this like a siege. Barricading herself in with research and willpower.

"Keep recording everything," I told her. "And if DHR comes back, call me first."

"Sure. I think I'll have plenty of time if I remember your number."

I glanced at Hoagy. He understood.

"Slide, I need to ask you something important," I began. "Do you know Honey Lane?"

"Sure, we've played together. Why?"

My eyes narrowed. "Just in the band? I heard …"

"Yeah. All right. We were a thing for a bit."

I nodded. "Understood. What happened? If you don't mind."

"Sure, Dekk. Honey's troubled."

"Creatively?"

"More than that." Slide's mask slid on. "But that's her business. I'm not discussing it without talking to her first."

I nodded. "Know where I can find her?"

Slide's shoulders dropped even more. "Yeah. In the bedroom."

"Thought you used to be a thing," I said.

She smiled sheepishly. "Every once in a while we give it another shot and remember why it never works. She showed up Thursday night."

"Mission accomplished?"

Slide shook her head. "That girl's so messed-up. Never seen her that bad."

"I need to talk to her."

"The door's open."

I stood. "Keep an eye out. Hang out with people." My eyes met hers. "Play, even if it is wrong. I think they're hunting you. All of you. And I think they're using Jacob's reviews as a shopping list or a log. Not sure which."

Slide's face tightened with worry. "Honey's current state ... She's been getting worse every day. I came here hoping some distance would help me think, but ..." She gestured helplessly at her trombone.

"Honey," I called as I entered.

Not a peep.

"We shouldn't go in," Hoagy said.

"True. But if we can help."

He grunted at me. "I think you're stretching the boundaries of help."

I winked at the kid. "That's how you find the boundaries."

Slide's kitchen was spacious with appliances older than I was. Holes in the plaster walls exposed the laths beneath, and a pipe hung from the ceiling above the stove where it disappeared into the wall. A narrow stairway led up just outside the kitchen.

The upstairs was a modified attic with steeply sloped ceilings. The floor had two small bedrooms and a bath. The bathroom was right above the kitchen, and the pipes came from the old iron tub. The closest bedroom was empty. The other had a king-size four-poster bed against the window. A comforter lay at the foot of the bed and the pillows on the right. A lamp lay on its side on the floor.

On the other side of the bed, a wide closet stood open, exposing wire shelves stuffed with clothing. In front of that rack, a tall mirror stood on the floor. In the mirror, I could see

Honey Lane lying on the floor, half wrapped in a bedsheet. I approached. Her face had gone slack, the warm brown skin now dull and lifeless. The vibrant Afro-Cuban performer I'd seen at the Hedgehog was now reduced to a hollow shell.

"Over here," Hoagy said.

I stepped around the bed. "Honey."

No response. Fearing the worst, I knelt beside her. Honey lay facedown, head turned toward the closet, and arms at her side. She wore a loose yellow tank top and no pants. She always wore yellow.

A beehive tattoo decorated her exposed shoulder, with writing in a language I didn't recognize. In the small of her back, a cluster of faded roses attempted to cover Slide's name, but you could still read it through the ink. Unfinished business, literally. Don't we all have that problem?

Leaning closer, my face an inch from hers, I shook her. "Honey."

Her skin was warm to the touch, but she hadn't blinked once.

"Dammit. Hoagy, call 911."

A faint grunt escaped her lips.

I leaned closer. If Honey had made a sound, there was no sign of it, but she was alive. The piccolo came out for a quick diagnostic riff. The room's energy felt chaotic with the residue of arguments and reconciliations, but that was just the emotional echo of their relationship. The real problem was deeper.

Most importantly, Honey was alive. Sliding closer to her, I hummed a healing note that would also help me find the issue, my fingers tracing the invisible energy channels that flow through all of us. Like the side notes, the harmonics of a violin.

Hoagy was still on the phone but standing beside me. "Are you being creepy?"

"Shh." Kneeling beside her, I continued humming, just above

a whisper, my fingers dancing an inch from her and tracing the lines.

Her pulse was thread-thin and irregular, like the final note of a symphony fading into silence. Honey's breath was so shallow I had to put my ear to her lips to detect it. But her skin remained warm, and when I shook her, she managed a weak "fuck off" without opening her eyes. Also, there was no sign of alcohol or drugs.

I stood to wait for the paramedics.

I ignored the kid's skepticism. "It's sort of like acupuncture. I was tracing her energy flow to see if I could isolate—"

"Sure," Hoagy said.

No matter what the kid thought, it was a trick I had learned from Maestro Park. I wasn't great at it, but when someone's life is on the line, you try everything.

The absence of Whimsy had left Honey in a creative coma. She must have been more sensitive to it than others. Her body lived, but everything that made her who she was had been drained away. If this was what happened when someone's Whimsy drained completely, the world had five days before everyone ended up like Honey. Less for some.

"What will the paramedics do if this is because of Whimsy?" Hoagy asked.

"Keep her in the hospital for tests and recovery." I glanced at Hoagy. "And keep the DHR away from her."

Forty minutes later, Hoagy and I stood outside with Slide while the paramedics wheeled Honey out on the gurney. The kid had remained silent the entire time, even avoiding his phone. If he wanted to see what it was like to be a Trovatore, he had had more than his fill in the past couple of days.

A CPD officer stepped up to the paramedics as they approached the ambulance. "Is she stable enough to wait?"

"Yes," said a paramedic.

The cop shook his head. "DHR wants us to wait."

I shot up. "No way."

"Not a Conservatory issue," the officer said.

"It is. This woman had the life sucked out of her by those people. She needs treatment."

Honey stirred, barely conscious, and muttered, "They promised they could fix me."

The paramedic shrugged. "Not sure what the docs will do besides dump fluids in her and perhaps a toxicology report."

I nodded. "Good enough."

The CPD officer clicked his tongue. "It's my ass, not yours."

Hoagy sniffled and wiped the corner of his eyes. "Please. I don't understand what the DHR is, but can't my aunt get to the hospital first? They can talk to her there, and I can call Mom."

The cop and paramedic exchanged a glance.

The policeman shook his head. "Get her rolling before they get here. They'll show up at the hospital eventually."

I wasn't sure if I should feel proud or guilty. The kid had just learned that sometimes you have to lie to do the right thing. Whether that made me a good mentor or a bad influence was above my pay grade.

CHAPTER 15
LOCRIAN MODE

LATER THAT NIGHT, I returned to the Hedgehog. Hoagy protested that it would be okay for him to go since he was with me or that I could whip up some Virtuosi magic to give him a bye. He didn't believe me that magic didn't work like that. But he relented and headed home to do whatever teenagers did these days. I was certain it was causing less trouble than I had as a kid.

After entering, I stopped at the bar, and the bartender gave me a sparkling water. Now was not the time to be drinking. To figure all this out, I had to keep my wits about me. Plus, I still had a piccolo in my pocket, and the last thing you want is a mean drunk who has magical abilities. Not that I was a mean drunk, but I was scrutinizing Cree more than I would have.

The barkeep told me that Ruby Blue was supposed to be singing, but she never showed up, so the band was winging it. Not too difficult if you're a jazz musician, though it was annoying when your singer didn't show up. But Ruby skipping out wasn't a surprise after talking to her.

Most of the crowd had skipped, too. I glanced at the bartender.

"Not much interest after earlier," he said, wiping the bar. "Been told that a couple of them are staking the place out."

"Figures." I smiled at him. "It'll get better."

"Will it?"

No. But I didn't say that. Or at least not without Whimsy.

Cree was playing tenor sax in the band instead of her usual alto. Perhaps she hadn't gotten her instrument back. She wore all black. I don't know whether I ever saw her in black in my life, but there was proof: a black blouse with two buttons undone and a blazer on top. Black pants, black shoes. But you couldn't tame the red locks.

Cree was a good player, but something was up. She was sticking out of the band on the rhythm and fading into the back on her solos. But she wasn't alone. The piano player, her boy Riff, was having similar problems. He appeared to be trying to compensate by simplifying his chords and having a little less rhythm in them. Syncopation would not be his thing today. Even then, he looked as if he was struggling, ash hanging from a cigarette, dropping onto the keys.

The audience, perhaps a dozen Statics, sat at their tables, talking among themselves. Not one of them was paying attention to the band. Hard to blame them. It was just noise at this point.

Interestingly, no one in the entire room was laughing. No winking, no smiling, nothing playful.

Leaning on the bar, I ordered some food. Bland, but that was even in the best of times. I waited for the set break.

Once that happened, the band scattered. Drinks, cigarettes, bathroom breaks. Cree slumped in her chair, still onstage, and gave me a tired half smile.

Riff approached the bar. He wasn't drinking water.

"Thanks again for the help," I said.

He tipped his head with a grim smile.

After finishing my drink, I walked over and straddled the

piano bench, resting my elbows on my knees. Cree half smiled at me.

"Not much of a show tonight," she said. "Hasn't been for a while. And after the raid, there might not be any more shows at all. They're shutting us down after tonight pending investigation." She looked at me and sighed. "Three nights ago, I tried to improvise during Reed's solo." She bit her lip. "You know I live for those moments when the music takes over and I'm just holding on for the ride." With thinned lips, I nodded. "But nothing came. I played the safest, most boring accompaniment of my career. The audience didn't even notice when I stopped playing entirely for eight bars."

I continued bobbing my head. There was nothing to say. So I deflected. "Hope Reed was in a better mood than when I saw him."

She smiled. "He said you were poking around."

"Cree, I need to ask you something, but I don't know if you'd rather talk now or wait until you're done for the night."

She met my gaze, then squeezed my hands, her soft fingers against the sandpaper of my palms. "Well, I'm sure you can guess what happens at the end of the night."

"Based on what I've seen tonight, some bad sax."

She chuckled.

I wasn't as upset as she wanted me to be. It hadn't been eight months since our last almost. I had finished a bad case, and she was lonely. We saved ourselves from anything happening.

Riff was improving in my eyes. "Okay, then," I began, "someone told me a story. A tip that you were giving information to the DHR."

Cree sat up, stiff now, and crossed her arms. After a moment, she unwound them and placed her hand on the neck of the saxophone on its stand beside her.

"About what?" she asked.

Now I sat up. "Well, I don't know, Lorraine."

Dredging up her real name from when we were in high school told her it was serious. No more pretense about the roles we chose to play in the world or with each other. In the end, she could be Cree, Locrian, or whatever was next, but to me she would default to Lorraine, eventually.

"What I know is I have two dead bodies," I said. "One we both used to care about. I also know that I have this woman from the DHR pushing in on this case."

"You mean his wife?"

"Ex-wife. Part-time wife. Whatever she is."

She nodded. "It makes sense she would push on you."

"Perhaps."

"Especially if she figures out how shitty the two of you left things with each other."

Rather than arguing about the rift between Felix and me all those years ago, I let it pass, repeating, "Perhaps."

"I'm sure you're antagonizing her, just like you are giving me grief about Riff." She moved close enough I could smell the sweat from being onstage in close quarters mixed with a floral perfume. "Don't you dare ever tell him about Lorraine."

As she leaned back, I saluted her. "How do you feel about Felix being the Guardian of Whimsy?"

"Apparently, it's a problem." Her eyes registered little expression. "You think my playing tonight is on account of feeling bad for Felix?"

"No," I said. "Your bad playing tonight, my lack of composition, the ridiculously pathetic chords your boyfriend's playing" —her eyes narrowed at me—"I think they're all related. To his death, but not because of him specifically, but because he was the Guardian of Whimsy."

She leaned forward and whispered, "I still don't know what that means."

Matching her movement, I gently grasped her lapel. Our heads were inches apart.

"This." I rubbed the cloth between my fingers. "I've never seen you dressed like this, never seen you without color. Never seen you play so badly."

"Thanks," she said. "I appreciate your support."

I threw up my hands. "Be mad if you want, but I assume your boyfriend plays better normally."

"He does."

With a nod, I moved away and continued. "All these people you were talking about before—Ruby Blue, Honey Lane, Slide Donovan. All of them are having problems, right?"

"Yep," she said. "Boomer Blake, too."

"Boomer Blake," I repeated. He wasn't on my original list.

"There's something else," she said, lowering her voice. "That DHR guy from this afternoon, Rimsky, came by the club twice last week asking about Felix."

I narrowed my gaze. "Are you sure? Before Felix's murder?"

She gestured in exasperation. "Before he attacked us." She waved around the club. I acknowledged my mistake, and she continued. "Yes, I'm sure. Said he was conducting a routine employee review, but he was asking strange questions."

"Like?"

"Whether Felix seemed worried about anything. If he'd mentioned feeling sick. If anyone had seen him with his wife recently." She glanced at the floor, then at me, eyes wide. "Then he asked if I knew anything about Guardian protocols. I thought he was nuts." Her eyes narrowed. "Why would DHR Internal Affairs care about that? And why would I know anything about your crazy Guardian protocols? I didn't know anything about them then or today when you're grilling me."

"Don't know," I said. "Anything else?"

"Ivory Fontaine is a little more off his rocker than usual."

"He's getting worse?" I asked.

"So you're saying that Felix affects all creative people."

"No, Lorraine"—she glared at me—"I'm saying that the Guardian of Whimsy dying means that Whimsy has gone and the creatives are experiencing the effects *first*."

She shook her head. "Look, I understand you and the Conservatory want to believe all that stuff. I really do, Dekk. It's part of you. But the fact is, Whimsy, as you say, has been dying for weeks, maybe months."

I sat back and stared at the ceiling. Something was missing in the timeline. If Whimsy had been dying for weeks, Felix couldn't be the cause. But he was still the key somehow. That would take some thought, but that wasn't the purpose of being here. And if Rimsky was asking about Guardians before the murder, he knew something.

"Are you telling me you didn't go to the DHR … Cree?" I asked.

"Dekk, I didn't," she said.

"So he was lying."

Riff returned just as I said it. "Who's lying?" he asked.

With a shake of my head, I turned to him. "Reed Holloway."

Cree stood, fists on her hips, and she glared at me. "Reed Holloway? That's your source that I ran off to DHR?"

Her hand came across my face faster than I could think to parry. In the years that I had known her in the various stages of our relationship, she had never struck me, and I had done plenty of things to deserve it. To be fair, I knew believing Reed Holloway would set her off. They were often like oil and water.

She stormed off the stage and out the front door, shoving it open.

Riff muttered I was an asshole and went after her. Probably true. I headed back to the bar. My cheek still stung. I deserved it. I'd weaponized Reed's lie knowing exactly how she'd react, and she'd called my bluff. The question was whether Reed had lied deliberately or been mistaken. Either way, I'd just burned a bridge I couldn't afford to lose.

The band was going to have a rough set, but I wanted to see if she came back and perhaps correct the problem with her.

When they returned, I watched Riff's hands settle on Cree's shoulders, gentle and steady. She leaned into him with a trust I'd never seen her show anyone besides me. Maybe that's what she needed. Someone who wasn't carrying twenty-something years of history and didn't disappear into Conservatory politics. Someone who was just there.

For someone whose life had been a series of brilliant, burning relationships with creative types, maybe ordinary was exactly what she needed.

I left the Hedgehog and walked into the bleak night. The confrontation with Cree had torn open something I'd kept sealed for twenty years. My left hand tremored. Not from the evening chill. From memory.

Twenty years ago, we'd made another choice outside another building. And that night changed everything.

CHAPTER 16
HARMONY HALL

CREE'S WORDS echoed as I walked home: "how shitty the two of you left things with each other." She was right. We did. Twenty years dissolved like smoke.

May 14, 2006. Eleven months into what everyone was calling the Eleven War, though most of Columbus had no idea it was happening. The Statics went about their lives while musicians fought for the right to create freely. Halfway in, they were joined by the writers, artists, journalists, and theater people. There were no internet content creators yet.

Cree, Felix, and I stood outside Harmony Hall with hundreds of other Dynamicists. The converted church loomed in darkness with its redbrick and Gothic Revival architecture, wrought-iron gates wrapped in chains.

Inside, the Compressionists held Professor Copland and sixteen other musicians. "Reeducation sessions," they called it. Harmonic torture. Breaking the connection between emotion and music until all that remained were hollow shells playing perfect scales with dead eyes.

The Compressionists didn't give a damn whether they were torturing Virtuosi or regular musicians. One was as good as the other because sometimes they might become Virtuosi.

Professor Copland had taught us that music without passion was organized noise. Now they had him in a chair with electrodes on his temples, playing the same four-bar phrase over and over. *Variation is chaos. Improvisation is dangerous.*

Cree peered over the wall, then dropped back beside us. "This is insane. There's hundreds of them."

"We chose this," I said.

"We chose to defend freedom. Not throw our lives away for a suicide mission."

Felix checked his watch. "Midnight. If we're moving, it's now."

The plan was simple. Cree creates chaos at the main gate with her voice. Felix and I go over the wall, through the old stage door, get Copland and whoever else we can, and get out.

My magic was the key. Sometimes when I played, I felt the world's musical patterns. Walls had harmonics. People had rhythms. Hit the right note at the right time, and things responded. It wasn't reliable—half the time it failed completely —but the Compressionists couldn't predict it.

"Remember," Felix said, voice tight. "We're here to save our teacher. Not feed a war."

Cree stood. "Speak for yourself."

She slipped into shadows. Felix and I waited.

His eyes locked on to mine. "You scared?"

"Terrified."

"Same." His smile was grim. "If this goes south, we look out for each other. Deal?"

"Deal."

"Use the code. B-flat."

"Damn trumpet players." I smiled at him. "B-flat. But I don't plan on needing it."

Cree's voice reached us—a wild, chaotic "Lullaby of Birdland" that made even me disoriented. Guards stumbled, confused.

"That's our cue."

We climbed the wall and moved toward the old stage entrance. I pressed my ear to metal and played a soft chord, feeling for the lock mechanism. Three tumblers, each at different frequencies.

"How do you do that?" Felix whispered.

"Practice."

Inside was a nightmare. Gray walls. Harsh fluorescent lighting. The concert space was divided into cells, each containing a musician hooked to headphones and machines.

I heard Copland before I saw him. His voice was raw from screaming. Electrodes attached. That deafening four-bar phrase on repeat.

"Variation is chaos," a gray-suited technician said. "Improvisation is dangerous."

I lost my temper.

Played the angriest chord I could think of, pouring rage and love for music into the strings.

Every piece of electronic equipment died at once.

Lights flickered out. Torture machines went silent. Emergency alarms screamed as backup power failed.

"What the hell—" Felix stared at me.

"Move!"

We ran through dark corridors toward Copland's cubicle. Compressionist guards shouted, unprepared for anything regulations couldn't fix.

Copland slumped unconscious in his chair. Felix grabbed him while I checked other cells. Sixteen more musicians in various states of trauma.

I played another chord—dissonant, unsettling. The musicians stirred. Eyes focused.

"Run," Copland whispered, rousing. "They can't catch us all."

Real forces arrived then. Elite units with harmonic disruptors, science emulating magic. Science overriding magic. Thirty seconds.

Seventeen escaped musicians and dozens of students burst through the gate. Copland stumbled beside us, checking faces.

"The basement," he gasped. "Did you get them?"

My eyes went wide. I didn't know there was a basement. I charged inside.

Students charged down the stairs with me. Two dozen more musicians in basement cells.

Cree appeared. "It's burning."

"What?"

"Someone set it on fire. Upstairs."

"Get them out," I ordered. "I'll sweep again. Make sure all of our people are out."

I released everyone and checked the entire floor twice. When I headed for the stairs, flames raced through the building. Consuming stations, climbing walls, devouring the timber ceiling.

I never saw what hit me.

———

My eyes opened to the building engulfed and Felix staring at me upside down, smiling.

"Welcome back, buddy."

He was dragging me out. Cree joined him. Together, they hoisted me up and helped me into the street.

Everyone scattered through the Arts District. Some made it. Some didn't.

By dawn, Compressionists had recaptured eight musicians and killed three who resisted. News called it arson. Dynamicist leadership called it a strategic victory.

Copland was never the same. He could still play and teach,

but something broke in those sessions. The spark that made him brilliant had been methodically crushed.

A week later, both sides negotiated. Compressionists became the Department of Harmonic Regulation. Dynamicists merged into the Conservatory, who had done their best to appear impartial while fueling the Dynamicists. Both claimed victory.

But listening to Copland weep for his lost students, we knew the truth. The Compressionists won the moment they made us believe regulated freedom was better than dangerous liberty.

That night cemented our futures. The siege led me to the Conservatory, Felix to Juilliard, and Cree to gig work.

We never learned who struck the match. One of ours in panic, or a Compressionist covering evidence. Maybe both.

The war never really ended. It just learned to wear better suits.

Twenty years later, I walked through Columbus streets, the chilly night air burning my lungs as if it were the fire that night. My left hand still tremored when I thought about that night. About Felix dragging me out of the flames. About the promise we made to look out for each other.

A promise I'd kept for less than a year before everything fell apart.

CHAPTER 17
WONDERLY

Sunday, May 24—Day 3

THE NEXT DAY, we took an easier route with a trip back to the Twelve-Tone Spin Zone to see about Billie. Sunday after church let out, and the place was packed. I doubted many of the customers were the church type.

Hoagy's parents were, however, so we didn't get started until after one. That was okay. I killed time proving my composition skills were still decomposing at the piano.

The two kids at the counter were the same ones: Sage and Riot. They had a line going halfway back through the room. Wedging through the crowd toward them, I'd have to buy something to get answers. So I grabbed a record without looking at it.

Hoagy was down with it and handed me another record. Ruby Blue's first self-titled album from five years ago. The cover photo was a sultry shot at the Hedgehog with Ruby in a red-sequined formfitting dress with her straddling the mic stand. Obvious choice. I smirked at the kid.

"Got a record player, do you?" I asked.

"Yeah. Do you?"

"I'll borrow yours."

Walking to the end of the line, I tripped on the uneven floorboards, but just enough to bump into a woman. With a nod, I apologized to her and got in line behind her.

The customer was tall and precise, mid-thirties, her chestnut hair pulled back severely with wooden pins. If she tied those chestnut locks any tighter, the whole lot of violin strings would snap. She wasn't my type, but something in those eyes made me think one little thing was dying to let loose. But if she came undone, if one button freed itself, she'd deflate like a balloon and flutter around the room. That juxtaposition was intriguing.

I must have not been thinking. It took me a full two minutes to realize it was the woman from the Archives. Noted. I thought back. The woman who ran out of Felix's building that first time at the scene. That was her.

She wasn't surveillance—too visible for that. She wanted me to see her. Question was: why?

Hoagy had noticed her, too, and whispered to me, using his hand to shield the sound. "That's the fourth time I've seen her. You think she's following us or we're following her?"

"Both, probably."

The kid frowned. "Is that a paradox?"

"It's an investigation."

Wait. I'd seen her at Felix's and at the Archives. The playground outside Ruby's. I glanced at the kid. I held up my fingers and mouthed, *Four times?*

Hoagy glanced at her. Not paying attention. He continued whispering. "Mr. Cantabile's. The Archives. Playground. And outside the Hedgehog. Across the street while we were looking at Jacob."

I'd missed that. "Good eye."

"Two even," he said with a smile.

None of which I should be thinking about, especially when I was still sore at Cree. Still unsure if she'd told me the truth. I gave her a smile like I was greeting her at church.

She stared back through the pince-nez glasses, playful, amused. Still had her Whimsy.

"Oh my gosh," she said. Quaint. "I almost forgot."

My line companion was talking to herself, but she excused herself from the line and hustled farther down the long hall. I watched her walk, stop, and flip through some records.

I shoved my record at Hoagy and watched.

It took her a couple of minutes, but she returned to the line with a new album in hand. Hoagy was between us. When she said nothing, I turned and tried to break the ice, but she ignored me, as she should. No doubt I was Whimsy-deficient.

With both records in hand, Hoagy looked up at me. *"Pirates of Penzance?"*

Shit. Pay attention to what you're doing. "Say what you will, but Gilbert and Sullivan understood musical structure."

"Really? That's your defense? I hope you don't do your mag—"

My hand shot to his mouth. I stared at the woman with the glasses. My hand dropped from Hoagy's mouth. He got the message. "Gilbert and Sullivan"—I swallowed hard—"were known for their patter songs."

Hoagy's eyes narrowed, darting between me and the woman from the Archives. "Something's pattering anyway," Hoagy said.

"Cute kid," the woman said.

"Not my kid."

When we arrived at the counter with my two favorite attendants, I asked again, "Billie here?"

The girl with all the piercings, Sage, frowned at me. Apparently, I was memorable. "We could only get one, and it's reserved."

They could only get one. Interesting. Billie wasn't a person. At least not the kind you'd meet.

"For whom?" I asked.

The girl turned to the boy. "Felix Cantabile," Riot said.

With a shake of my head, I stared at her. "Felix is dead."

They looked at each other, not knowing what to do. Every time I saw these two, I was announcing dead bodies.

"When did he reserve it?" I asked.

Sage checked something under the counter. "Three weeks ago. Paid in advance."

Three weeks. A constant thread in this case.

"So, how about it?" I asked. "How much for Billie?"

Hoagy perked up. "Billie Eilish?"

The clerk and I both stared at him.

The librarian behind me was antsy, like the kids had the key to the restroom and she was too polite to cut.

Sage dug into the shelf under the counter and pulled out an album. The edges were worn, and the cover art was muted. With a grunt, I wanted to shoot myself. Billie Holiday. Ridiculous. So this would mean absolutely nothing.

I paid for the album anyway, more than I should have. I told them I didn't want Gilbert and Sullivan, but I was stuck with the record for the kid. I didn't own a record player. I could create music or play it through magical means.

After I stepped aside to let Prim and Proper complete her transaction, we exited with our purchases. The doorbell chimed as I stood on the pavement, examining my purchase. Perhaps I should go back to Felix's and figure out if he had a record player, and I didn't see it. In his memory, I could listen to it retro-style.

With the album in hand, I tapped it on my leg and stared down the street. Hoagy looked impatient. A couple more names remained on the list. But we were getting nowhere. Armando wouldn't let my leash get too long before I had to report. Even if the kid was reporting already, I would have to as well.

A moment later, the glasses girl exited empty-handed. She stepped beside me. The whole sidewalk was open, but I had the ideal spot, I guess. Hoagy leaned forward, checking that the three of us were lined up like an album cover.

"Well, hello," I said.

"Hello yourself," she returned.

"Gave up on your album?"

She smiled. "You have what I want."

I held up Billie Holiday. "This or something else?"

She wasn't biting. Hoagy groaned under his breath.

She smiled. "Yes, that album. I would like it. So please tell me how much."

"Don't think I can sell it. Turns out I'm a big Billie Holiday fan."

"No, you're not," she said.

Interesting woman. "How do you know?"

"You were surprised that Felix Cantabile ordered a Billie Holiday record."

"Eavesdropping, eh?"

"Yes," she began, "because I really need that album, and you went in expecting a person named Billie."

I lifted the album, looked at the cover, then at her. Smart suit, skirt to her knees, reasonably sized mortal heels. Not a stitch out of place, not a button unbuttoned, not a hair attempting escape.

Through the rimless glasses, her eyes met mine. "Never understood those." I pointed at them. "Isn't it a pain without having arms on the glasses?"

The woman cocked her head at me. "It is not. In fact, it's more convenient. Now, how about my album?"

With a chuckle, I shook the album. "My album?"

I flipped it over and looked at the back. There was nothing special about it. I mean, yes, if you were a Billie Holiday fan, it was probably a first pressing or something, given the price I paid for it. But it wasn't worth a fight over it.

"Hoagy." I handed him the album. "You're the record expert. What do you make of this?"

Prim and Proper stepped closer as Hoagy studied the art. She put her arm on mine. "Please. Name your price for that album."

Something about her intensity reminded me of student resistance groups from my college days. People who'd risk everything for what they believed in. But those days were long past. I was reading too much into a vinyl collector's enthusiasm. Still, the business card said "Ask for Billie." Was it just to pick up a reserved antiquated album?

"There's something," Hoagy said.

He reached inside to pull the record from the jacket only to find that the sleeve had notes scrawled all over it. And these were not part of the original album. Someone thought they'd start their novel on the sleeve of a record.

The sleeve wasn't halfway out when Miss Prim and Proper reached out, grabbed the record in the sleeve, and bolted down the street, leaving Hoagy with only the jacket. The Ruby Blue album fell to the ground.

"Not cool," Hoagy said, picking up his record.

"Agreed."

The kid looked offended, like she'd violated some sacred record store code. I wasn't gonna chase her, but I headed that direction. As we walked, I pulled out the piccolo and assembled it.

"What are you going to do?"

"Find her. She can't run far."

The smaller instrument was better for tracking work. Less power, more precision. I played a simple search pattern in G-sharp minor, watching as faint magical traces became visible to me, like footprints made of moonlight. The trail led down two blocks and turned into an alley, but there was something odd about it. The traces flickered, as if whoever I was following knew how to mask their magical signature.

Hoagy ran into me as I halted. "She's been trained."

"She's Virtuosi?"

"No. I don't think so. She's a rookie, though. Some people can do nonmagical things for us. She obviously has some connection. Still, masking her path is a good skill to have." I glanced at the kid. "For us."

She'd run two blocks and turned into an alley where the path ended. She was still there. I crept along the wall, using shadows for cover, keeping my feet quiet. Hoagy got the idea and stayed behind me.

Three-quarters down, a doorway was recessed into the brick wall. She stood there, looking at her prize. When she noticed us, she stepped back into the doorway.

I held up the empty album jacket. "Missing something?"

She moved toward the street, but I stepped into her path. "Just want to talk. You don't look the thief type," I said.

"I'm not," she replied.

"All evidence to the contrary."

Defiance burned in her eyes. "You don't look the creep type."

"Not usually," Hoagy answered.

"I'm not." I stepped back after snatching the sleeve, then slipped it into the jacket. "Have a name?"

She crossed her arms. "Of course I have a name."

"So, I have a question for you."

The woman stared at me, curious, without intent to run.

I delivered my most disarming grin. "Do you want to talk about this here in the alley, like this? Or do you want to go sit down and have a cup of coffee to discuss it?"

A smile came across her face after her eyes searched my face. Full Whimsy on that one. "Yes, I would love to have a cup of coffee."

I leaned in closer. "You're going to do it, too. You're not going to take off?"

"Of course I won't," she said.

I stepped back and gestured toward the street, extending the crook of my elbow for her to take. I'm polite like that, and I wanted to make sure she stayed with me.

Prim and Proper broke free once we hit the street, snagging the album. That was okay. She wouldn't run. And she halted and waited for us to catch up. Hoagy watched the interaction with interest. She handed the Ruby Blue album to me.

"Sneaky," she said.

"You're getting quite the workout today," I said.

"Yes." The woman smirked. "Let's have our little talk so I can go rest."

With a nod, I pointed down the street. "There's a coffee shop about six doors down. If you want to run ahead, I don't mind."

She glared at me, and we walked to it. She appeared not to trust me. Reasonable, given I had confronted her in a murky alley. This was a consistent attitude with the Conservatory. It was safe to assume she knew that.

The woman smiled at Hoagy. "How'd you get stuck with him if he's not your dad?"

"He's my mentor," Hoagy said.

The look on her face screamed pity for the boy. "What are you training to be?"

"I've got a summer internship to see if I'd like to be—"

My arm went around his shoulder and pulled him closer to me. "Let's not get him started. This kid will talk your ear off if you let him."

Inside the coffee shop, she got a croissant and cappuccino while I stuck to coffee. Black. Hoagy got some foo-foo drink that was going to cost Armando more than he'd like in expenses. After weaving through the dining room, we sat next to the window. The place was about three-quarters full, but we could talk without too much trouble.

The kid pulled out his phone and started scrolling while we settled in.

I set the album and the sleeve on the table. She pulled it closer to her but didn't attempt to flee.

"Do you have a name?" I asked.

"Wonderly," she said, extending her hand.

I shook her hand and released it before the handholding became too long. "Wonderful."

"No. Wonderly. Eliza Wonderly."

"Eliza Wonderly. Is that your real name?"

"Yes, why would I lie to you?"

With a shrug, I smiled at her. "You are a record thief."

"Attempted record thief." Her fingers pressed the album so hard she might break the table. Long, strong fingers. Free of defects.

"So, what's so important about Billie Holiday here?"

She sighed and studied the room. "It's a special signed edition. I am still happy to pay you for it."

I laughed. "Signed edition. Only if the signature is written in whole paragraphs." Wonderly smiled back at me as if I were an idiot, and she was nudging me to bother someone else with her eyes. "My first question is: do you know Felix Cantabile?"

She exhaled sharply. "Yes, I knew him."

"So you know he's dead."

"You said so in the store."

"You did," Hoagy added.

I grimaced. "Thanks. Are you upset about it?"

Her coffee hit the saucer hard as she set it down. "Of course I'm upset about it." Her eyes even agreed with her words.

"Any idea who might have wanted him dead?"

Wonderly sipped her coffee and stared out the window. "I'm afraid I don't have experience with the seedier side of life like you do."

My eyebrows shot up. "You think I have that experience?"

Wonderly frowned at me. "You're looking for info on dead

people and cornering helpless women in alleys to get what you want."

I laughed. "Touché. But helpless isn't the word I would use. If I were so scary, why'd you stop in the alley instead of continuing to run?"

"To make sure it was the right one."

With a nod, I leaned forward. "Eliza, you knew it was the right album."

"I knew it would take a great deal of effort to get away from you."

I pursed my lips. "Yeah? Think I'm a track star?"

Wonderly's eyes narrowed. "I know you're Virtuosi."

"That's what I'm training to be. Maybe," Hoagy said.

"She knows that." Leaning back in my chair, I chuckled. "Had some trouble with us?"

"You're all trouble," she said. "Virtuoso, Virtuosa, the whole lot of you." She leaned forward. "You use artificial means to create your music. Real artists create with their souls."

"Artificial? Our magic comes from the music."

"Yes, but it's not creative, it's … it's something else outside of you."

"Ouch. How very DHR of you," I said. "Felix was a Virtuoso."

"And one of the kindest people on earth." Wonderly smiled. "He wasn't like the rest of you. Felix was going to break free. Then one of your people did him in."

Hoagy's head snapped up from his phone, eyes wide. The kid was hearing that his potential future profession might be full of murderers. Not the best recruiting pitch.

"One of my people?" My eyes narrowed. "You're saying someone from the Conservatory killed Felix?"

She threw her hands up. "Of course. He was no longer needed. Whimsy was fading already. He was a liability. Time for the replacement."

"That sounds more like a job for the DHR," I said.

Wonderly shook her head. "Why? He had lost the Whimsy a while back, and now he was harmless to the DHR. It's your type that were threatened." She leaned forward. "And he knew the Harmonic Council was compromised."

"How did he know it was compromised?"

"I don't know. He didn't tell me."

Who? I wondered. Some of the Council were a pain in the ass. Some were difficult, but they had all been part of the Conservatory for so long.

"Why would a Council member suddenly switch sides?"

"I think that's your job to find out, not mine," she said. "Now how about my record?"

I drank the last sip of my coffee. "How 'bout if I sell the record to you as soon as I investigate the scrawl across it?"

"I have a better deal," she said. "How about I keep it? You go see if I'm incorrect about the Conservatory. Then I'll make sure to leave you magical little bread crumbs so you can find me to read the inscription."

"You're suggesting you're immune to my magic."

"Deal?" Wonderly held out her hand.

No wonder she'd attracted my attention at the Archives. I was certain she'd let me find her again. What was I saying? She was getting inside my head. I was certain my skills could find her. "Deal."

CHAPTER 18
SFORZANDO

HOAGY WAS silent as we walked toward the Short North. I liked that about the kid. But the gears were grinding in his head.

"Hungry?" I asked. Stupid question. When was a teenage boy not hungry?

"Sure."

I steered him down Spruce Street to get to the easy entrance to North Market with all the construction going on. The place was not a market in the traditional sense but a two-story culinary carnival. The building used to be a warehouse, now a busy, loud place to get Vietnamese, Polish, pick-your-favorite food or snack place.

It was a Sunday, but the streets felt abnormally empty. We stepped into the market and it was empty, too. But it was open and all the vendors were waiting on customers or doing prep work.

We stepped back onto the pavement. The entire street had no cars.

"There!" Hoagy pointed into the construction zone.

Two DHR officials wearing their usual tactical cosplay jackets with the DHR logo on them walked someone out of the work site and into the street. A third ran up to them with an acoustic guitar in his hand.

"Just destroy it," one of the DHR goons said.

When their captive protested, I recognized that it was Eric Mueller, a web designer by day and a street performer in the Short North by night. The third man slammed the guitar onto the sidewalk and jumped on it, crushing it. He hurled it into the construction zone.

He glanced at Eric. "Another one gone. I suggest you stick to your day job."

Eric continued his protest, but as the guitar flew from sight, he deflated. A DHR van pulled up to the curb. I hustled over, leaving Hoagy to catch up.

"Eric, you all right?"

"Shove off," one of the goons told me.

"It's okay," Eric said. "They're going to help me."

"Doesn't look like help to me." I leaned forward to find his eyes. "You don't have to go."

"Step back," the goon ordered.

"This is a public street."

The goon lurched forward, shoving me. Not hard, but definitive. "I said, step back."

Those instincts from the war flared, my hands balled into fists, and every instinct in me was screaming to fight. The war had taught me how to fight. Harmony Hall had taught me how to lose. I centered myself and stepped aside. Not time yet.

As Eric was being loaded into the van, he mouthed, *Sorry*.

And then something snapped. I lunged at the goon, but he was expecting it. He seized my arm, wrenched it behind my back, and shoved me to the sidewalk. My face was smashed into the concrete.

Hoagy stood a dozen feet away and started toward us, but a look from the enforcer caused him to halt. My face was being dragged against the concrete as the goon put his knee on my neck and pressed. Nothing serious. A warning.

"You're off this case, Kohl. Stay off it."

The goon released me. Slowly, I sat up while he towered over me, hands on hips. My piccolo had fallen out of my pocket in the struggle, and the two pieces rolled toward the goon.

He picked up the pieces and then worked on each with all his strength until he was able to break them in half. Then, if it weren't enough already, he hurled the pieces into the construction zone. After a fake laugh, he jumped into the back of the van and sped off like they had just robbed a bank.

My cheek was burning, scraped, and had some blood on it. Hoagy approached. "Are you hurt bad?"

"Only my ego."

As I stood, he helped me up. "I didn't know what to do."

"You did exactly the right thing. No sense in both of us getting beat up."

I brushed myself off. A little extra dust on my jacket added character, so I waved the kid forward. "Still feel like eating?"

"Not so much."

"Good. Me, neither."

We got back on High Street and headed toward the Short North. I was curious to see if the streets were barren there as well or if it was just the North Market.

It was empty. With a glance down Poplar, I saw a van being loaded. Not DHR goons this time, but Boomer Blake loading up a drum set. I dragged the kid in that direction.

"Hey, Boomer," I said.

"He's not *that* old," Hoagy mumbled.

"It's okay, kid. It's his stage name."

But Boomer didn't answer. There was a small music store there where Boomer and some others gave lessons. You could buy a guitar or drums, too. Lots of old, used stuff.

There was no storefront window, but the glass in the door,

the kind with the metal grill behind it, had been shattered. The metal framework kept the spidered glass in place.

"Boomer, what's up?"

He didn't even look at me. "Getting out before they come for me."

I didn't have the heart to tell him that in a couple more days it would be worldwide. Worse. Once Whimsy was gone, he wouldn't care that he couldn't play anymore.

I reached out and grabbed his shoulder. Boomer whipped around, drumstick raised like a weapon. Paranoid. Terrified.

"Stay back! I don't know you. I don't know anyone."

I raised my hand. "It's me, Dekker Kohl. You know me."

"They sent you. You're one of them." He backed toward the van, wild-eyed.

"Boomer, we're trying to help."

He swung at me with his drumstick. I blocked the attack, and pain shot up my arm. Bruising from kissing the concrete. But in the moment, Boomer recognized what he did.

"Oh God, Dekk. I'm sorry." He shook his head. "I thought you were … They're everywhere. Can't trust anyone."

But he didn't wait for my reply. He shut the van doors and drove off, leaving the front door to the music store open.

Physical pain was nothing compared to the helplessness that I felt. That's what burned. Not hurt enough to stop. Hurt enough to be angry. Sometimes getting beaten up is permission. Permission to stop being nice.

I sent Hoagy home.

By the time I limped back to Italian Village, dusk was settling. My face throbbed where the concrete had scraped it raw. My piccolo was in two pieces somewhere in a construction zone. I needed sleep. Tomorrow I'd deal with the Council and whatever fresh hell they had planned.

I had no idea how right I was.

CHAPTER 19
CASE DISMISSED

Monday, May 25—Day 4

AT THE CORDIAL invitation of Il Consiglio Armonico, I arrived at the Conservatory the next morning, Monday, without an instrument. All formal documents from them used the full Italian naming conventions. Following the invitation title: "Report *allegretto con urgenza.*" So I chose to report "*andante con ritardando*" and maximized the slow walking, no matter how painful it was.

This time the Custode ushered me into the Council chamber, which was as mystical and ridiculous as it sounded. Without concern for my boredom, I was left alone, perhaps to ponder the greatness of the Council. In front of me was a long table with seven chairs for the Council members. Behind them was a giant clock, except that it was on a giant metronome, the pendulum keeping the beat, swinging nearly the width of the room.

Why they wanted to build towering halls underground was beyond me, but knock yourselves out.

Scaffolding was erected around the perimeter of the room because it is a law that all historical landmarks must be under renovation at least six months of the year. I'd have to remember to ask Sonny if she had a regulation for that.

In this case, I hoped they would never finish it. They had paid a troupe of artists to paint the arched ceiling with Renaissance-looking paintings with all the angels holding a giant, magically glowing Circle of Fifths with the zodiac mapped onto it so that C Major was Aries etc. all the way to F Major being Pisces. One problem, though. The painters were not from the Conservatory or any music school. Their painting was more the Circle of Thirds with an occasional fifth.

Under each spoke in the wheel of theoretical fifths stood a marble column with a bust of a composer on it. All of them were famous composers except the last one, which was Armando.

Normally, I didn't mind being left alone with my thoughts, but today felt different.

The door at the back opened, and the Seven strode in, wearing fancy purple robes with enough gold trim to bankrupt a small duchy. They took their seats, the heavy chairs scraping the floor in an unmusical fashion. Armando was at the center.

Armando spoke first, as was his right. "Mr. Kohl, how are you today?"

"Sharp around the edges, flat in the middle."

"What is wrong with your face?"

I reached up and touched my tender cheek. "The sidewalk jumped up and bit me."

"Yes," Armando said. "I have heard that you've been busy."

"Following orders," I said.

"And have you solved the case?" he asked.

I frowned. "Not yet. I need more time."

"How much time?" Councilor Foyle asked.

"I don't know. Hopefully, less than three days."

Armando read from a paper on the table, then looked at me.

"It is my understanding that you have been chasing down musicians that one Jazzy Jacob wrote bad reviews about."

"Yes, Jazzy Jacob was murdered in the alley next to the Cinnamon Hedgehog."

Another member, this time to my right, spoke in a low gravelly tone. "And this Jazzy Jeff is somehow tied into the death of Felix Cantabile?"

I corrected him. "Jazzy Jacob. I don't know. Following the trail."

Emily Contralto, the Council member on the far left, stared at me through glasses half the size of her head. "The trail seems to be leading you away from the Guardian, which was, I believe, your mission."

Under normal circumstances, Ms. Contralto was prone to take my side of things or provide me with more leeway. It didn't feel like that today.

"It was." I swallowed. "It is. It's complicated."

"How about you simplify it for us?" Armando said.

"Felix was murdered. Whimsy has been failing."

Armando interrupted. "We expect Whimsy will be gone in three days." He glanced at Foyle, who gave a barely perceptible nod. Something unspoken passed between them—some decision already made that I wasn't privy to.

"Well," I continued, "it didn't start fading when Felix died. It started weeks before."

Artur Berko, a blond-headed Councilor who sat a head taller than everyone else and at the right hand of Armando, spoke. "You are suggesting that someone or something else had control of Whimsy? How could that be? It was not conferred on anyone else."

"I'm uncertain, but I'm working on it."

"By investigating leads about some music critic?" Berko asked.

Armando raised a hand. "Let us pause this." He looked around the table at his fellow Councilors. "Regardless of the outcome here, we have three days. We've already set larger matters in motion. This"—he gestured vaguely at me—"may become irrelevant. Admit the guests."

The giant doors behind me groaned open. I turned to see Sonny entering the hall. For a moment, I wondered if she would go up in flames. She was dressed in purple as well, but more formfitting and elegant, with angled pleats running from hip to shoulder. Sonny carried a matching purple bag over her shoulder.

She didn't give me so much as a glance as she stopped beside me.

"Well, hello," I said.

No response. Blending in with the statuary.

A moment later, Hoagy entered, polished, uncomfortable, and avoiding my gaze. Armando gestured at him, and he took a seat behind us.

"You have met Sonny Mordent," Armando said.

"Yes."

"Ms. Mordent, welcome to the Harmonic Council. Please make your presentation."

"Thank you," she said with a bow. "As the Head of Special Projects of the DHR, I personally got involved in this case when your Guardian of Whimsy was the victim."

I spoke out of turn. "You don't believe in the Guardians."

Sonny didn't look at me. "I do not. However, I do know the importance of them to the Council and the Conservatory as a whole. It is in all of our best interests to solve this crime."

"We agree," Armando said. Other members nodded.

"Mr. Kohl doesn't trust me," she continued, "mostly due to my being part of the DHR. Perhaps a little due to the fact that Felix Cantabile was his former friend."

"And your former husband," I added.

"Mr. Kohl!" Foyle said.

Sonny continued. "But regardless of his beliefs, I want the case solved more than most. Professionally and personally, I need to resolve it."

I didn't know why she was in such a hurry. Felix was a musician. She wasn't going to inherit anything besides that piano, some poorly written music, and a cat.

"As I'm sure you are aware," Sonny said, "Mr. Kohl has sidetracked from solving the case of Felix Cantabile to the case of some washed-up music critic in a dumpster."

Poor Jacob. So mistreated.

"It is my belief that Mr. Kohl's irregular methods of detection have rendered him a detriment to this case," Sonny said.

"How so?" Armando asked.

"May I approach?" Sonny asked.

He gestured her forward.

Sonny stepped to the table and pulled an envelope from her bag. "Mr. Kohl has been tracking me. And watching me."

The envelope contained eight by ten glossy photographs. Was this some kind of AI job being done on me? After flipping through them, Armando held them out for me to look. I accepted them and flipped through.

Dammit. Not AI. Security cameras with time stamps over the past three weeks. But I hadn't been following her. Yet it was clearly my face.

I looked up. "I don't even know where you live."

"The end of Warren Street," Sonny said evenly. "High-dollar condos. I called it my apartment in our conversations. Perhaps I should have been more specific."

Warren Street. One of my regular walking routes between the Conservatory and Italian Village. The photos weren't fake—they were just taken whenever I passed by. Surveillance cameras on a building I walked past anyway.

"These prove I walk through the neighborhood," I said. "They don't prove stalking."

"They prove a pattern," Sonny replied. "Three weeks of you appearing near my home. Sometimes twice a day. You have had significant antagonism with me since the day I met you. I don't know if it's me you don't like, the DHR, or that Felix didn't tell you about me."

"Why limit it to just one?" I asked.

The busts of the composers must have gasped along with the Council. That was soon followed by the pit of my stomach hitting the floor like a kettledrum.

"He should be dismissed," one of the Councilors muttered. I couldn't tell who.

"Wait," I said. "You want to dismiss me based on surveillance photos showing I walked through a neighborhood? On my normal route home?"

"If personal harassment of a grieving woman is not sufficient for the council," Sonny said, pausing to look each member in the eye.

"The appearance of impropriety—" Berko began.

Sonny shook her head. "Then impeding a DHR investigation and assaulting an officer of the DHR should be sufficient for the purpose."

"Whimsy dies in three days," I cut in. "And you're benching your only investigator over appearances?"

"And assault," Councilor Foyle said.

Emily Contralto shifted in her seat. "The timing does seem—"

"Ms. Mordent has brought serious concerns," Foyle interrupted. "We must consider them. And you are, to be fair, close to the case. Armando should not have assigned you."

I looked at Armando. "You know me. Eighteen years with the Conservatory. You really think I've been stalking Felix's widow?"

Armando's face remained impassive. "What I think is irrelevant. The Council will deliberate."

The chairs of the Councilors scooted back, and the members huddled together like they were racing to hit the final cadence before the music stopped. Sonny remained close to the table. I was alone in the world, unable to explain this story.

Through the murmur of their discussion, I caught fragments. Foyle's voice: "Cardinals have agreed to an emergency convocation." Berko: "The seventh day—that's all we have." Armando: "Every Guardian. Every Keeper from every delegation. At Isola Sonora." Contralto: "There's no precedent for this."

Isola Sonora. At least they knew it was important to go have a powwow at a Mediterranean island. It was nice, though. Been there once as Armando's Novizio.

A Custode slipped in through the side door, whispered something to Armando, who nodded grimly and gestured for him to continue with the summons. The Custode bowed and disappeared back through the door.

Within a minute, the members returned to their seats with all the appropriate noise-making.

Armando remained standing. "The Council has voted six to one. Given that the case to solve the murder of Felix Cantabile has derailed and that Virtuoso Kohl appears to have invested personal stakes in the case, the Council orders that the investigation be immediately ceased. We will review all the conditions and results. Virtuoso Kohl, you are to cease and desist. Enjoy some time off, but remain in the city."

"Who voted to keep me on?" I asked.

Armando's expression didn't change. "Council votes are not disclosed. We have other pressing matters; then we will resume."

Emily Contralto wouldn't meet my eyes. That told me enough.

He addressed Hoagy. "Novizio Porter, you are to have no

contact with Virtuoso Kohl. You will be reassigned to Tuning. My understanding is that you are good with your hands and repair instruments well."

So that was it. Dismissed from the case while they scrambled to assemble every Guardian and international Keeper for an emergency convocation at Isola Sonora on the seventh day. The legendary island where Guardians were chosen and unmade. Where the Cardinals sat in judgment. The Vatican of magic itself.

Yet somehow I was the one who needed to enjoy some time off.

Case closed. Case dismissed. Whatever they wanted to call it.

But it wasn't closed. The photos existed—that much was real. Warren Street security cameras had been recording me for three weeks every time I walked my normal route. Coincidence? Or had someone been setting this up for longer than I realized?

But the thing that ate at me most was the DHR goon grinding my face into the pavement, saying, "You're off this case, Kohl." Like he knew. A day before I did.

I was still processing my dismissal when I spotted Rimsky outside a coffee shop two blocks from the Conservatory. He wasn't drinking coffee. Instead, he was watching the building through binoculars.

When he saw me, he lowered them slowly. "Mr. Kohl."

"Inspector. Admiring the architecture?"

"Studying patterns. Your Conservatory has been remarkably quiet since the Guardian's death." Rimsky tucked the binoculars inside his coat. "Almost as if they expected it."

Something in his tone made my skin crawl. "What's that supposed to mean?"

"Ms. Mordent believes magical creativity is dangerous. I believe she's more dangerous than the magic." He started walking away, then paused. "Be careful who you trust, Mr. Kohl. Sometimes the person warning you about wolves is the one sharpening their teeth."

I walked away, hands shaking. Eighteen years with the Conservatory. Gone. Just like that. I needed to hit something. I needed to move. I needed to not think.

I headed for the Fencing Academy.

CHAPTER 20
OUT OF MEASURE

A REASONABLE MAN ought to be pissed that they shit-canned me. True, I had been wandering around asking questions about a music critic, and Jazzy Jacob was also known to criticize the Conservatory as being full of nonmusicians. I was sure the deaths were connected, but I had been ordered off. And Rimsky gave me cryptic warnings.

Going home would have been smart. Perhaps it was my lack of Whimsy, but I didn't care. Rather than dwell on professional failure, I sought the familiar comfort of physical combat. The kind that would let me feel the discomfort of my pain without kicking me in the gut with it. Fencing.

Stress demanded its usual remedy: stabbing people with swords. Royal Arts Fencing Academy had two branches: one downtown and one on the east side. I could walk to the one downtown in Italian Village, so decision made.

Naturally, we just called it the Academy. Fencing had several things in common beyond the heavy Italian/European influence, maestros, and a dedication to managing time. Tempo applied to fencing, music, and magic. And "measures" applied to fencing, music, magic, construction, and—if you were really having a bad day—undertakers.

The fencing club was another redbrick former factory converted into high-cost offices and then eventually high-cost offices on one end and a fencing academy on the other. The good thing about old factories was the high ceilings and long rooms for our fourteen-meter fencing strips.

The landlords weren't generous with the width of the place, only allowing us to get about twenty-five feet wide. On the other side of the wall were a couple of oddball stores: a dry cleaner and an occult bookstore where you could buy charms that supposedly warded against people like me. I preferred they do the evil-eye thing, but everyone needs to spend their money to taste.

The floors of our part bore the scars of a thousand blade-fights, wood scarred and pitted like an old boxer's face. I stood in the cramped changing area as other members moved between the strips. The floors were so springy that when a fencer bounced up and down, the ripples made us all bounce a little.

Along most of the walls, a notched shelf held weapons every few inches, and hooks held masks a foot above. The entrance had benches for personal items and cubbies for the members to keep their gear and a few for the nuggets wanting to get stabbed repeatedly to see if they liked it. A spiral staircase stood in the corner, heading to the second-level loft. The rickety spiral stairs violated several safety codes, but nobody seemed inclined to test its limits.

I had a cubby in the place as a perk of being a member since the days when Felix and I were running around pretending we had good futures ahead of us. At least one of us had survived to see today.

I dressed in my full fencing whites with my knee-high breeches, demonstrating that I was a walking anachronism. Trovatore, magician, fencer. What was next? Calligraphy? At this rate, I'd be hand-binding books and insisting fountain pens had more character than keyboards.

Cree was there, too, and had suited up, inspecting the tip of her sword. When she looked up and saw my face, her expression shifted from irritation to concern.

"Jesus, Dekk. What happened to you?"

I touched my cheek gingerly. The swelling had gone down a bit, but the bruise was spectacular. "Long story. Involves a DHR enforcer and my piccolo."

Her eyes narrowed. "You need to see a doctor."

"I'm functional."

"Functional isn't the same as smart." She returned to inspecting her épée. "You sure you should be fencing?"

Walking over, I eyed her sword. "Not sharpening it, are you?"

"I oughta." She sneered at me. "Might put you out of your misery."

"Well, keep your claws in. The case is over."

Her eyes narrowed. "You figured out who killed Felix?"

"No, the Conservatory and the DHR finally agreed on something. They don't like me."

Cree smiled. "Some days I understand."

"Want to take it out on me with a sword?"

She put her hand on my chest and stepped closer, looking up at me with those eyes that told me I wasn't going to like what she was about to say. "Riff is getting dressed."

Before I could piss her off, I was saved by the bell—the doorbell, which was a series of horns stolen from an organ and repurposed to play a mostly out of tune trumpet fanfare. Three seconds of one, anyway.

I spun, and what to my wondering eyes should I see but Ms. Wonderly, everything in its place, and one of the old-timers greeting her. She was buttoned up tighter than a banker's wallet, every inch of the navy blue fabric speaking of control and buried secrets. No other colors, no dangling things on her wrists, no rings on her fingers. The only accessory was a matching oversize bag over her shoulder.

"Are you here to fence or put up fences?" the old man asked. "Because we get a lot of confusion about that. Every other language has a unique word for what we do." Wonderly stared at him. "Stabbing? Or building?"

Her face had all the warmth of a coroner's table. "The stabbing kind, obviously. Though if you're offering to help me put up barriers between myself and tedious questions, I'm listening."

The old-timer's mouth dropped open enough to drive a one-hundred-piece orchestra with full percussion through and still have room for the choir. However, I was beaming.

"I was hoping to find Dekker Kohl."

Riff stepped out of the changing room, fully suited for fencing. He moved with the controlled precision of someone who'd been training for years. When he saw Wonderly, his expression shifted: recognition, maybe even respect.

"Fenced long?" I asked Riff.

"Since I was eight. My father insisted." Riff adjusted his mask. "Said it would teach me discipline. Focus. All the things music apparently couldn't. Been a while, though. There wasn't a club nearby in my last town."

The bitterness in his voice made more sense now. Another musician with something to prove.

I walked away to greet Ms. Wonderly. "Well, hello," I said.

Her eyes inspected me from head to toe. "Let me guess. You raided the theater costume department for a Jane Austen adaptation?"

I smiled at her. "No, I time-traveled from 1750 and couldn't find a change of clothes."

The barest hint of an upward-turned lip appeared before it retreated to 1750. "Mr. Kohl, I am here to fulfill my promise."

"How'd you find me?"

"Maestra Flanconade told me."

"You know her?"

"I'm here, so obviously."

"Why are you here?"

"So I can fulfill my promise?"

I hoped Cree was close enough to hear that comment. "Let's step into my office."

Gesturing upward, I led her to the spiral staircase. Wonderly climbed the rickety stairs while I watched her for safety. Then I bounded up them, trusting that I'd catch myself if a step fell through.

The upstairs level looked over the main floor. Each end had windows, which let in the only light in the place. A few feet from the railing was a kitchenette. Six wooden tables sat next to the edge with chairs so you could overlook the action below or get a whiff of old leather and sweat.

With a wave, I gestured for her to sit.

"Back there"—I motioned to the rooms behind our kitchenette—"is where Maestra Fleurette Flanconade lives."

Tea seemed like the kind of civilized gesture that might impress someone who looked like she alphabetized her emotions. Evening timing saved me from attempting cappuccino foam art, a skill notably absent from my repertoire.

"Did you fence?" I asked.

Wonderly cocked an eyebrow. "You assume I quit?"

"I'm sorry." A shrug accompanied the admission. "But I haven't seen you around here."

"I don't fence. But is fencing creative?"

I couldn't tell if she was serious. "Of course it is. A different kind of creativity, but—"

"So had we stayed downstairs, I wouldn't have seen you at your full potential," she said with the edge of her lip curled up.

I opted to not answer.

Wonderly's hand disappeared into her bag like a magician's

assistant, emerging with my Billie Holiday record. The vinyl slid across the table with the finality of a signed confession, while she sipped her tea like she held all the cards and knew exactly when to play them.

"Where's your intern?" she asked.

"Picking a new mentor."

I flipped the album over and looked at it as if I were inspecting it for damage. I slid out the inner sleeve. The record was intact, no scratches, but I didn't know whether it had had them when I made the purchase. What had changed was the sleeve. Pristine white now, with nothing written on it.

"No 'signature,'" I said.

"Of course. That was the part I required, as you recall."

"Kind of lessens the value of my album now."

Wonderly smiled thinly at me. "Not really. It was all gibberish."

"Mm-hmm. And I don't suppose you'd like to tell me what was on that sleeve?" I asked.

"I suppose I might."

That was unexpected. She stared at me for a long time, breathing slowly and studying me.

"How long have you been at the Conservatory?" she asked.

"Eighteen years or so."

"When was the last time you saw Felix Cantabile alive?"

"Twenty years, maybe."

Wonderly bobbed her head, then took a sip of tea. "And you did not know he was the Guardian of Whimsy."

"I did not." This lack of knowledge was not a good selling point for investigations, closed or otherwise. I frowned. "In my capacity at the Conservatory, I'm not privileged enough to know any of the Guardians."

"Would you be betraying your job to tell me what you know of them?" she asked.

With a shrug, I threw up my hands. She already knew something. Most of the time the Statics blew off any hint of magic, but this one seemed to be collecting hints. "Nothing too secret. The Guardians of the Virtues are what they're usually called, but their actual title is *i Guardiani delle Virtù*."

Wonderly pursed her lips. "Why Italian?"

Every ounce of her said she didn't know that, but the slight variation in her voice told me she did. She was stringing me along.

"Most musical terms are Italian, right?" I asked.

"I think that music has borrowed many words from other languages like French, German, and English."

I smiled at her. Was she testing me? "Well, it wouldn't surprise me that the Conservatory chose Italian because of the long history of music in Italian. It probably sounds more pretentious."

"I see," she said. "Please continue enlightening me."

Now, I had little doubt that I was not enlightening her at all. "The Guardians protect the most important virtues in humans. They encourage their growth and work to strengthen them when circumstances weaken them."

"Like Whimsy," she muttered.

"Like Whimsy."

"Who's protecting Whimsy now?"

I shook my head. "No one, I guess. They'll have to appoint a new Guardian."

Wonderly smiled at me. "Maybe it will be you."

I laughed. "Go downstairs and ask around. No one would accuse me of having Whimsy." I shook my head and stared out the window. What was her game? "The Four Cardinals will select a suitable candidate and tell the Council. Then together they will determine who will take the mantle."

Wonderly finished her tea. I asked if she'd like more, but she declined. My cup was still a third full, so I worked on catching up to her.

"Who are the Four Cardinals?" she asked.

"Wisdom, Justice, Courage, and Temperance."

Her eyebrows rose. "You know them?"

"Of course not. They are more important than the Guardians."

She leaned forward. "So you could be one."

"No."

Wonderly smiled. "So I could be one."

"Certainly not."

She sat upright, and her brow furrowed. "And why not?"

"You're not a member of the Conservatory."

"Bothersome," she said. "So you can't tell me who the Guardians are, who the Four Cardinals are, or why Whimsy died."

"Not yet." I shook my head. "Sorry. Not ever. I was removed from the case." She had a genuine look of shock, so I preempted her question. "The case was closed. The Harmonic Council was displeased with my lack of progress on the case, and Sonny Mordent protested my being on the case on behalf of the DHR."

"Why did she do that?"

Staring across the Academy, I shook my head. "She believes I've been stalking her."

"You did corner me in an alley."

I frowned at her. "You know that's not true."

"Why didn't you do a little spell with your lute to prevent her from telling the Council?"

"Doesn't work like that. And it's not a lute. It's an ossia. And I didn't have it with me."

"So no ossia, no magic. You are, as it were, unarmed."

I shivered for a moment. "It's not a weapon. Normally, I carry something, but the Council asked me to come, as you say, unarmed, to meet them."

Wonderly leaned forward. "So I can say or do whatever

I want and you can't determine if I'm honest or yanking your chain since you appear disarmed as we speak?"

She was playing me like a fiddle, and we both knew the tune by heart. "You have it all wrong. I don't need the instrument. The Virtuoso can use many things to attune. We are trained from the beginning to use what we have available. The ossia or any instrument can aid in that process, like an antenna."

She nodded and leaned back, relaxed but still not. "It's a shame you didn't bring your lute. Whatever kind of bard will you be? Your jokes will fall flatter than usual."

"Bards do not tell jokes. And I'm a Trovatore, not a bard. Leave the bards to RPG nerds."

"Trovatore don't tell jokes?"

I shook my head. "Not in the way you mean. We are keepers of the lore, highly attuned, and that's why people like me are assigned in cases like Felix Cantabile."

"Except not anymore," she said.

"Except not anymore," I repeated. "Oh well, not my problem."

I stood and took both of our cups to the sink. "Well, Ms. Wonderly, thanks for returning my record, mostly as it was. I won't take any more of your time."

Wonderly stood and smiled at me. "That's it?"

"I'm off the case, and I have plenty of time for other pursuits." I looked down at my fencing whites. "I should go cross blades for a while. I don't wear this for the fashion."

She stepped close to me and looked up at me. "Oh, I don't know. I'm sure they're just fighting to get a hold of a man in knee-high pants, one glove, and a blob of white."

Ms. Wonderly picked the record off the table and studied the jacket. "The thing I don't understand is that you have been accused of not doing your job, stalking a woman from the DHR, and you remain unmoved. Instead, you want to run downstairs, sweat buckets, and stick people with swords, but you have no fight for your real-world situation."

"Not much I can do."

"Can do or would do?" I didn't respond, so she continued. "You have no desire to figure out why Whimsy died? Why your friend died? Why every night the band at the Hedgehog sounds like they're killing cats?"

"I can't do anything about any of it."

Wonderly headed to the stairway. "Let me know if you change your mind and want to make a difference."

I heard her last footfall on the bottom step of the stairs when curiosity overcame me. My feet pounded the same steps, leading me to charge out the door after her.

She turned when she heard the front door slam open.

"What did you mean by 'make a difference'?"

She smiled. She was glowing. "You're not dressed appropriately to be out in public. Go fence, Mr. Kohl. I'll meet you here at ten o'clock. I need to check with the others first to make sure we're not walking into a trap."

"Certainly not one from me."

Wonderly turned to walk away but stopped herself short and faced me. "Mr. Kohl, do not bring any instruments with you tonight. I will have to search you. We prefer you disarmed."

Pretty sure I was disarmed every time I met this woman. Good thing Hoagy wasn't here for some witty remark.

CHAPTER 21
LUTED

IT WAS JUST past four when I arrived at my apartment. My neighbor nodded. "Be careful. They made a lot of racket in there."

"Where?"

"Your apartment. Never saw them leave."

I raced upstairs and unlocked my apartment door. From the hallway, everything looked normal. Then I stepped inside.

The living room looked like a hurricane had auditioned for a percussion section.

Sometimes you know how it's going to be when you go somewhere, but you refuse to accept it. It wasn't like my apartment was a great work of art or stirred powerful feelings in me, but to see it in such a state pissed me off. Only I had the right to make it look like a slob lived there.

At this moment, I was glad to face it alone, without Hoagy.

The looters hadn't just tossed the place. They'd thrown it on the rocks and served it shaken, not stirred. Someone had worked out his frustrations in my living room. Fine. Spring cleaning a bit late, catching up for the past ten years.

The front door showed no signs of forced entry. Whoever did this had a key or knew their way around locks. I ran my fingers along the doorframe, looking for scratches, tool marks, or magical residue. Nothing. Inside, the destruction followed a pattern. They'd started in the living room, worked methodically toward the bedroom, then hit the kitchen on their way out.

The balcony door was open. Easy exit.

This wasn't random vandalism or a desperate search. Someone had been looking for specific items while sending a very clear message to a stubborn Virtuoso.

The piano bench had been knocked on its side, sheet music scattered like they'd played fifty-two-card pickup with my creations. Now they were out of order. Perhaps that was an improvement. But the piano itself was untouched. Whoever did this knew the difference between destruction and desecration. They wanted to humiliate, not destroy what mattered most.

As I worked, I couldn't help reflecting on how the apartment had served me well for a decade. I didn't mind the character adding chips in the plaster or the giant black stain on the walnut-colored floorboards. The neighbors appreciated the thick walls smothered with a layer of plaster. It made great sound dampening so that they didn't hear me as I hammered out the same phrase over and over, never being sure that I liked it.

I got the place cheap, too, because the day before I moved in someone had been murdered in the hall outside my door with an axe. My former neighbor said the man had been a druggie and committed suicide with that log splitter. Soon afterward, the neighbor was arrested for witnessing someone commit suicide with a splitting maul in front of him. Tough breaks.

This wasn't the first time someone had broken in.

"Dekker, you had some party."

Bianka, my Polish upstairs neighbor, stepped inside the apartment. She was short and pretty with her long hair pulled up on top of her head. She held a garment bag over her shoulder and waited for my answer.

"Yeah. Wasn't a party I was invited to."

Her eyes roamed around the room. "Wasn't me this time."

"I know."

Bianka had come to the US just in time for the pandemic as a costume designer. And only weeks before she was out of a job.

Twice she had tried to make rent by searching my place for some dough. Unfortunately for her, she didn't find a Franklin or a Pillsbury in the place.

During the pandemic, she had started streaming on Twitch, showing people how to make costumes and play games. Perhaps she used all the platforms. Now she was making more than most people I knew, with all her funnels.

"New costume?" I asked.

"Commission piece for a client hitting SDCC. Paying me four grand for a screen-accurate Samus suit."

She squatted in front of me. "Sorry about your place. I have a stream in an hour, but I can help you clean up after."

"Thanks, Bianka. I got it. I need to atone for my sins apparently."

She kissed me on the forehead. "You're a dork."

"Says the girl who spent six hours last week arguing about whether a halfling rogue could hide behind a torch."

"It's called rules layering, and I'm the DM, so I'm always right."

She headed toward the door. "You're still welcome to join the campaign. No magic, though."

She meant my kind of magic.

Bianka knew what being Virtuosi meant. Nice girl. I had convinced her a year ago to let me ward her place so that her anonymity remained. Online footprints were so hard to hide. Periodically, I checked to make sure it was all in good shape, like checking mousetraps to see if you caught something.

I continued my assessment of my place. Someone had dented my tenor sax, snapped the E string on my guitar, and left my accordion in the middle of the floor on its face, examining the stains.

I knelt beside the overturned accordion, studying the scuff marks on the hardwood. Boot prints. Size ten or eleven, distinctive wear pattern on the ball of the left foot and the outer edge ground down more than the right. I'd seen that pattern before. Recently. A fencer. Probably a new one that didn't know me well. The realization hit like a crescendo. Cree's pianist. The one she'd brought to Columbus. The one with access to her apartment, her keys, her trust.

In the bedroom, dresser drawers had been pulled out and dumped, but not randomly. Someone had riffled through my clothes with purpose, looking for hidden pockets, secret compartments. They'd found my backup phone with an alternate number in the sock drawer, a cheap one I kept for emergencies. Gone.

To outsiders, it would seem odd, but I kept a tenor sax tucked under a spare comforter in my closet. The intruders had taken a hammer to the bell like they were blind Christmas elves making a toy that wouldn't work. Maybe the dents would add character to the sound. Perhaps they'd remind me of this violation every time I played.

The bathroom medicine cabinet hung open, contents scattered across the sink. Odd choice for a burglar, unless they were looking for something specific. Or trying to make it look like a drug-seeking junkie had done the job.

That's when I noticed what they'd missed, or what they'd left on purpose. Tucked behind the fallen picture frame of me and Cree at graduation was a single sheet of music paper. Not mine. The staff lines were hand-drawn, slightly crooked, and the notes were written in a style I recognized but couldn't immediately place. The melody was simple, almost childlike, but something about the harmonic progression felt familiar. I hummed it under my breath, and the hair on my neck stood up. This wasn't random music; it was a message. Someone who knew I'd find it, someone who wanted me to understand something specific. I folded the paper carefully and slipped it into my pocket. First rule of investigation: never let the other side know what cards you're holding.

In the kitchen, the cupboards were strewn about the floor. There I found the case to my ossia on the kitchen table, open and empty. I slid my hand into the pocket of the case. My notebook remained, too. They got what they came after, the instrument.

Without my ossia or piccolo, I had to improvise. The old harmonica in the kitchen junk drawer would have to do. Harmonicas were not ideal for magical work, but desperate times called for desperate measures. I played a simple seeking melody, trying to read the emotional residue left by whoever had violated my space. The harmonics were muddy, confused, but I caught traces of something familiar. Guilt, yes, but also righteousness. Whoever did this believed they were justified, maybe even doing me a favor. That narrowed the field considerably. Most professional burglars didn't carry moral convictions about their work. There was something else, too. A harmonic signature I'd felt before, recently. Someone from my immediate circle, someone I'd been in close contact with in the past few days. This wasn't some DHR operation or Conservatory politics. This was personal. All confirmation.

Finally, I took the broken pieces of things downstairs and out back to the dumpster. There I found the ossia, in pieces.

For a moment I considered informing Dash, but what would he do? I could demonstrate to Sonny, but at this point she wouldn't care if it was a setup. She got what she wanted. The Conservatory was off the case. She also had the backup photos of me "watching" her.

Who cared?

Armando wasn't going to let me into the workshop to have

a new one made for a while. Hell, perhaps he'd fire me. Too bad I didn't drink much, because this was a great day to drown my sorrows and forget that the Conservatory found me or the day I met Sonny Mordent. Who cared about that? She'd find who did it. Let her and Rimsky battle it out. True, she'd give some crazy DHR explanation, but I had little doubt she'd find the killer on her own with Rimsky smiling over her shoulder.

I couldn't stay here. Not with the enforcer's threat still fresh, not with my ossia in pieces. I left the apartment unlocked. Let them come back. There was nothing left worth taking.

CHAPTER 22
RIMSKY

I WAS WANDERING. That's what I told myself. Not running, not hiding. Wandering. The Arena District was only a thirty-minute walk from my apartment, and the night air felt good on my scraped face.

At the edge of the park stood a Roman-style arch and four columns beside it. During games at the arena or the nearby baseball stadium, wall-to-wall people packed the streets, migrating in herds.

The Arena District wasn't my normal hangout, but that's where I ended up. Today it was like an empty glass with enough bourbon left in the glass to recognize what it was but not enough to taste the melting ice.

Across from the park was a restaurant with tables outside and a nice-sized expanse of brick sidewalk to accommodate all the spectators to whatever event transpired.

Today, the plaza stretched out like a graveyard for good times, empty as my bank account and twice as depressing. Even the pigeons had given up hope. A group of them would land, look around for suckers with breadcrumbs, then fly off to find a city that still remembered how to feed its birds.

I felt for them. The outdoor tables were empty. The perfect place to sit and think.

The sound of heels clacking on the plaza bricks interrupted my brooding silence. Sonny was crossing the plaza at speed and ducking into a pedestrian walkway. We were less than a five-minute walk from the DHR. Made sense.

Also not my problem.

More shoes pounding pavement. This time, Rimsky charged faster than he should have for his age. He stopped in the middle of the plaza and looked around. He saw me, so I waved at him out of courtesy, acknowledging that he existed. Rimsky spun around, searching as if he'd lost his child, then smacked his hand on his leg.

After a minute, he decided I wanted company, which was in error. No matter what face you put on, someone's always going to read it as the exact opposite.

"Strange place to hang out with no one around," he said, like a man who'd never sat alone with his mistakes for company.

"Strange place to run around in a suit."

Without an invitation, he sat. Rimsky had the look of a man who collected other people's secrets like some folks collected stamps—carefully, obsessively, and with a patience that made honest citizens nervous. Perhaps that made him good for Internal Affairs. Petulant and annoying.

Rimsky's eyes flicked to my face. "Someone hit you."

"Someone tried to deliver a message."

"What kind of message?"

"The kind that comes with a fist and a threat." I touched my cheekbone and winced. "Turns out I'm a bad listener."

His expression didn't change, but something shifted in his eyes. Calculation. "Was it Sonny?"

"Wasn't a woman."

"Description?"

"DHR paramilitary type. Like your friends at the Hedgehog." I watched his reaction carefully. "Yours?"

Rimsky's pause lasted a heartbeat too long. "No. But I can guess whose." He stared at me. A bead of sweat ran down his forehead from all that running. "Did you see where she went?"

"Who's that?"

He clenched his jaw. "Don't play games with me, Mr. Kohl. You know who. Sonny Mordent."

With a shrug, I threw up my hands. "Wasn't looking for her. She just got me fired."

"You'll recover." He glanced around. "Your sidekick is gone, too?"

"Hoagy? Yes. Ordered not to come within ten feet of me." Rimsky's eyebrow shot up. I didn't bother to tell him I was BS-ing him.

A cool breeze whipped through the plaza, so I pulled my jacket closer. Rimsky seemed unfazed. He was still on a mission.

"I've been investigating her for months," he said.

"Between bar raids? That seems more like a thing Internal Affairs would do."

He sneered at me. "The reason might be interesting to you."

"All right. I seem to have a lot of free time right now. The server isn't very attentive."

Rimsky scooted his chair closer even though there was no one within half a mile that could overhear our conversation. "Ever wonder why a woman who works for the DHR married a Guardian, as you call them?"

"I'm guessing you don't think it was love."

Rimsky laughed. "She seems just the loving type, right?"

I shrugged. Was it love? I didn't know. She seemed uptight for the way I knew Felix, but perhaps I didn't really know him. To be fair, the only thing unattractive about Sonny was her atti-tude, but that was always the kicker.

I'd had plenty of experience in that department. My tastes

ran to strong women. The problem was that the line between strong-willed and intolerable was thin until you learned where it was drawn. It took me longer than it should have to find that line. On the other hand, perhaps Sonny was all sunshine and roses at home with the creative genius.

"I didn't know he was a Guardian to have time to wonder," I muttered.

Rimsky sighed. "You're no longer on the case. Sonny caused that, right?"

"Sure. I didn't suggest that she was a saint. I was told when I arrived at the crime scene right before you, she was difficult."

"And cagey."

Somewhere in there was a story with more rests than notes. What Sonny said, what made her difficult, and what she wasn't telling anybody. Perhaps vindictive given recent events. Not my problem.

His eyes fixed on mine. Whatever his deal was, he was deadly serious about it. "Like I said, I've been on her for months. Digging into her past. Following her."

"Looks like you need help in the following department."

"I do." He smiled at me. "You could help."

"Why would I bother? I'm off the case, and Armando isn't happy with me at the moment about it. She claims I was stalking her."

Rimsky nodded and tapped his fingers on the table. "Were you?"

"No. And now somebody broke into my apartment and destroyed my instruments."

"Your guitar you had at the Guardian's apartment?"

I frowned at him. "Ossia. Not guitar."

"What's the difference?"

"A lot really, but I don't have enough time to teach you."

Rimsky laughed. "Okay. You're a Trovatore. Isn't your job as a 'lore keeper' to educate me?"

That was why I avoided telling people about my job. You had one of three responses: sneak away, try to counterhex me, or try to laugh it off. And you could never yell back at them about the days when Trovotari were how information got around. Think we were singing songs for your entertainment? No. We were the original source of communication before books, the discovery of magic, cellular phones, the internet, whatever.

Regardless of the sore spot, I answered, "At the moment I'm a failed Trovatore."

"I actually believe that Sonny has latent magical powers, and she is hiding them."

My eyes narrowed. "Why would she if she did?"

"Because I think the thing with Felix Cantabile—"

"You mean her marriage?"

"Yes. It was him training her."

I threw up my hands. "Don't believe in love, do you?"

"Waste of time. Look what it brought them. For that matter, look what being a Guardian of Whimsy brought to him. Regardless, I think that she has secretly trained and is working against DHR."

I laughed. "You think Sonny Mordent is a double agent working with the Conservatory and against DHR?"

"Yes."

"Have fun with that."

"Don't believe it?"

"No. I have dealt with Sonny a few more times than I would like. Not a single time did I sense any latent magic in her."

"She hides her emotions. Why not her magic?"

"You can hide physically. You can't hide the essence of the harmonic spectrum."

"Maybe. Help me prove it."

"No, thanks. I'm full up with misery at the moment."

Rimsky stood. "When you're done sobbing and trying to be a tough guy, consider it."

I nodded. "I'll put it on the to-do list right after 'become a decent human being.'"

His eyes fixed on mine. "As I said, I've been investigating her for months. Following her movements. Tracking her contacts. Perhaps even one of the twelve."

"Sounds like Internal Affairs work."

"It is. And what I've found ..." He paused. "That raid at the Hedgehog? Sonny was briefed beforehand. She knew it was coming. Those target lists? I've traced them back to her communications with Jacob. She's been using his reviews to identify vulnerable musicians."

I already suspected this. "Why would she do that?"

"That's what I'm trying to determine." He shrugged. "How many people do you think it would take to coordinate something like this? To identify targets, plan raids, manipulate evidence?"

"You're the investigator. And the raider as I recall."

"I am. But you're the one who's been in the middle of it." His eyes narrowed. "What have you observed? What patterns have you seen?"

"I observe that you're asking a lot of questions for someone who claims to have been investigating for months."

Rimsky smiled thinly. "And I observe that you're deflecting. Which makes me wonder. What exactly did you find at Felix's apartment that got your instruments destroyed?"

He straightened his jacket. "Look me up. And perhaps look her up. She lives at the end of Warren. I'm sure you know the high-dollar condos down there."

"Yeah."

Rimsky wanted me to work for him. He was doing something dirty. Sonny was setting me up. Time to fight. Time to roll up the sleeves and get dirty.

"Wait," I said. "Twelve? Officials? DHR? Who?"

"Not for the curious. Scratch my back ..."

I shrugged. "Fine. Then I can't help. I was just curious how many crossovers we had on our lists."

"Your list?"

It ate at him. Too bad there wasn't a list. Troubled musicians, yes. Twelve officials? Not yet.

"Three Council members. Two DHR administrators to start with."

"I think that tracks," I said.

I guessed that Rimsky was on that list, too.

Rimsky walked away like a man who'd just lit a fuse and was waiting to see what exploded. In my experience, that's when smart people duck. Too bad I'd never been accused of being smart.

I checked my watch. Eight p.m. I had time to make it back to the Academy for Wonderly's meeting. I started walking.

CHAPTER 23
RIPOSTE

THE THAI PLACE on High on the way to the Academy was still open, light spilling onto the sidewalk like a promise of normalcy. I ordered pad Thai and spring rolls.

The kid behind the counter tried to make small talk while boxing it up. "Bad day?" he asked.

"Bad week."

"Sorry, man." He handed me the bag. "Fortune cookie says it'll get better."

I paid cash and headed home with the bag warming my hands against the unseasonable late-May chill. Even Mother Nature felt Whimsy slipping.

I didn't open the fortune cookie. Some lies you don't need in writing.

The walk to my apartment building took twenty minutes. Long enough for my mind to catalog everything wrong with the case. Riff had been in my apartment. Cree's boyfriend—or whatever he was—had broken in on somebody's orders, ransacked the place, and destroyed my ossia. All to shut me down.

The streets were wrong. Not empty—worse. A dozen people walked past, but none of them looked at each other. No eye contact. No nods. No acknowledgment. Like they'd all agreed to pretend they were alone.

And then there was the twelve.

In the distance, the LeVeque Tower's colored lights—usually steady, reliable—flickered and died. I stopped walking. One full minute of darkness at the top of the Art Deco spire before the lights stuttered back to life.

No one else stopped. No one else looked up.

My mind returned to the case. Not case. Cree had given him the key. Or he took the key?

Back at my apartment, I climbed the stairs, my footsteps echoing in the stairwell, pad Thai going cold in the bag.

I shouldn't have come back. I knew better. But I'd left my notebook in the ossia case, and somehow that felt important. Just five minutes. In and out.

I felt something. One of those lingering harmonics that dwell around people like me.

The door was still unlocked from earlier. I should have locked it. The war had taught me that, if nothing else. Locked doors buy you three seconds. Three seconds to reach for a weapon, to plan, to survive. Or perhaps in my case to grab an instrument and play a defensive tune.

I set the food down on the hallway floor, quiet as prayer. My hand went for the piccolo in my pocket. Crap. That DHR goon had destroyed that.

Hand on the doorknob. Listening.

Nothing.

Complete silence.

Silence is worse than noise. Noise means amateur, kids looking for electronics to pawn, junkies after pill bottles. Silence means professional. Silence means someone who knows what they're doing.

I opened the door slowly, my fist balled up as a nonmusical

weapon, like the only thing between me and whoever was waiting in the dark.

The apartment was darker than I'd left it. Someone had closed the curtains, killed the LED strip lights I let provide perpetual ambience. The streetlight that usually bled through the window, shining on the ceiling, was gone, leaving only shapes and shadows.

I stepped inside, back against the wall, letting my eyes adjust. Old habits. War habits. The kind that keeps you breathing when breathing isn't guaranteed. Follow what Maestro Park said. Center. Silence the internal music. Rests are preparation, not nothing.

Then I heard it.

Breathing in the darkness. Not my own. I was holding my breath. Someone else's rhythm. Steady. Patient. Waiting. Never alone when you want to be.

A figure moved from the kitchen shadow. Tall. Broad. DHR gray suit caught what little light existed.

Not Sonny. Too tall. Not Rimsky. Wrong build. Someone new. Someone sent.

The voice came low and professionally calm, like a doctor delivering bad news to someone who couldn't afford treatment.

"Mr. Kohl. Don't make this difficult."

I kept my back to the wall, wishing any instrument was nearby that wasn't big and bulky. "Breaking and entering. That's a crime."

The figure took a step closer. I could see the outline now. Military posture, controlled movements. "Some people don't know when to quit."

"I was fired. Officially dismissed. There's nothing to quit."

"The dismissal was a courtesy. This is the period at the end of that sentence."

I didn't move. "Who sent you? Sonny? Rimsky? Or someone higher up the chain?"

The figure stepped into a shaft of ambient light from the hallway. I saw the face now. Scarred cheek, dead eyes, the kind of expression you get from doing ugly work for too long. Not a bureaucrat. An enforcer.

The enforcer's smile was cold. "You think too small, Kohl. This is bigger than a wife."

"Still—"

"Doesn't matter who," he said. "Matters that you stop."

He lunged without warning.

No theatrical windup, no announcing his intentions. Professional. The kind of attack that ends fights before they start.

I sidestepped on instinct, muscle memory from the Academy, from fencing drills, from the war. I tumbled into my media center with the unused TV. But there was a useless recorder there, the plastic kind from sixth grade. Magically inert, but it was a solid stick.

As the enforcer reached for me, the plastic instrument connected with his elbow with a comforting crack.

He didn't flinch. Used the momentum instead, drove me backward into the wall.

Air left my lungs like a kicked dog. Vision sparked white at the edges. My ribs screamed protest loud enough to hear it.

Breathing hurt. Moving hurt. Not moving would hurt worse.

His knee came up, a textbook move, aiming for the groin. I twisted, caught it on the thigh instead. Still hurt, but hurt I could walk away from.

My hand found the lamp on the side table. I swung without thinking. Connected with his shoulder.

The lamp shattered, ceramic shards everywhere, and the darkness got deeper. One less source of light. But darkness was my friend now.

I brought the recorder to my lips and tossed it aside. Reflex. Instead, I whistled three sharp notes. A wind gust spell in E minor. One of my favorites. Worked on Reed Holloway.

The spell—desperate and sloppy, but functional in close quarters.

The air moved. The enforcer staggered back. Furniture toppled, sheet music scattered.

Magic in close quarters is stupid. Stupid keeps you alive.

I charged while he was off-balance, tackling him into the piano.

The keys crashed discordantly. Wrong notes. Violent music. Chaos made audible. The sound rattled my teeth, but it rattled him, too.

His elbow caught my face. My cheekbone exploded in pain. Right on my sidewalk burn from the DHR goon abducting Eric Mueller.

I tasted blood, too, familiar and unwelcome, but I spat and kept fighting.

My fingers wrapped around the mouthpiece of the recorder the way you're taught to, with a roll of quarters to add some oomph to the punch. Not as solid as quarters, but I swung wild and connected with his temple.

He dropped. Heavy. Final.

Silence again.

My breathing was harsh in the darkness. I was on hands and knees, shaking. The enforcer was unconscious but not dead. Still breathing. Pulse steady under my trembling fingers.

I should call Dash. Should report the attack. Should do something official.

But I was off the case. Dismissed. And this wouldn't help.

I stood slowly. Every muscle screamed. Ribs definitely cracked. Maybe broken. Hard to tell the difference when it all hurt the same.

I found the light switch and flipped it.

No way to tell the destruction this time from the previous one by Riff. But this time there was a message carved into the piano's fallboard in rough capitals: "STOP."

Not spray paint. Not marker. Carved with a knife. Deep gouges. Permanent. Bastard.

A photograph lay on the piano keys. I picked it up with shaking hands. Cree at the Velvet Room. Telephoto lens. Surveillance shot. Professional quality.

A red *X* was drawn over her face in marker. I flipped it over.

"First the lute. Then her."

"It's not a fucking lute," I muttered at the unconscious man.

The threat was clear enough. They'd destroyed my ossia. Next would be Cree. Unless I stayed quiet and stayed down. What had I run into?

The fear that hit me then was different from fight fear. This was cold. Personal. Targeted. Escalating. The enforcer groaned, stirring.

I checked his pockets. No ID. No wallet. No phone. A professional ghost, just like I'd thought.

The enforcer was waking. I made sure I had my phone and fled my own apartment.

Couldn't stay here. Not safe. Not tonight. Maybe never again. The streets outside were cold and empty. I leaned against the building, catching my breath, trying not to pass out. My ribs screamed. My face throbbed. Blood had dried on my chin. I looked like hell and felt worse.

Couldn't go to a hospital. They'd ask questions I couldn't answer. The Conservatory was out of the question. I was fired. Well, not fired, but not in favor.

I pulled out my phone, considered calling Cree. Then I remembered the photograph. The threat. Calling her put a target on her. I already had one. She didn't need mine, too.

I texted Hoagy to make sure he didn't show up anywhere without explanation.

Seconds later, a response. *I don't care what they say.*

Teenagers. I fumbled with the phone and sent another text. *Not about that. Stay away for now. Not safe.*

He sent me a pile of emojis showing he agreed. I assume. I didn't know what all of them meant, but he seemed to understand I was serious.

Royal Arts. Maestra Flanconade wouldn't ask questions. She never did. Shit. I had the meeting with Wonderly.

I headed toward the Academy on foot, staying to shadows, checking behind me every half block. Three blocks. I could make three blocks without passing out.

Two days left. I kept repeating it in my head. Two days. It occurred to me that might be the point. Just another two days and all of this would resolve. I wouldn't care who beat the shit out of me, and the world wouldn't know it had lost something. Bastards.

We were doomed.

The loft was dark when I climbed the stairs at nine, but Maestra heard me coming. She took one look at my face and pointed to the couch without a word. That was the deal. She cleaned the blood, wrapped my ribs, handed me a half-empty bottle of Stoli, and went back to her room.

I drank until the photograph of Cree with the red *X* didn't make my hands shake anymore. Someone didn't want me looking into things.

Too bad. I'd just decided to look harder. Now it was time to meet Wonderly. Good thing I was already there.

CHAPTER 24
THE UNDERGROUND

THE BELLS at Saint John the Baptist tolled ten o'clock. Three bells. Not ten. Odd. Pretty sure there was a law against banging bells around when normal people were thinking about sleep. Also unusual to hear them so clearly.

The Academy had been closed since before I arrived. Practice ended at nine, and even the die-hards had called it a night. The maestra hadn't reappeared. I went back outside to meet Wonderly.

The streets were dark, not from lack of light but from lack of life. Faux Victorian streetlamps lined the apartments across the street, and small lights mounted on the Academy's walls provided enough illumination for ambience. Fine by me. The shadows suited my mood.

I stood far enough from one of the Academy lights to be in shadow, waiting to see if Wonderly would appear. Then I saw a silhouette walking the sidewalk toward the club. She wasn't in a hurry.

She stopped in front of the Academy and looked around. I stepped from my shadow and approached her. She had donned a light jacket and a longer skirt to ward off the chill.

"Hello there," I said.

"Is that your only line?"

With a shake of my head, I frowned. "Yes, I'm afraid I'm linguistically challenged."

Wonderly grunted at me. "I don't think linguistically is the principal challenge."

"I see," I said. "You didn't have dinner, so you decided to snack on me."

Her eyes locked on to mine. "I'm taking a great risk with you. Please don't disappoint me."

"It would be my goal to never disappoint you."

Wonderly ignored my commentary. Not an issue for me. I had plenty of it running through my head all the time.

"I have something to show you. You will keep it secret."

"Intriguing. You know where we're going. Lead the way."

"The Academy," she said, pointing. "Inside."

I shook my head. "Well, I'm afraid we're about an hour too late."

Wonderly reached into her coat pocket and pulled out a key. Interesting. She didn't fence, yet ...

With some concern, I reached out to the door and stopped her. "The Maestra may be asleep."

"We won't disturb her."

Curiosity won out over caution.

"Did you bring an instrument?"

"No."

"Good," Wonderly said.

"And someone saw fit to break my piccolo and destroy my ossia."

"Tough."

If she felt surprise that the door was already unlocked, she didn't register it. Without another word, we entered the main fencing room. The two lights mounted on the wall outside created a long spot on the floor resembling the lattice of the window, providing enough light to walk the length of the room with reasonable certainty. Her footsteps were muted on the old hardwood floors.

At the back wall, Wonderly lifted a mask from its hook in the corner. She twisted the peg hook, and I heard a soft click. But instead of opening whatever was back there, Wonderly froze, head tilted.

"What is it?" I whispered.

"Protocol," Wonderly murmured. "If this door opens and the wrong harmonic signature is detected, everything down there burns."

So her magical knowledge was more than I had suspected.

"Only downstairs?" I asked. "Must be magical fire."

"Yes. No one up here would know. Takes about ten seconds to burn through the evidence. Or so I was told."

Wonderly pulled out a small silver tuning fork, but I caught her wrist.

"Wait. Magical fire that burns through evidence in ten seconds? If that fork hits the wrong note, everything gets erased."

"Then don't startle me." She held up the fork, that slight smile playing at her lips. "Still want to see what's down there?"

I stepped back. "After you."

With a smile, Wonderly struck it against the mask and held it near the door. The tuning fork sounded a pure F-sharp. A faint musical tone emanated from behind the wall, a harmonic response, like a password being accepted in the key of F-sharp resolving to B-flat. The earthy tone made sense to me, but I wondered if Wonderly understood it or followed directions.

"Clear," she breathed, and pushed the door open.

The stairs descended into darkness, but I could feel something humming in the air below. Not sound, but magical resonance. Like standing next to a power line you couldn't see.

"The dampening field," Wonderly's voice echoed softly as we descended. "It doesn't just block magic from getting in; it stores what it absorbs. Twenty artists work here in magical isolation for months. All that creative energy has to go somewhere."

"Is that necessary?"

She glanced at me. "Did you hear the bells?"

"Yeah. It was weird."

"Three days left until we've lost all Whimsy. Shelters like this will be necessary."

"Closer to two now," I said.

At the bottom, I understood. The basement wasn't just a safe space. It was a battery charged with stolen inspiration. The air felt thick with potential, like the moment before lightning strikes. Every breath tasted of half-formed melodies, snippets of unfinished symphonies pressing against my skin like invisible cobwebs. Creativity under pressure, compressed and concentrated until it hummed with its own frequency.

I grunted. "You're concentrating creativity."

To Wonderly, I must have looked shocked. Our eyes met. "I expect you to never tell your fellow fencers about this."

"Of course," I said.

"Even Cree."

I nodded. "Cree's a bit preoccupied right now."

Wonderly pushed the hidden door open and flipped a switch. A bare lightbulb was mounted on the wall. A wooden staircase descended into the basement. We stepped inside, and I pulled the door shut behind me.

At the bottom of the stairs, a room spanned fifty feet with support poles holding things up every dozen feet. The joists from the fencing floor were above us. At the back was a kitchenette, and five round tables with six chairs each sat in the room. Four bare bulbs were mounted to the joists, casting stark shadows across the room.

A dozen people sat at the tables staring at me. Another dozen. They were silent. Two of them got up and approached as my foot hit the concrete floor. A seventy-something-year-old man lifted his chin at me.

"Arms out," he said.

I followed directions, and he patted me down. Then he nodded at Wonderly. "You sure 'bout this?"

Her eyes met mine. "Pretty sure."

"It's on you, doll, if it goes south."

I winked at him. "She was one wrong note from vaporizing all of you."

The old man returned to his seat.

"I'm not going to bother to explain it to you," she said. "Please don't antagonize them."

She directed me to a table. A man in his thirties brought me a rocks glass and poured two fingers of something amber. "You're gonna need this." He stuck out his hand.

Wonderly remained standing. "Mr. Kohl, we are risking a lot to bring you here. This group is some of your fellow creatives."

A woman objected, causing Wonderly to raise her hand. "Creative artists," she said. "They are not Conservatory members."

"Understood," I said.

She continued. "They are not DHR." Someone grumbled about that one. "I assume you know none of them."

With care, I searched the faces of the twelve. Eight men, four women. I had never seen any of them that I recalled.

Wonderly leaned forward, putting one hand across my shoulders and waving the other across the room. "They are artists, writers, musicians. For now, you will not know their names."

That was when I noticed that in the shadows lining the basement were two easels, a couple of desks, and a couple of cabinets.

"They live here?" I asked.

"No, but they visit often," Wonderly said.

"Careful," one woman said.

The woman who had spoken sat hunched over a notebook, sketching frantically. Paint caked her fingernails in blue and gold. "Mr. Kohl, this basement under your fencing club is magically isolated. After the raid on the Hedgehog, it's one of the few safe spaces left. The DHR didn't just target musicians; they broke the network that keeps creativity alive. Without gathering places, without community, Whimsy decays faster than we ever imagined."

Those sharp eyes assessed me before she continued. "You don't seem surprised that this is possible."

"No." My eyes roamed around the room. "Sonny Mordent showed me a room at the DHR that was magically isolated. A woman named Vittoria was playing the violin there. It was beautiful until it wasn't."

"That's what happened to her," one man said. "Is she all right?"

"As far as I could tell," I said. "She was playing, creating something great. Then she stepped out of that room and nothing."

I glanced at Wonderly. "Are you telling me this room is the same?"

"Opposite. Protects instead," she said.

Wonderly sat beside me, with one hand on my chair and one on the table.

Glancing across the faces, I bobbed my head with understanding. "So you come here because your creativity flows when it won't out there."

"Yes," she said. "Whimsy can linger here longer."

"I understand." The artists stared at me as if they were starving and I was food. Really they were creating a new drug. It wouldn't last in two days. "But why the secrecy?"

"Do you know Ruby Blue?"

Keep it close to the vest. "Interviewed her. Ruby didn't show up for her gig at the Hedgehog."

Wonderly nodded. "She is at DHR in one of the isolation rooms."

"And you know what are they doing in the isolation rooms?" I asked.

"They are deprogramming. This room"—she waved her hand around the room—"is more dampened than isolated. Magic can't seep in. Magic can't find this room."

"Except to get inside," I said.

Wonderly frowned at me. "Inside here creativity flourishes and Whimsy flows, but when these people leave here, they can still create. For a while."

"So you're claiming that this is the opposite of the compression chambers? But it's still modifying creativity."

"No, it's allowing it to flow. DHR's mission isn't to enhance creativity; it is to remove it."

"Yes," I said. "They believe the Conservatory is ruining creativity."

One man spoke up at the table next to us. "Not so much ruining as making it too easy."

"How so?" I asked.

"Please don't be offended, Mr. Kohl, but we all learned our craft the hard way through sweat and toil. We did not have the benefit of magic to simplify the process."

Ah, the usual old belief. The Conservatory are nothing but hacks entertaining for laughs in taverns and bat mitzvahs; our Virtuosi gifts allow us to create without effort.

With a chuckle, I half smiled at the man. "I'm afraid you have a misunderstanding. Our musical and magical gifts are separate. Sometimes we're good at one and not the other. If we're lucky, both. Right now I couldn't compose my way out of a wet paper bag."

"We heard you couldn't compose. That is true?"

"Unfortunately true. But I've got plenty of time on my hands now to fail at it properly."

Wonderly smiled at me, then addressed the woman. "Mr. Kohl was removed from the case. He is no longer inspecting the death of Felix Cantabile."

"Or Jazzy Jacob."

"Jazzy Jacob was incidental," the woman said.

"He was not," Wonderly protested.

The woman continued. "When did you start losing your composition skills?"

"Don't know," I said. "Weeks ago, I think. Time keeps slipping by."

"Yes," the woman said. "And it wasn't all right away, correct?"

"I suppose not." In truth, I knew it wasn't, but rule one of pretend detective was to not give away everything you thought.

Wonderly leaned in. "While Felix Cantabile died rather suddenly, the Whimsy had been draining for some time."

"I hadn't seen him for years. Better ask Sonny Mordent."

The man that had spoken before, sitting fourth from the left, so let's call him Juror 4, said, "Given what you have told us about Vittoria and now Ruby, it seems like talking to DHR will accomplish nothing but to inform her."

I shrugged. "Well, I'm off the case, so I can't get the Conservatory to help."

"The Conservatory is just as bad," he said.

"Then I think you're out of luck," I said.

"Eliza is going to help you," Juror 4 said.

"Thanks, but I work alone." My eyes drifted to Wonderly. Wouldn't mind if she were around more, but not for this. "Like a cat with trust issues."

The proof was that a sly smile crossed her lips, imperceptible if you were more than two feet away from her.

"You had an assistant," Juror 4 said.

"Yeah. Good kid. Bad mentor. He's off the case, too."

A young man with a full head of hair spoke up. "Mr. Kohl, we insist."

"I'm afraid I have a job already. Plus, I'm on administrative leave at the moment, so I'm booked solid."

This time Juror 2, a conservative-looking blonde, piped up. "So you have no interest in what happened to Felix or, in a much larger sense, your Whimsy? Or the Whimsy in all of us?"

"Not much I can do about it," I said, and I meant it, too. Add to that, it pissed me off just a little that they were getting on me about it. "What exactly are you doing about Whimsy sitting here in a basement hiding?"

Juror 9 didn't like my implication, which was good, because I didn't intend it to be a mystery. "We are the Improvisationists. We provide places like this for creatives to continue to thrive. For you see, Mr. Kohl, our arts are the soul of the human race. People learn to create, to love, to get along, sometimes to hate because artists model it for them, let them play it out safely. And if Whimsy is dying in us, it is dying in them. They just don't know it yet. You have seen them walk the streets in a daze. They get sidetracked by meaningless things. Our fellow citizens forget to stand in the sun, breathe the air, sit in a café outdoors with their friends. Instead, they hide in the caves of their homes like trolls and then lash out at others because that has been modeled to them without us."

Hell, he should be promoted from jury to head prosecutor with a speech like that. But I wasn't buying it.

"Better be careful," I said. "You're too young to remember the Eleven War, but Improvisationists sounds dangerously close to Compressionists and Dynamicists."

Juror 9 was still on his stump. "When Whimsy finally fades in just over two days, you'll wish there were more Improvisationists working to make things better."

"Or, as you say," I began, "I'll just forget Whimsy ever existed and won't miss it."

The juror nodded. "And what's next, Mr. Kohl? Love? Joy? What others are you willing to sacrifice for your cynicism?"

Wonderly stood; she kept her hand on my shoulder. "I don't think Mr. Kohl is ready. It hasn't yet settled on him that he is a part of this already. He has just lost his job."

Juror 2, a brunette grandma, spoke. "Did you tell him who you are?"

I glanced up at her. "You're not Eliza Wonderly?"

"I am." She pulled her arm from me and clasped her hands in front of herself. "What she means is that I was the contact for Felix. He couldn't be seen with us directly. I've been organizing creative resistance cells for three years now, ever since I watched the DHR 'cure' my brother of his musical abilities. Felix reached out to me six months ago when he first sensed something was wrong with his connection to Whimsy. He knew the Conservatory wouldn't believe him until it was too late."

My brow furrowed. "Why would he reach out to you? You're not Virtuosi. How would he even know about you?"

"I am not Virtuosi. Nevertheless, I walk in your circles. And I have ways to let people find me when the need arises."

Outside the Twelve-Tone Spin Zone, she must not have been hiding her trail. She was showing it, and I dove straight in. Perhaps she did the same to Felix.

"And we didn't want to give up our secret creative spaces," Juror 7 said.

My eyes narrowed. "Felix was from the Conservatory."

"He was the Guardian of Whimsy," Wonderly said. "Anyway, he was also one of us. We couldn't risk him accidentally saying something to his Conservatory coworkers or to his estranged wife, the Head of Special Projects of DHR."

"I understand. We're the special projects."

"There's more." Wonderly reached out and urged me to stand.

"It's a lot, I know," she said. "Consider helping us find a solution."

"Simple," I said. "The Conservatory will just appoint a new Guardian of Whimsy." An outright lie, but they didn't know the process that the Conservatory forsook. They would have their little meeting to agree to have meetings; then the world would forget. Improvisationists, too.

"It is not that simple." Wonderly tugged at my arm, pulling me deeper into the room, into the shadows. A small table hugged the wall with two chairs. A small LED lamp sat on the table along with a small record player. Wonderly tapped it and gestured for me to sit.

I glanced at the rest of the room. The twelve had migrated to easels or manuscript paper. They were the modern group walking around reciting memorized books for a future that might not be savable.

"You already know your cases are linked," she said. "Jacob was working with us and with Felix. I often relayed messages through Jacob."

"So he was a messenger boy?"

"No. He documented the cases. Interviewed people. He was logging the entire decline of Whimsy. The night they both died"—she squeezed her eyes shut and put her hand to her mouth before recovering—"Jacob was supposed to be doing a big interview with Felix. The capstone." She looked away. "Then this."

"I'm sorry for you," I said.

"Be sorry for the world, for we all lose. I lost my brother to this. Cured by DHR. But essentially, a zombie. No soul. No spark, although technically proficient." She exhaled. "Remember the two teenagers at the Spin Zone?"

"Yeah. Sage and Riot."

"They were arrested today." Her eyes locked on to mine.

"They wouldn't divulge to the DHR who took the record. Said they didn't know."

She pulled the Billie Holiday record out and set it on the table. "Your record."

Crap.

The correct liner sat in front of me with all the scrawl. "Read it if you want, but that is a distraction in case the DHR found it. The real message is on the record." She placed the record on the player. "You'll have to attune to it to hear it."

"Can you attune?"

"No. I had help."

Billie Holiday played quietly on the record while I zeroed in and found the right harmonic. To outsiders and perhaps to Wonderly it sounded like I was humming along with the music, keeping my own harmony, but to me the message became clear.

Felix's voice. Tired.

"If you're hearing this, I'm probably dead. The Conservatory wouldn't listen. I told the Council three times that Whimsy was dying, truly dying. They said I was being dramatic. Guardians don't 'feel' their Virtue dying.

"But I felt it. Every day. A little less Whimsy in the world. Children playing out of habit, trying to prevent boredom when boredom is one of the great teachers. Boredom shouldn't be filled with more things to do. It should be embraced, the solution found by our own hearts and minds, not fed by algorithms, another sport, binge-watching ...

"I felt it everywhere. The insidious insertion into culture, bleeding spontaneity out of existence. And the creative artists? The ones who still try? They suffer most. No creativity flows naturally anymore, or the DHR drains it away like draining your soul.

"But they've drained more than souls. They've left something

behind. *Dissonant energy, lingering where creativity was ripped away. It's creating something else, something that wasn't there before. You'll have to deal with it. I won't be here.*

"*Eight months ago I made myself the proof. I started taking thallium in low doses. People might be losing Whimsy, but as the Guardian was losing it, the Conservatory would have to notice. The goal was to create an undeniable sympathetic drain through the Guardian bond that the Cardinals would feel. As I die, Whimsy dies. Measurable. Impossible to dismiss.*

"*Jacob's been helping me. His 'Silencing' reviews aren't criticism. They're documentation. Every musician and artist losing creativity. Every note flatter than before. Proof the Council can't ignore.*

"*I'm not suicidal. I'm desperate. The only language they understand is crisis. So I'm creating a crisis they can't dismiss. Jacob will publish this after I sit down with him in three days to explain it all. He'll distribute it, though not without risk. The DHR gets closer every day. They suspect something the Council ignores. The Council will have to act. They'll have to choose a successor, as I've requested many times. Whimsy will transfer and I'll recover.*

"*If not ... my death will mean something. It will save the Virtue I've sworn to protect.*

"*Tell my beautiful wife, Sonny, I'm sorry. She never wanted to marry a martyr. She walked into the middle of a conflict, and I don't begrudge her choosing the DHR side. Funny thing is ... I think she knows something is up but can't put her finger on it. I've seen her so many times lately, almost like we were dating again. She doesn't know that the DHR is one of the biggest investors in the world in AI, the next best thing to compression chambers.*"

The music swelled back in, and I was speechless. Poisoning himself. That explained it. I had wasted so much time solving a crime that wasn't a crime. But Jacob was. Someone murdered him, and it had to be related to this.

"Okay," I said, fighting tears trying to find my eyes. My voice cracked a little. "I'll figure out who killed Jacob." I paused. "And needlessly double-killed Felix. Rushed what was already happening." I shook my head. "I'm in."

She smiled at me, comforting. I stared at the record.

Her hand reached across the table and grabbed mine. Wonderly smiled. "Welcome to the resistance."

As I rose, I looked over the room. Everyone was staring at me. Twelve artists plus Wonderly in a city of a million. This wasn't a resistance to the death of Whimsy. They were a statistical error.

CHAPTER 25
DHR RECRUIT

Tuesday, May 26—Day 5

SOMEONE HAMMERED on my door like they were serving a warrant. Through the grimy window, Tuesday morning looked as gray as my prospects. Seven fifteen a.m.—the kind of hour when only bad news comes calling.

I should have stayed at the Academy, but my recliner was more comfortable.

I threw the blanket off me and climbed out of the chair. My shirt was only tucked in on one side, and I lost a sock somewhere. Whatever. My ribs were killing me.

The door groaned about the hour, too, only to reveal Sonny Mordent.

"Good morning," she said. "May I come in?"

With a sigh, I gestured inward and held the door wider. "Sure. Why not?"

Sonny stood in my living room and surveyed the mess with obvious disdain. I was too tired to compete with her in posture, so I flopped back into my chair and grimaced at the bad idea. My clothes from yesterday were making up for the lack of wrinkles in her blue dress. I wondered if the woman ever dressed casually.

"I came to apologize," she said.

My eyes widened, and I sat up. Perhaps I should take notes. "Apologies not necessary. I was getting tired of the job anyway."

"Did they fire you?" she asked.

"No, but may as well have. Might yet." I stood and stepped into the kitchen. "Coffee?"

"No, thanks."

Sonny followed me into the kitchen, looking at the floor as if she were afraid she was about to step in a pile of dog shit at any moment. But I didn't like dogs. Particularly, I didn't like having to take them outside, walk them, or pick their shit off the ground, especially in winter.

The freshly brewed coffee tasted like I had licked the bottom of a birdcage, but I drank it anyway and leaned against the counter. "Well, now, I didn't think I'd see you again after my stalking you and all."

She looked away and closed her eyes for a moment. "I had Felix cremated. Thought you might want to know. Simple service."

"Yeah. He wouldn't have wanted anything big."

Her eyes met mine. "No music. No improvisation. I thought it best for the DHR to keep it private."

"I understand."

Sonny smiled grimly at me. "I came to apologize for reporting you to the Conservatory. I was mistaken about your neglecting the case. So, either I can go back and correct my mistake, restore your standing with them, or you can work for me instead."

Rimsky. Sonny. Now I was popular. Interesting that she apologized for reporting me to the Conservatory, but not for the destruction of my ossia. But I didn't have proof for that. That omission told me everything I needed to know about the DHR's "standards."

"I don't think I have much to offer the DHR."

"You'd be surprised what desperate people find useful," she said. "But more importantly for today, I want you to finish the case. Your Conservatory seemed like they were distracted and barely had time to deal with my request."

"The case was closed on account of you."

"It is officially still. It is for the Conservatory. But I discovered who did this"—she glanced around the apartment again—"although I don't know how they found anything in here."

"Yeah, it's a mystery," I said. "Who?"

"Perhaps you should sit down," she said.

"I'm a big boy."

Sonny crossed her arms, studying me, and stepped closer. Her perfume cut through the stench of bachelorhood, providing a three-foot bubble of stale flowers. Or perhaps that was me projecting onto her.

But she was not deterred. "Did you know that at least three times the woman you call Cree tried to see me at the Department?"

With a groan, I nodded. "At least three times?"

"Perhaps you should ask her if she ransacked your apartment."

"Why? She still has a key."

Cree. The one person I'd trusted with a key. The one person who could walk in without breaking anything.

Sonny's smile was sharp as broken glass. "Keys unlock more than doors, Mr. Kohl. They unlock secrets. Why did you let her keep it?"

My hands shot up, and I shook my head. "I don't know. In case I ever got a cat and took a vacation and I needed somebody to feed the damn thing. They oddly like eating."

The reality was that I didn't want closure. A sliver of me

hoped, even though I knew better. That hope should have died the same day as that poor bastard in the hallway, axe buried in his skull. But I'd never been good at letting dead things stay buried.

No forced entry. No broken locks. Because she didn't need to break in. Cree. Cree and Riff. Christ. I thought about all those nights I'd imagined her walking back through that door, apology on her lips, that old spark in her eyes. Instead, she'd been riffling through my things like a common thief. Looking for what?

"What did she take?" I asked.

"I don't know what she was looking for," Sonny said. "But I'd like you to find out. She visited the DHR three times over the past month. Each time, she asked to speak with me specifically."

"About what?"

"I refused to see her. But someone who wants to speak to the Head of Special Projects that badly is very brave or very desperate." Sonny's eyes narrowed. "Or both."

"Speaking of DHR visits," I said, "Rimsky's been making his own rounds. Been asking questions about your marriage to Felix. Your work schedule. Your access to him."

Sonny's face tightened. "What kind of questions?"

I hid my smile behind my coffee cup. "The kind someone asks when they're building a case. Almost as if he wanted to establish your opportunity and motive."

"That bastard," she muttered. "I knew he was gunning for my position."

I'd give her one thing. Sonny was an expert at the fast turnaround as she took us back to Cree. "Your friend Cree knows Felix?"

My coffee hit the counter harder than necessary. "Yeah. We were all in school together."

Sonny uncrossed her arms, slid her hands into her pockets,

and stepped closer. "When was the last time she saw him?" Too casual. Too rehearsed.

"Don't know. I hadn't thought of him for years, so I assume she hadn't, either." My eyes met Sonny's. "No offense."

A thin smile crossed her lips but avoided her eyes. "One of the things about this job is that you have to be able to compartmentalize." Sonny held out her left hand, palm down, like she was showing me the height of the box. "This box is my job." She repeated this with her other hand. "This is my relationship with Felix. I've always had to push them apart for sanity."

Half listening, I bobbed my head. Without the ability to get a little musical assistance, I had to trust my instinct. Her body was open and relaxed; her face was the most emotionally accessible I had seen it yet. She had ventured to me in this hellhole.

"So, by finish the case, you mean what exactly?" I asked.

"I mean, follow the trail and see where it leads." Sonny put her hands on her hips.

"Follow the trail where, exactly?" I asked. "You want me to shake down Cree? Find out why she's ransacked my apartment if she did?"

"I want to know what Felix was really working on," Sonny said. "The Conservatory claims he was just composing. But Felix never just composed. He was always three moves ahead, always planning something." Her jaw tightened. "And I think Cree knows what it was."

"You think Cree and Felix were working together?"

"I think someone murdered my husband, and the official investigation is protecting someone." She met my eyes. "I want to know who. The DHR will compensate you. And you can submit expenses to me. I'll ensure that you are reimbursed."

Someone murdered her husband when he was already dying. Let's not mention that.

I frowned at her. "Some people won't take it well if someone like me works for the DHR."

"Some people" meaning every musician I'd ever respected. Meaning every student I'd taught, every colleague who'd watched me defend the old ways against DHR regulations. If word got out I was working for Sonny Mordent, I'd be radioactive. The Conservatory would drop me faster than a wrong note in a concert hall.

But the Conservatory had already hung me out to dry. And my rent was due the day after Whimsy was gone.

"Just you," I said. "Not the Department. This stays between us."

"Agreed," Sonny said. "As far as anyone knows, you're consulting on Felix's estate. Private matter. Nothing official."

"One more thing," I said. "My ossia was destroyed. I want it replaced."

Her lips tightened. "Unfortunate. But I can't replace unsanctioned instruments, Mr. Kohl. Department policy."

She knew something. But she wasn't saying.

"Unsanctioned? You mean magical."

She grunted at me. "Perhaps your compensation will be sufficient to get you a new one. Appropriately regulated, of course."

"Of course. I am a strict follower of the rules."

Sonny reached into her pocket and pulled out a slip of paper. After a glance at it, she handed it to me.

The paper had a series of numbers written on it, with spaces separating them into groups.

"That's my cell phone. Private. Not a DHR phone."

"Of course."

I slipped the paper into my pocket, but something about her tone made me look up. For just a moment, her mask slipped, and I saw something in her eyes that chilled me more than the May morning.

Fear.

Not of me, not of the case. Something else lingered at the edges.

CHAPTER 26

SWEET LORRAINE

EVEN THOUGH I didn't need to, I shaved and brushed my teeth. I made breakfast, ate, drank a cup of coffee, brushed my teeth again, then thought about a second shower before I told myself to stop thinking and do the job. Finally, I glanced at my phone. After Sonny had given me her number, I knew I wouldn't call it. Waste of time.

Looking at my phone was another stall tactic. Get the work done. I sat on the piano bench and sent a message to Cree telling her I needed to talk to her without her beau around. Her response came fast and said *Come on over. Lorraine.* That signature told me the place was one hundred percent safe. She'd never tell someone like Riff Parker her real name. I was pretty sure there were only four people in the world left who knew it, and one of them had died.

Cree lived a dozen blocks from Hedgehog on the fifth floor of a redbrick building that used to be a warehouse before the housing crisis. I knocked, and she yelled for me to enter. Rather than luxury apartments, it was a space to call home that wasn't three thousand a month in rent.

The apartment was bigger than mine, but what she gained in size she lost in acoustics. The walls were brick, the floors concrete, and the windows were single pane with stripped wooden frames. Cree had thrown rugs on the floor and hung more on the walls to kill the reflections, but it was only moderately successful. That was why she always practiced at the Hedgehog.

Moving around the apartment with that familiar restless energy, she cleaned and straightened.

"Still can't sit still, can you, Copper Top?" I said.

She'd earned the nickname in high school—when she was still Lorraine—not just for the hair, but because she seemed to run on some internal battery the rest of us lacked.

Cree smiled at me. "Sit. Give me a minute."

I plopped down on the couch with the casual abandon of my youth. It was one of those L-shaped things, gray, a part-time black hole that sucked you in and made it difficult to escape. On the upside, the massive number of cushions and pillows would help kill some of the reverb in the room. There was a blanket and pillow on the couch, so I tossed them to the end.

Cree ducked into her bedroom and closed the door.

We'd been through a lot together. I was responsible for her choosing the name Locrian, aka Cree. By then we'd already been best friends, bandmates, mutual consolers. It was the last night Felix, Cree, and I were together. Sure, I'd stay friends with her, but Felix was off to Juilliard, I was about to be indoctrinated by the Conservatory, and Lorraine was going to improv her life.

Felix had already passed out that night, leaving Lorraine and me side by side in a drunken stupor. I told her out of the blue that Lorraine was such an old-fashioned name when she was such a free-spirited thing I chose not to remember because, well, twenty-something guy and inappropriate.

Right then she decided: no more Lorraine Morgenstern. She would be Locrian Morgenstern in my honor. The Locrian mode of music is unstable by nature. Classical composers often avoided it, but jazz musicians love it. It creates an unsettling tension that keeps you a bit off-balance.

Perfect name for a sax player who had magic of her own. It wasn't my kind. It was a special kind of chaos she created, untamable. That was how she played. That was how she fenced.

And Cree became the nickname rather than explaining it every time to the Statics.

But that night on a different couch in a different place was when the band broke up—the day our music died. It was August 18, 2006. Hot as hell outside, even at night. Sweat rolled down us as she slipped her hand into mine, squeezed it, then stood. She bent back over and kissed me on the forehead. She handed me her beer bottle and walked out the front door as a creative, free-spirited soul.

As if mirroring my thoughts, Cree opened the door of her bedroom and returned to me. Baggy bronze pants, canary-yellow turtleneck, oversize sport coat of red, black, and orange plaid— she was an explosion of color that made me smile just looking at her. The hair was as wild as ever, and the lipstick matched the red part of the jacket.

She smiled at me.

"Going somewhere?"

She plopped down on the ottoman in front of me and leaned forward, elbows on her knees. "Nope. I thought I'd prove to you I hadn't lost my color, contrary to what you believe."

"You didn't have to dress up for me."

Cree looked at the floor for a moment. "Your message sounded ominous. I wanted you to feel better."

Plausible, but not convincing. Because she had a sense of these things, particularly my discomfort, she dropped beside me on the couch. When I didn't react, she grabbed my arm and pulled it around her shoulders while I studied the room.

Cree elbowed me. "Don't be so morose. What's gotten into you?"

Clearing my throat, I began. "I'd like you to explain your visits to the DHR."

She sneered at me, put her hand on my face, and pushed me away. Cree stood, walked a couple of paces, then spun, hands on her hips. "So this is official business again, is it?"

"No. I was taken off the case."

"Were you? Seems like you're still on it. And we had this discussion already."

I shrugged. "Stubborn asshole."

"True."

I stood and approached her. "And I'm a little bothered that our friend was murdered."

She shoved me back. "Don't be so full of yourself. I bet you planned this whole thing to—"

Cree stepped back to me, grabbed my hand, and yanked me along as if she just realized that we stood in a jungle full of predators and she knew the way through, and I was too busy staring at the animals to realize I was lunch. She dragged me into her bedroom.

"Look. Look all you want. That's why you're here." I didn't move. She released my hand, went to her dresser, and opened it. "Come on, detective. Nothing of Riff's here."

She gritted her teeth and shook her head. I could bring that out in her like no other. "Riff moved to Columbus because his playing dried up in Chicago," Cree said, answering the question I hadn't asked. "Same as everyone else. I thought a change of scene might help. It didn't. But at least he's here."

I yelled back at her, "Stop deflecting!" I caught my breath. "Did you or did you not go to the DHR?"

Cree stormed out of the room. We both needed a minute. She was mistaken that I came to detect signs of Riff. Deep down, she knew that. But the signs were there. Maybe not clothing, a toothbrush, or anything meaningful, but small things. Scraps of sheet music on a grand staff, scribbled with piano parts. The two chairs at her kitchen table were closer together instead of opposed. Two sets of towels in the bathroom instead of one.

I turned to go after her. By the time I reached the doorway, she spun, stopping me. She exhaled with a grumble. "I went to the DHR, if it is even any of your business. Does that satisfy you, or do you want a whole libretto of the experience?"

"No, just give me the overture."

She laughed. I stepped toward her, and we embraced. After an extended hold, she pushed away and wiped a tear from her eye. Then she shoved me again. "You dumb brute. I'd kill you if I didn't love you so much."

That was a loaded response, not the best one when I was investigating a murder. But I took it as intended because of our long history.

Cree sighed. "I went four times."

"To see Sonny Mordent?"

"Hell no." She shook her head. "I went to see Dr. Phrygian. The first three times he wasn't there, but I caught him on the fourth visit."

She was fudging the details a bit. A twenty-something-year-old relationship was far better than magic at detecting that.

"I saw him, too," I said. "Not the way I remembered him."

"People age."

"Still have the rubber chicken?" I asked.

"I don't think so."

Cree removed her jacket and walked toward the bedroom. "I guess I don't need to impress you anymore."

"You never did."

She threw her jacket onto the bed and disappeared into her closet. A minute later, she came out with a jacket matching her pants.

"I thought Dr. Phrygian might be able to help. If anyone

could get people out of a slump, he could," she said. I must have looked suspicious, because she added, "He inspired you, right?"

"Years ago."

"You think it goes away?"

She said it, but she didn't mean it. Cree knew it went away for her, for me, for Felix, for everyone we knew.

"That was a good idea," I said.

"Was it? Because he had already lost it. He was there because his daughter had died. He said from dangerous magical dreams." Cree threw her hands up. "His daughter was seventeen." Cree continued, her voice soft. "Samantha. She was a painter, magical realist stuff. Phrygian showed me her work once." She wiped her eyes. "God, Dekk, she was brilliant. But she tried to paint her dreams into reality, literally. The magical backlash ..."

Cree couldn't finish. She didn't need to. I understood.

"Whimsy may have died, but you're still the eternal optimist," I said.

Her return smile was grim. She wasn't finished.

"What?" I asked.

She opened her mouth and closed it several times before finally getting the words out. "You want to know why I really went to DHR?" Cree's voice was barely above a whisper.

"You told me."

"True. But ... incomplete. I also went because I knew something was wrong with Felix months ago." Cree swallowed hard and looked away from me. "He called me, Dekk. Three times in the past couple of months. Said he felt like something was draining out of him, like a slow leak in his soul."

She wrapped her arms around herself. "And I told him it was just stress. I told him to see a doctor. I never thought ..." Her voice broke. "I should have told you. Should have insisted the Conservatory take it seriously. Something. I don't know what."

"I hadn't heard from him in years. Why didn't you tell me you had talked to him?"

Her eyes met mine. "Really? The way you two left things with each other? There was no way I was telling you anything, even if I should have."

"I suppose you're right."

The front door of her apartment opened. I expected Riff, but was surprised to see Hoagy. He froze in his tracks.

My eyes went to Cree's.

"He found me at the club and asked for help."

I glanced at the blanket on the couch. "He's been staying here?"

"Yeah."

Hoagy closed the door and approached.

"How's Tuning?" I asked.

Hoagy's brow furrowed. "They're like a bunch of grumpy dwarves tinkering with screwdrivers and miniature hammers, grumbling about how the Virtuosi treat their instruments."

"They are a special breed."

"I'll let you two catch up." She leaned close to me and lowered her voice. "He reminds me a lot of you at that age." She gave me a toothy smile. "Eager and clueless." She kissed me on the forehead.

Cree headed toward the door. "Be sure the door is locked when you leave."

"Sure," I said.

She glanced at Hoagy. "Don't worry. No one will know."

Once she had gone, he plopped down on the far end of the couch with a massive exhale.

"Why aren't you at home?" I said.

"I told Mom I was staying at a friend's house for a few days. It's summer, you know."

"Okay. Did you tell her your friend was an older woman?"

His face contorted. "Gross." He shook his head. "It's not—"

"I know. Just messing with you."

He leaned forward. "She's nice and let me stay here and all, but weird. You know she sleeps on top of the blankets on her back, lying on the bed like a corpse?"

"I wouldn't tell her you've been watching her sleep."

"Bro. Gross." His face contorted again. "The first night she was making all kinds of noises, so I was worried. She sleeps with the door open, so—"

I held up my hand. "I don't need the details. Why'd you ask to stay with her?"

"To help you with the case."

"There isn't one. Remember?"

"Oh, but there's no way you followed those orders."

"You think you got me figured out, do you?"

He smiled. "I found her at the Hedgehog, and then she helped me meet Eliza."

My eyebrows shot up. "Why did you want to meet Eliza?"

"She was helping you. I wanted to help, too."

"You'll never have a career if you hang out with me, whether I'm on the good side of the Conservatory or the bad."

"What's our next step in the investigation?" the kid asked.

CHAPTER 27
SONATA ALLEGRA

LIFE CAN TAKE you down some strange paths. I understood Dr. Phrygian abandoning his soul to work at DHR after what happened, but it didn't sit well with me. The question also nagged at me: did Sonny know him? It was a big department, so he could be a small cog in a basement doing meaningless crap. Still, it felt like a betrayal. Not against me. Not against Cree. Against all the students he ever had. Never mind the excuses.

Hoagy still couldn't be seen with me, so I left him at Cree's. After wandering the streets aimlessly, I returned home and sat at the piano intending to create something new, but my fingers only found the tune "Sweet Lorraine." Cree's answer was appropriate for her.

I slammed the keyboard cover down and rang Dash. He was reluctant, but he agreed to meet me outside Felix's. Then I called the kid at Cree's place.

"Okay. Remember the apartment at three-twenty Sycamore?" He grunted that he did. "I'm headed there."

"Good idea. The cat is probably starving."

"Yeah," I said.

But no. I wanted another look. But the cat wasn't a bad thought.

A cab ride later, I met Dash outside the apartment. He shook hands with me as he approached. "You shouldn't be here," he said.

"Can't help myself."

My eyes roamed the street. Quiet. But there were two silhouettes in a car one hundred feet away. Dash didn't seem to notice. Could be his?

The detective frowned at me. "DHR and the Conservatory both informed me you were off the case. So …"

"I'm off the case."

To keep him out of trouble, I needed to give him something —a way to be here and help me without helping me. "Who's got the cat?"

"Nobody. We haven't seen her. The neighbor hasn't seen her."

I stared down the street, then back at Dash. "Well, I came to take the cat. It needs a good home, and the wicked witch of DHR doesn't want it."

Dash chomped on another sunflower seed. "Mm-hmm." He stared at me. "I shouldn't let you in."

With a shrug, I pointed at the door. "I'll find the cat and take her."

He gave me a curt nod and opened the door to three-twenty Sycamore. "Don't wreck my career, Dekker."

"I only destroy my own life."

Hoagy bounded up the stairs behind us. Dash glared at me. "I supposed he's helping to find the cat, too."

"How many CPD officers couldn't catch her?"

Dash frowned and let us into the apartment. It looked the same, of course. No need to have it cleaned.

The detective spat another sunflower carcass on the carpet to match all the ones from the last time we were here.

"Landlord's got an itch to get this all moving," he said.

"Imagine so. What's the holdup?"

The detective grabbed my arm. "Buddy, I'm gonna tell you something, but you never heard it from me."

"Sounds ominous. Shoot."

"Felix Cantabile may have died by strangulation, but he was gonna die anyway." The detective studied my face for a reaction. I did my best shocked-but-still-hiding-it face.

"So the killer didn't need to go to the trouble," I said.

Dash shrugged. "Unless the killer wanted to hurry it up a bit."

"So toxicology confirmed this?"

"Yeah."

Check. At least part of Felix's story was true.

With new thoughts rumbling in my head, I wandered around the room. To the right of the piano was a stand for Felix's trumpet. With a heavy sigh, I picked up the horn. It wasn't my instrument of choice, so I was sure I'd be flat on the trumpet.

"You're not a good actor, Dekk," the detective said. "You knew?"

I frowned. "Yeah. He was poisoning himself. Left a note of sorts. Thallium."

"Why?" He seemed unconvinced, suspicious even.

"To get the attention of the Conservatory." I shook my head. "The thing I wonder is, did the killer know he was already dying and want to speed it up?"

Dash shrugged. "Damn bummer if impatience sent you to jail."

The detective spat out another seed. "I'm going to let you two find the cat. You're the only person it's come out for, so I'll step out. There's one of those cat cages on the kitchen table." His eyes met mine. "Stay on task and don't make trouble for me."

I agreed, and Dash stepped out, cracking the door. With

a nod to Hoagy, we began our search in earnest, looking under the bed, in every cabinet, and everywhere I thought a cat might go. Ironic that I had just told Sonny that I let Cree keep the key to my apartment in case I ever got a cat. Be careful what you put out into the ethers. It has a tendency to bite you in the ass later.

"You really want the cat?" Hoagy asked while I was on my hands and knees reaching inside the piano. Journal back where I put it but no cat.

"For now. If it's a pain in the ass, I'll drop it off at your house."

The closet door in Felix's bedroom was cracked open. I pulled the door and flipped the switch. This was a walk-in closet that was more for storage than wardrobe, but Felix had enough sports jackets that were so loud they ought to have given decibel warnings. He and Cree agreed in that department.

That and five hundred sticky notes on the back wall.

But sitting on the top shelf, tucked between shoe boxes, sat Mixolydian. I reached up, and she let me grab her. In the process, I knocked the boxes and a pile of papers to the floor.

The cat was in my arms, and I stroked her back. She purred like a slow timpani roll, but something about the vibration felt off. Like a chord where one note was microtones flat. Her six legs shifted as she settled into my arms, and for just a second, the movement reminded me of those AI-generated images from a few years back: technically correct but fundamentally wrong in ways you couldn't quite articulate. I shook off the thought. Grief does strange things to perception. Felix was dead. His cat was weird. That was enough strangeness for one day.

"Let's get you out of here," I said.

It didn't matter that I knocked everything off the shelf, but I squatted to straighten the mess a little. It was a pile of paperwork. But the thing that grabbed my attention was the wedding certificate.

I gave the cat to Hoagy. "Don't let her get away."

I picked up the marriage certificate with a sticky note attached, reminding him to file it with the Conservatory. A few years too late, buddy. The certificate said "Joined in the holy state of matrimony were Felix Nicolo Cantabile and Sonata Allegra Mordent on this 27th day of January …"

I stared at the date—Mozart's birthday. Funny. A very Felix thing to do. But it was the name that was the shocker. Sonata Allegra Mordent. Whispering the words aloud, I repeated it.

Shaking my head, I looked at the wall. More of those damn sticky notes. Dozens of them, overlapping like scales: "Grocery list," "Change strings," "Library—return by 15th." How did he keep up with these? But one interested me, stuck apart from the others. It read "DR knows about thallium. Says it won't be fast enough. Meeting to discuss."

I set it on top of the marriage certificate, contemplating both.

"Look at this," I said to Hoagy.

For a moment I thought the paper was trembling in my hand; then I realized it was something that hit the back of my head. Gravity reclaimed me.

The lights went out, and I didn't realize that it was only in my head until I felt the sandpaper tongue of Mixolydian licking my face. Felt like sandpaper on a violin bow. Had to be Mixy.

I lay on the closet floor contemplating what had happened, my mind wandering like a sailboat anchored in a tropical bay, bobbing up and down, carefree. Beyond the rhythmic lapping of water against the hull and the breeze in my hair, the only sound was someone swimming in the turquoise water, their voice reaching me like an echo through cathedral acoustics.

It sounded as if they were calling me to dive in with them, but I kept thinking about how January 27 was Mozart's birthday, and we ought to celebrate. Birthday cake with … with Felix? Sonny laughs, but that's wrong; she doesn't laugh. Never laughs. Why was someone swimming in my apartment?

"Dekker, get up," the swimmer called. "Come on, buddy, snap out of it."

My eyes opened for me to realize I was lying on a pile of papers, and I'd assume it was me drooling on them and not the cat.

Dash rolled me over. "How many fingers am I holding up?"

"Two," I said. "Though I'm sure you prefer one."

"All right, funny guy." Dash sat me up.

"Caught the cat," I said.

"Looks like more than the cat."

I stood with his help. The cat jumped onto me, and I cradled it while it hissed at Dash.

My wits were finding me again. "Where's Hoagy?"

"Nursing a good-sized knot on his head with a bag of ice. He woke first and came for me."

With a nod, I stared at the floor. The certificate was gone. "There was a marriage certificate."

Dash had his arm around my shoulder, leading me out. "Who? Felix and Sonny?"

"Yeah."

"All right. We'll look it up downtown if we need to."

Sharp focus hit me. I glanced like a madman at Dash. "We need to. The certificate said Felix Nicolo Cantabile and Sonata Allegra Mordent."

"That's not new information," Dash said.

"Uh-huh." My eyes roamed over Dash, detective turned nursemaid. "By the way, where were you when I got hit?"

"Got hit?" Dash studied me as he helped me out of the room. "I assumed you fell, but if you're worried it was me, I was getting a latte and pretending that I didn't know you were here."

We stopped in the living room, and Dash sat me down.

My eyes went to Hoagy's. "All right?"

"Yeah. Fun job you have."

"How'd you figure out how to find Dash?"

"Aimed for the stereotype first. Figured you would."

I laughed outright.

Dash spat out a seed. "What's the joke?"

"Coffee and doughnuts."

"Kids today." Dash shook his head. "A lot of people like coffee, and they don't like doughnuts."

I was only there for a beat before I jumped up and handed Mixy to Dash. "Hold her." Then I told the cat to tolerate it.

Then I stumbled to the piano over twenty feet away, and I was sluggish. Otherwise, I would have sprinted to the piano. When I made it, I grabbed the sheet music.

"What's gotten into you?" Dash asked.

I didn't answer. Finally, he said, "Don't run off."

The detective dipped into the bedroom and came out a minute later with the cat in the portable carrier. She was meowing in protest. Meanwhile, I was flipping through the sheet music.

Dash gave the carrier to Hoagy.

"Look at this, Dash. 'Sonata Allegra in G.'"

"Meaning?"

"The song title Felix wrote. His last piece."

"You can keep it if it means something to you," Dash said.

"It means something to you." I walked to him and pointed at the title. No bells ringing, so I showed it to Hoagy.

"Sonata. Sonny," the kid said.

"That's not just a song title. It's his wife's name encoded in music. Sonata Allegra Mordent."

Dash put his hand on my shoulder. "Okay, there. You've had a shock. Sonata's a type of music, right?"

"A form, yes."

"And Sonny's parents were—"

"I'm not crazy," I said. "Sonata Allegra in G. Should've been G-sharp like her personality. But it was probably for Guardian.

Felix knew what she was doing to him, and he encoded it into the title."

Dash frowned. "And the G-string murder weapon?"

I shook my head. "Probably coincidence. Felix was dying slowly from thallium poisoning—he couldn't have known she'd strangle him in a moment of rage. His mind was probably not what it was. But G? That's deliberate."

"Why don't you leave the detective work to detectives, Dekker? You're creating things that don't exist. You know that there was some attempt to strangle him and that gloves were in the dumpster with Jazzy Jacob."

"I'm right."

"I'm afraid you're wrong. Toxicology says good ol' classic arsenic." Dash shook his head and looked at Hoagy. "Can you walk him home?"

My eyes were wide, and my heart was pounding. "Look at the tempo."

Dash read where my finger pointed on the sheet of music. "*Andante non vivace.* Sorry, Dekker. I'm not a musician. Not getting the urge to learn."

"'Walking not lively,'" Hoagy said.

"Right. There could be hundreds of tempo markings. I wouldn't write it this way. *Andante ma non troppo,* maybe. But not 'walking not lively' or 'walking not alive'?"

Dash whistled. "Whew! Talk about grasping at straws, Dekk. We might want to have you checked out. Let's take you over to Grant Hospital."

I was determined, and I was not crazy. Felix was not composing his final piece; he was writing his own death certificate and telling us who it was. A failed musician overshadowed by the Guardian of Whimsy? Was it professional resentment or personal failure? Her work at the DHR made sense. Special Projects.

My eyes roamed across the score. How had I not seen it?

Then I realized something else. I reached into my pocket and pulled out the slip of paper Sonny gave me with her phone number. I held it against the sheet music.

C-sharp | G-sharp | B | C | C | C | D | D-sharp | A-sharp | A

Note for note a match with our cipher.

I showed it to Dash, explaining it in detail.

The detective bobbed his head. "That's … actually pretty clever. But it's circumstantial."

"Maybe. But it's also a dying man's confession written in the language he lived in."

"A preconfession. Not as he was being murdered. Let's get out of here," Dash said.

"Are you going to arrest her?"

Dash laughed. "The head of the DHR Special Projects? Not a chance. Clever idea. I'll look into it. But you're also recovering from … a fall? A hit? And you said he already confessed to killing himself? What did the guy do, go around leaving notes for everything? Who would find such things?"

"I'm fine. And I would understand it."

The detective shook his head. "Someone you haven't talked to in decades leaving you notes?"

"He knew I was Virtuosi. And I'd bet money he knew I was a Trovatore."

"That again." He looked at Hoagy. "Son, get away from this crowd before they make you bonkers, too."

I turned away from him and folded the first sheet of the score and Sonny's phone number, and stuck them in my pocket.

Hoagy seemed to take the detective's side on this one. "How would he know you were Trovatore? Does the Council tell everyone who does what?"

I smiled grimly. My eyes met Hoagy's. "Cree had talked to Felix several times over the past few months. What are the odds she didn't at least mention me? She could say something to him because she was annoyed with me."

"True," both said together.

"Okay, Dekker," Dash said. "Sonny's not going anywhere." He pushed me and the kid toward the door. "Take the cat home. Feed it. Go see a doc. I'll check in on you later. Then we'll talk."

CHAPTER 28

RESISTANCE IS FUTILE

DURING THE HOUR walk from Felix's apartment, I tried to make Hoagy understand that he was risking his future by associating with me. He was certain it would work out. Nice to have optimism. I lost it decades ago and can't remember where I put it.

I didn't want to go home to the mess. We should have stopped to drop off Mixy, but I had a feeling that might tip off the DHR or the Conservatory that the kid was with me.

We walked to the second-best place to be, the Fencing Academy. The trumpet fanfare sounded as I stepped inside, which made me realize something. It hadn't gone off when Wonderly let me in after hours.

Maestra Flanconade was almost at the top of the dilapidated spiral staircase. She stopped and squatted. Her silver-streaked hair cascaded to her shoulders and framed her angular face. While laugh lines and crow's-feet had appeared, she looked younger than her sixty years. No doubt it was all that fencing and giving lessons that kept her fit and healthy. Dealing with stubborn, less-than-perfect fencers like me may have assisted in the arrival of the gray hair.

"Dekk, you're hours early," she said.

"The door was open."

"There's no one to fence."

With a nod, I smiled at her, pleading. "I'm a bit out of sorts, Maestra. Mind if I stab something that can't stab back? Teach the kid a few moves?"

Hoagy was smiling. She waved us on and continued upstairs.

In the *salle*, I set the cat down on one of the fencing strips, then picked up an épée from the wall. I gave Hoagy a foil. I showed him how to make a touch. I pounded on the target for a while as if I were in a war against the entire DHR on my own, feeling each touch in my ribs as if the target were stabbing back. Perhaps because I was hitting the wall more than the target, chipping the plaster. I needed to focus. Hoagy had given up. A lot of kids think target work is boring.

Like a moth drawn to the flame, I glanced to the corner where the secret door was. Down there, the dampening field couldn't reach me. I could think clearly, and I could blot out the thoughts rattling around in my head and figure out a plan.

I didn't have a tuning fork on me, but I remembered the tone and the harmonics, so I could whistle it and avoid Wonderly's warning of destruction. F-sharp to B-flat. Done.

Once downstairs, I flipped on the light. The place was abandoned. I placed the cat carrier on the counter and unzipped it, demanding that the cat not run off. She had to go home with me. Her mom and dad were lost to her now, and she was stuck.

I glanced at the kid. "Secret location. I expect it to remain that way."

"No problem."

The cat stretched, indifferent. I opened the fridge and found some plain yogurt, which I put out for the cat. While she ate, I paced.

But pacing didn't clear my mind, either. I kept wandering

back to the darkest corner of the room, as far away from the front door as could be. An old upright was there.

The yellow bench had seen better decades, showing layers of paint chipped away like archaeological evidence. Red underneath blue underneath whatever optimistic color had started this journey. The piano looked about as trustworthy as a campaign promise. This thing was a restoration project that would cost more than buying a new one. I didn't care.

The keyboard cover squealed as I flipped it open and pressed the D4 key. In tune. Lingering a little longer in the air than it should. My breathing slowed. I closed my eyes and listened to the harmonics as I held the sustain pedal and struck the key again.

Mixy jumped on top of the piano and lay down at the edge, her tail hanging down. My left hand started working a simple rhythm. The cat meowed at me.

"You're right," I said.

Hoagy understood that nothing exciting was going to happen and sat at one of the tables to doomscroll.

I thought for a moment; then I sat at the piano hammering out a three-note motif. I intended it to be for Cree, an apology maybe. In my head, I heard words. But they weren't for Cree. They were ...

"Won-der-ly. Won-der-ly. Lov-e-ly Won-der-ly. Where are you?"

It happens. Words stick in your head and make up your melodies. Sometimes an idea is like a rock that gets stuck in your shoe. You take the shoe off, and you keep hunting for that rock, but you just can't find it. Ideas are like that. Even when you try to get rid of them sometimes, they won't let go.

But those were the kinds of things you didn't tell Statics. The minute you pointed out that a melody matched its title in phrasing, it ruined it for them.

I kept repeating the pattern, adding a nice bass line, and felt joy run through me as if all music and magic had come from inside me and radiated outward.

Mixy sat on top of the piano, her tail twitching in what I would swear was 4/4 time. When I hit a wrong note, the cat turned and gave me a look that said, "Really? After decades of composing, that's the best you can do?"

Of course, cats always look like they're judging you. This one just happened to be right. I continued ironing it out, the persistent words in my head, the harmonies morphing as the tune tried to find a home, as I rediscovered my ability to compose.

"That's nice. What is it?"

My fingers froze, and the notes hung in the air. I turned to see Wonderly with her hand on Hoagy's shoulder, looking at me. She instinctively had good timing. Good skill for a musician or a fencer.

"Nothing worth copyrighting. Just seeing if my fingers remember they're attached to a musician instead of a tone-deaf accountant."

She approached the cat, which graciously allowed her attention. That was perhaps the first reasonable decision anyone had made all day. "Sorry for the break-in. Nowhere else felt safe."

Her questioning look said it all. "Home?"

"Right. Where someone had already attacked me and tossed the place and broken my ossia. Hoagy thought it was a mess before."

Wonderly sat beside me. "Play it again."

I did, being careful not to make a mistake. Then I apologized. I had worked out the A theme but hadn't gotten to B. Perhaps an analogy for my life, ever repeating the A theme without variation.

"It's lovely," Wonderly said. "Does it have a name?"

"Still in the experimental phase. Like most of my relationships."

I stared at her for a long moment, my fingers still holding down the last chord although the notes had long since faded into the ethers. The world was a black-and-white movie full of Dutch angles, and she was the only thing in color. But also slightly out of focus, like looking at something beautiful through tears you don't want to admit you're crying.

"Write it down," lovely Wonderly said. I shook it out of my head. It was stress. It'd been a rough few days.

"I don't need to. My memory's like a steel trap—mostly rust, occasionally functional."

That smile could have powered half the city's streetlamps. When she moved to fetch pencil and paper, I wondered if I was about to compose my way out of this mess or deeper into it.

"Write it down," she said again. "In a world without Whimsy, we can't trust ideas to remain if not written down. That is the first step in fighting. Tell our tales. Remember them. Share them."

I scratched down the notes, only the melody. Wonderly's melody.

"There's something else," Wonderly said, pulling out a folder from behind the sheet music. "One of our members works in maintenance at DHR. After Felix died, we had him watching everyone who'd been in contact with Felix in the weeks before his death. Rimsky's office was one of several we monitored. Found these yesterday morning before the regular collection. Rimsky must have thought they were safe to discard once the investigation closed."

Inside were notes in precise handwriting:

Subject FC deterioration slower than projected. Timeline compromise unacceptable. S emotional attachment becoming liability. Acceleration may be necessary. Consider alternative containment.

.   .   .

"Rimsky was monitoring Felix's decline," I said. "And he wasn't happy with how slowly it was happening."

Finally, I looked at her again and paused. "Felix knew his power was waning." Wonderly didn't respond. "He also knew his death was imminent."

She nodded. "He knew his ultimate killer, of course. Rimsky must have suspected something."

Wonderly closed her eyes. "Whimsy is almost gone." She opened her eyes and stared at me. "It's obvious now on the streets. People are reacting to the loss of Whimsy. The world is reacting. The skies are gray. The children are morose. People are getting in fights and they don't know why."

I nodded. There was little I could say.

She lifted my fingers from the piano and closed the keyboard cover. "I have something to show you."

She had me sit at the table with Hoagy while she retrieved something. Then she sat beside me and laid my record sleeve, with all the writing on it, in front of me.

I started to read it; then she covered it with her hands. "Not yet." I looked at her. "Felix knew he was dying. He formed the Improvisationists. Yes, likely choosing a name related to the experience the two of you had in the Eleven War."

My eyes stayed locked on hers, and I swallowed hard. "Why did he form it?"

"So that we would start preparing for a world without Whimsy. He was afraid that without Whimsy the world would forget and then war, hate, and life without happiness. Without rainbows. Without love."

I searched her face for falsehood. Found none.

I spoke before considering my words. "He also knew he would be replaced. The Conservatory would choose a new Guardian."

"He did. Guardians were always chosen before the current one died," she said. "They retire before they lose it. Sometimes someone clings too long to it, and history books will tell you when those times were."

"I saw the notes about it in the Archives." I shook my head. "Why wouldn't they believe him or fix it? It's their job."

She lifted her hands. "Read it"—she pointed at the sleeve as she removed her hands—"but know this. It was always meant for us, the resistance. 'Ask for Billie' was for us, not him."

"And I took it from you," I said.

Wonderly smiled at me. "You were fighting for it so hard in the Spin Zone I mouthed to Sage, the girl at the counter, to let you have it."

"Then you stole it from me."

"I did."

She sighed and continued. "The poisoning wasn't just killing Felix," Wonderly explained, pointing to a passage into his hidden message. "It was creating a sympathetic drain on Whimsy itself. That's why everyone started struggling weeks ago. His power was being slowly siphoned through his trust. Jacob was putting the information out there, hoping to get someone to notice."

"You said this was gibberish."

"It is for the most part. You'll know what isn't."

The record sleeve beckoned me. Felix wrote at a frenzied pace. It was gibberish except for odd phrases in the middle of sentences like "my old friend will be able to hear the message."

I glanced at Wonderly.

She nodded. "That's how we figured out there was a hidden message. He recorded the message but wrote the gibberish at the last minute before taking the record to the Spin Zone."

"But why Billie Holiday?"

Wonderly smiled. "Because we often talked about my father. He played with Billie Holiday. So I have deep ties to her music."

I returned her smile, then returned to the notes. They devolved into ramblings about music theory, many of them flat-out wrong. Then I made it to the end. I read the most relevant section aloud: "I hope they find another. I'm glad Dante encouraged me so much. Variation is chaos. Improvisation is necessary."

"Dante?" I asked. "As in the *Inferno?* Or someone Felix knew?"

Wonderly frowned. "Dante Rimsky."

With the last recorded words, he talked about how happy he was that his wife had returned to him in his final weeks, even if he would not live to enjoy a true reconciliation. His last written words wanted the resistance to fight harder. He took the record to the Spin Zone for Wonderly to get once he died. His last line said he would leave clues if he could figure who or why.

"How did you know to find the record?" I asked.

"The business card on his piano. You damn near caught me."

"So you weren't following me."

She smiled. "Not then."

Tears were in my eyes, so Wonderly reached out and placed her hands on mine. Warm. Comforting. I pulled away and wiped a tear.

"I don't know that we have enough time before Whimsy has decayed beyond repair," she said. "That's why I wanted you to write down your tune. You may never have another."

"Sure I will," I said.

Wonderly smiled. "We will fight. And if you can say anything to the Council, it might help."

I nodded. "Felix told us who killed him."

With relief, I relayed the entire thing. Hoagy backed me up.

And now one more person on this earth looked at me and didn't think I was a nut job. She wrapped her arms around my head, pulling me to her shoulder, and told me I was right. I had solved it.

But to what end?

She let go of me but kept her hands on my shoulders, holding me in place. "Great job, Mr. Kohl. You're a genius."

"Dekker, please."

Wonderly smiled. "Dekker, any idea in that brain about how to save us?"

Looking away from her so I could focus, I pondered it for a long moment. Then I noticed the Maestra had walked halfway down the stairs.

"Everything okay?" she asked.

"Yes," Wonderly said. "Dekker's figured it out. He's about to complete the puzzle."

I was about to protest the idea that I would come up with anything when I suddenly got it. Then a shock wave hit me that Wonderly's enthusiasm seemed to have spurred my brain. Her belief remained firm when so many had faded. She inspired me in so many ways.

The Maestra had said something, but neither of us heard it. She returned to the fencing room. Now I understood that energy, that certainty I'd sensed in Wonderly at the record store. She wasn't just passionate about music; she was part of something bigger. Something that had been preparing for this moment long before Felix died.

My mind raced, and I spewed my thoughts to Wonderly. "The DHR used the crackdown to fuel expanding their dampening fields. They've been testing them on musicians. They used Jacob's murder as the reason. Plus, it deflects from Sonny."

Wonderly was with me, but she was testing the theory. "But Sonny is an administrator. Non magical. She would need someone with some ability to help her. Jacob had what?"

"Irrythmia."

"Magical?"

"Yes." I contemplated for a moment. "Either she hides her

magic or her helper has it. But a spell that stops the heart requires significant magical training."

"Who would help her?"

I thought about the dampening chambers. About Phrygian's daughter. About revenge wrapped in bureaucracy. "I have a theory. Dr. Phrygian."

"Who?"

"My old English teacher turned DHR bureaucrat. Nothing says 'follow your dreams' like crushing them professionally." Seeing that I had lost her, I rephrased. "He was a huge influence on me as a kid. And Lorraine. And Felix. And—"

"Who's Lorraine?"

I closed my eyes, regretting the slip. "Cree. Don't repeat it." But I knew she wouldn't. Nor would Hoagy. I had to get it out of me. "Phrygian lost his daughter."

Wonderly nodded, comforting, lost.

"Cree met him at DHR to get help. She thought he could help bring back creativity." Wonderly stayed transfixed on me, and I soaked it up. My voice dropped to a whisper. "He told her that his daughter had died because of dangerous magical dreams."

She nodded. "And Sonny believes that suppressing magic and the Conservatory is best for the world. Don't waste time on frivolities."

"Right." I held up a hand. "It's speculation. But it fits. Phrygian has the magical knowledge, the motive, and access to Sonny. If I'm wrong, we'll find out soon enough." The words tumbled out like a jazz riff I couldn't stop. "And now you and I have to stop them." I stood and paced to the window. "It's not enough to tell the police about Sonny." Turning back to face her. "We have to stop them from killing Whimsy permanently."

"How?"

"Working on it. Improv."

Wonderly stood with a smile. "I'll call the others."

"No time." I stood and lifted her chin so I could see into the depth of her eyes. "It's us together, Wonderly. Just two people against a magical conspiracy."

Her smile said she liked those odds. Hoagy's cough said, "Don't forget about me."

Ah, moment ruined.

CHAPTER 29
PHRYGIAN SCALE

CREE MET WONDERLY, Hoagy, and me a block from the DHR building. She didn't understand the rush, but she complied and met us, having told no one. After a brief greeting between the two women, I told her it was imperative that we talk to Dr. Phrygian.

"So talk to him," Cree said.

She eyed Wonderly with suspicion even though she was the one who had led Hoagy to her. Not that Cree didn't believe Wonderly was important to the mission, but more that I was being an ass and Riffing back at her. But Wonderly had a way, a wonder, I guess, and Cree was soon sold on it. She understood I would not be permitted to talk to him.

I also wanted her to be a part of the solution.

"Wait," Cree said, grabbing my arm as we prepared to enter the DHR. "Riff told me something when he was drunk. About why he really helped Sonny." Her eyes were hard. "He said she promised him she could make his playing 'matter' again. She's been recruiting musicians who've lost their creativity, turning them into weapons against the ones who still have it. I'm sorry, Dekk."

"I understand."

The two women and Hoagy entered the building and headed to the information booth. Walking in a minute later, I rushed as far away from the counter as I could. I jogged up to a man, put my arm on his back, and acted as if he was a long-lost friend. Poor bastard probably thought he'd won the lottery until he realized I was broke.

Meanwhile, the two women and my protégé had finagled a meeting with Dr. Phrygian. I caught up with them at the elevator.

"What does the good doctor think?" I asked.

"That Eliza is struggling to cope with a loss because of the Conservatory, and I thought he might be able to help."

Phrygian worked three floors below ground, as far from Sonny's office as the building allowed. He opened the door. The doctor rated somewhere between janitor and actual importance—no secretary in sight.

Time had played him in a minor key—all the high notes gone, just the bass line of regret remaining. But I would not be winning any beauty contests myself. His remaining hair looked more frazzled than the last time I saw him.

Student art from dozens of projects, poems, and sketches covered the office walls. But dominating one wall was a large painting in an ornate frame. Even from across the room, I could see the joy in the brushstrokes.

The desk was cluttered with papers and a closed laptop. His cell phone sat on top of it, but no landline phone. I guessed upper management wasn't going to be calling him. Or maybe his line was on permanent mute.

"Samantha's work?" I asked.

His face folded like sheet music in a strong wind before he smoothed it back into professional composure. "Her last piece. 'Dreams of Tomorrow.' She was trying to paint a world where magic and creativity weren't at war." He stared at it for a long moment. "The irony wasn't lost on me when I took this job."

"Dr. Phrygian," I began as Wonderly closed the door behind us. "You remember me."

"Of course, the cafeteria."

Squinting, he studied my face, then pulled glasses from his shirt pocket for a closer look. Those tired eyes closed for a moment before finding Cree. Recognition dawned as he pointed the glasses at me, then her, like a conductor marking time.

"Musician," he muttered.

I smiled grimly. "Yes."

A heavy sigh escaped him. "That was before I learned what the world does to dreamers."

Dismissing my words with a wave, he turned to his desk drawer, rummaging through it absentmindedly.

The words died in his throat. Whatever he'd intended to say crumbled like sheet music left in the rain.

He looked to Cree. "Ms. Morgenstern, you have deceived me."

With my hand in the air, I confessed, "I made her do it."

The professor's face lit up. "Of course." He pointed his glasses at me, then Cree. "You two were in school together. Even—"

"Yes." Right now was not the time to dredge any of that up. "You taught me that music could change the world."

His voice had none of the warmth I remembered. "Before I watched my daughter chase the very fantasies I'd filled her head with."

The doctor gestured for us to sit. There were only two chairs. Wonderly remained behind Cree and me, close enough to the desk that I wondered what she was planning. He sat at his desk. Hoagy hung behind the two women, peeking through.

"What happened to the man who carried a rubber chicken in his pocket?" I asked. "Who made us stand on desks to feel Shakespeare?"

"So," he began, "this adventure is about missed dreams? You're blaming me for them?"

I shook my head. "No. This is about reclaiming them. Reclaiming the Whimsy in life."

He waved dismissively. "Good riddance. You'll appreciate it when it's gone. Sure, you'll be sad for a few days, maybe a few weeks, but life will be better."

Cree smiled at him. "We're worried that you're inflicting your pain on others." Phrygian didn't respond, so she continued. "When we were young"—she pointed at me, then herself—"we loved you. You were an inspiration to both of us. And when I had my pain and couldn't sort my feelings, you talked to me and you gave me a book that helped me to deal with it. I wouldn't be who I am today without you."

The old bastard believed his own propaganda, refusing to acknowledge what Cree said. "I'm saving you from pain."

"Did you save Felix Cantabile from pain or Jazzy Jacob?"

"My superiors explained the Guardian situation to me. Best to be done with it." His old, calloused hand moved toward his desk drawer. "Jacob wrote about her in the *Arts Weekly*. Called her a 'visionary who painted dreams into reality.' Said her work showed 'the dangerous beauty of uncontrolled magical expression.'" The doctor's voice was hollow. "Three weeks later, she read that review to me over dinner. She was so excited, so proud. She said Jacob understood what she was trying to do."

He pulled out a newspaper clipping, yellowed and worn from handling. This was long before Felix had taken the first drop of thallium or arsenic. Whatever. Before Jacob had switched from print media.

"That night, she went to her studio to work on her masterpiece. She wanted to paint something worthy of Jacob's praise. Something that would prove magical art could change the world." His hands shook. "The neighbors heard the screams around midnight. By the time the fire department arrived ..."

But he couldn't continue. The newspaper clipping fluttered onto his desk. The article was Jacob's review, read so many times the words were barely legible.

"Professor," I said carefully, "you taught during the Eleven War. You remember what the Compressionists did."

His hands shook. "I remember colleagues becoming hollow shells. Playing perfect scales with dead eyes."

"And now you've built the same rooms for DHR."

"Not the same!" He stood abruptly. "These rooms let creativity flow safely. The Compressionist chambers crushed it."

"Do they?" I gestured at the folder. "Because it looks exactly like what we fought against. Just better branding."

He collapsed back into his chair. "After Harmony Hall burned, I thought we'd won. Proven creativity couldn't be controlled." His voice broke. "Then Samantha ... Then I learned uncontrolled creativity destroys, too. So I tried to build something better. But Sonny, Rimsky—they perverted it."

His voice broke. "I read every word Jacob ever wrote after that. Every review that filled some kid's head with impossible dreams. I couldn't stop what happened to Samantha, but I could stop him from destroying other families."

Cree shook her head. "So you decided to kill Whimsy itself?"

The doctor smirked. "I decided to save people from the delusions that destroy lives. Felix was spreading the same poison I once did. Jacob's death proves how dangerous emotional magic becomes when it fails. Someone had to stop it before more innocents died."

I nodded. "Did you kill Jacob?"

"I'm an old man. You think I can do that? I'm so blind I couldn't hit him if I tried. You think I killed your Guardian, too?"

"Sonny Mordent killed Felix Cantabile," I said.

His voice cracked like a dry reed. "She couldn't have." The words came out flat, no vibrato.

"She did."

Dr. Phrygian opened his desk drawer and pulled out a thick folder.

"It's not just Sonny," he whispered. "The DHR has been planning this for years. Look."

The folder contained correspondence, memos, and budget allocations. All pointed to a systematic plan to identify and neutralize magical creativity.

"'Project Silence,'" I read from one memo. "'Phase One: identify targets through cultural criticism. Phase Two: isolation and study. Phase Three: permanent neutralization.'"

Another memo caught my eye:

Site Selection for Phase One:

Columbus, Ohio recommended.

Criteria met: (1) Active Conservatory presence,

(2) Significant DHR infrastructure,

(3) Guardian residence confirmed,

(4) Sufficient creative population for testing,

(5) Geographic isolation from primary Isola Sonora
   oversight.

They hadn't chosen Columbus randomly. We were always the target.

I handed the folder to Wonderly.

"This is actually insane," Hoagy muttered, looking up from his phone. "Like, not hyperbole insane. Literally a conspiracy."

"Jacob wasn't just writing reviews," the professor continued. "He thought he was saving the world, but he was creating target lists. Ruby Blue, Slide Donovan, Reed Holloway. All of them were being studied. Sonny was just the most aggressive implementer."

I glanced at Hoagy, knowing he would react. He didn't say anything, but I could see Ruby Blue's name hit him hard.

"How long has this been going on?" Cree asked.

"Too long," I said.

"How many others are involved?"

Phrygian grimaced. "At least a dozen DHR officials. Maybe more. They call themselves the Harmony Initiative." Phrygian pulled out another document. "Look at this timeline. Ruby Blue was the first test subject." Phrygian's fingers traced the document edges. "They isolated her, studied how creativity could be suppressed and—"

"Christ." Cree's face had gone white. "No wonder she's missing gigs."

"Not missing." His voice barely above a whisper. "Recovering. Then came Slide Donovan." He looked up at our horrified faces. "You want to know the worst part? Each musician thought they were getting help."

I felt sick. "They volunteered for this?"

"Honey Lane's in there now. Each one a different experiment in controlling artistic expression." The professor's hands shook as he flipped pages. "But Felix—Felix wasn't just Sonny's personal project."

"His wife? Why?"

"Who knows what goes wrong in any relationship?" Phrygian asked.

Wonderly stepped closer. "And now Felix was the ultimate prize."

"If they could kill a Virtue itself ..." Phrygian couldn't finish.

"They think creativity is a disease." My voice came out harder than I intended. "And they're looking for a cure." I felt sick. "So Sonny wasn't acting alone."

"No. But she was the only one with direct access to

a Guardian. That made her the prototype. If she could kill Whimsy itself ..." He didn't finish the sentence. We both knew what came next. Hope. Joy. Love. All the Virtues systematically destroyed by people who saw them as diseases to be cured.

With a heavy sigh, I stood. Cree followed. The professor leaned back in his chair. "You opened my eyes when I was a kid."

He slumped farther into his chair. "I did nothing."

Wonderly dropped Phrygian's folder on his desk, covering the laptop. Her hand moved quick, palming the cell phone.

"You taught me that teaching meant taking risks for your students. What happened to the man who carried a rubber chicken in his pocket? The man who inspired hundreds of students? I understand your pain about your daughter, but did Jazzy Jacob really kill her? And did he deserve it?"

Glancing at Wonderly, I felt a swell of energy. It was almost as if she ... no. Not possible without my ossia. But I felt something, like the notes arranging themselves before I could play them.

I leaned forward, the pieces clicking. "You read every review Jacob wrote after Samantha died. You said you wanted to stop him from destroying other families."

Phrygian nodded slowly.

"But you're an old man who can't see straight. Someone else had to be your hands." My voice hardened. "Someone young and angry enough. Someone who knew exactly how Jacob had 'destroyed' your family."

The professor's face went pale.

"Which of Jacob's targets did you tell about Samantha? Which musician did you convince that Jacob killed your daughter with his praise? Ruby Blue? Slide Donovan? Someone who'd already lost their creativity and needed someone to blame?"

He closed his eyes and squeezed them tight. "It's possible

you might be right. But it's too painful for me. I can't stop it now. Everything is in motion. Whimsy is gone."

"We will stop it," I said. "The three of us are going to undo it."

Phrygian shook his head. "You can't. Felix died before his replacement was trained. That was the idea. Natural order."

"Even if it ends in another plague? A war? Worse?"

The professor didn't budge.

The eyes of my companions remained firm, so I leaned into the professor. "Please help us rectify it. Which musician did you tell about your daughter?"

"None," he said. "I only told my boss."

"Sonny Mordent?" I asked.

"Yes."

"Perfect. Nice and tidy." I didn't believe it for a second, but we had what we needed. "Thanks, Prof."

We turned toward the door.

We stepped out of the office. Before the door closed, Phrygian yelled back at us, "Hey, kid."

I opened the door and peered in. Hoagy poked his head in, too. That one was my fault.

My old mentor opened the drawer in his desk, reached in and pulled a full-size rubber chicken from it. I smiled back.

"You know what she would have wanted?" he called after us. "Maybe she would have wanted me to keep teaching kids to dream." His brow furrowed for a moment; then he realized something. "Yes. She would have. Even dangerous dreams. Especially dangerous dreams."

The old professor's eyes held something I hadn't seen since high school—hope wrestling with decades of cynicism. The rubber chicken sat on his desk like a promise he'd forgotten how to keep.

"The compression chambers have a side effect beyond the individual."

"What's that?"

"Energy can't go away. It must transform. What the chambers cleanse them of lingers, then escapes. Forming something else I can't explain. A problem I couldn't solve, and they wouldn't let me have more time to do it."

Hoagy looked up at me, eyes wide. "And?"

"And what?"

He looked at Phrygian. "Who's next on the list?"

"Roland Tomasi."

My eyes squeezed shut. Roland Tomasi—the fake name I'd given Sonny to make her think I was cooperating. If I needed another nail in the coffin, there it was. "We'll be in touch, Prof."

As we headed for the elevator, Wonderly held up his cell phone. "At least he can't call ahead."

"You are a thief," I said, watching the floors count up. "Good. Because Sonny's about to discover she's not the only one who can play games with other people's lives."

CHAPTER 30
FORTISSIMO

TEN MINUTES LATER, we rushed into Sonny's office. The office lights cast everything in that flat, institutional glow—the kind designed to drain personality from a room as efficiently as the DHR drained joy from music.

"Who the hell do you think you are?" Sonny spewed her words without looking. When she spun her chair and recognized us, she stood and pulled her skirt down. "Dekker."

She used my first name for the first time, and it sounded as if I was about to be chastised like a two-year-old who didn't know his place.

Her gaze shifted to Cree, but she addressed me. "I see you've been busy. Why didn't you take her to the police?"

Sonny smiled at me. "Doesn't matter. Detective Handler is already on the way. My staff called him when your friend entered the building. He might be a little sore at you for violating your orders and coming directly here."

"He'll get over it," I said.

"I know," Sonny replied with a smile. "Just in case, DHR security will be here in a minute, too."

"Perfect."

"In fact, Mr. Kohl, may I speak to you alone?"

Back to the usual. I shook my head. "Sonny, I think it's best if we all stay here. We need to not provide any opportunities."

"Quite right." She tipped her head toward the windows overlooking the city.

With silent agreement, we met at the windows, staring through the narrow view to the city.

"Don't worry," she whispered. "I can see all three of them in the reflection."

She was right. We could.

"Good," I said.

Sonny put her hand on my back—warm, but not comforting. Fingertips only. "Your secret will remain safe with me when Detective Handler gets here, but I don't think it was a great plan to bring her here."

"I had to adapt to the circumstances, which led me here."

Sonny glanced over her shoulder at Cree. "She was coming here?"

I didn't answer, but I saw the concern on her face. "I recognize your little sidekick, but who's the other one?"

"Someone who helped me put the pieces together."

Sonny nodded. "Oh, good. If you have any expenses related to her, let me know."

"I will."

A knock rapped on the door. Wonderly opened it, and Dash came in with the DHR security goons.

The goons headed toward me, but Sonny held up a hand, stopping them. All doubts were erased from my mind. "He's not a problem. Dekker here is giving a gift to the detective."

Dash's eyes flickered between us, uncertain of the situation. Sonny and I maintained perfect poker faces, waiting to make our move.

Trying to break the tension, Dash said, "I hope it's not the cat."

I shook my head.

"Dekk." Dash glared at me. "Did you get medical help like I asked?"

"Wasn't needed."

It was time to serve things Sonny-side up.

I moved a few steps to stand in direct line with the door. Wonderly sensed my thoughts and adjusted so she had an angle to the door, too. Hoagy stuck to Cree like glue.

"Sonny," I began, "what is your full name?"

Her eyebrows shot up.

"Dekker, don't," Dash said.

"I'm afraid I don't understand." Her hands went to her hips. "It's not a secret. Sonata Mordent."

"Uh-huh. Middle name?" I asked.

"Allegra, but it seems that you know that. It's on every legal document."

I pulled out the sheet music. "Remember what we discussed at Felix's? About his last composition?"

Dash nodded slowly. "Dekk, careful."

"Right. The tempo of the piece says, *'Andante non vivace'*"—walking dead." Sue me. Close enough. I turned to Sonny. "Felix didn't just know you were killing him. He encoded your full name, the method, and your identity into his final piece. In the only language he had left. And one I could figure out from our time together in school."

I pulled out the music and spread it on Sonny's desk. "The piece is in G major. That's the cipher's root. Count chromatic steps from G: G equals zero, G-sharp equals one, all the way to E equals nine."

I wrote the notes in a line on the sheet music for those in the room who couldn't read sheet music.

C-sharp | G-sharp | B | C | C | C | D | D-sharp | A-sharp | A.

Hoagy was counting on his fingers. His eyes went wide.

"Ten digits," I said quietly. "And I know whose number it is."

My eyes shot to Sonny's. "He encoded your phone into the melody. Every note was evidence. Every tempo marking was testimony." I held up the sheet music. "This wasn't a composition. It was a death certificate. And he signed your name on it."

Sonny shook her head. "You're beginning to sound like some kind of pulp detective."

"Bear with me," I said. "Now look at the second word. Allegra."

Cree gasped. "That's Sonny's middle name. Sonata Allegra Mordent. That's why it's 'allegra' instead of 'allegro.'"

I whispered to Sonny, "Those dime-novel detectives always have one that reacts."

"So Felix wrote a piece for his wife," Dash said slowly. "Already covered. And out of bounds."

"Not just any song. Look at the key—G major. G for Guardian."

Hoagy muttered, "That's dark," but kept his eyes on Sonny. "Why 13/7 time signature?"

I felt something catch in my throat. "That one is for me. And the key signature."

Dash frowned. "Meaning?"

"July thirteenth. The day we invented the cipher." I looked at the sheet music. "We met at band camp the summer before college. Felix and I used to write it as 13/7—European-style."

"So he left you a reminder," Cree said softly.

"He wanted me to know this message was personal. That he trusted me specifically to find it and understand it. Despite ..." My hand trembled. I didn't want to relive our bad parting. "The whole composition is not just evidence. It's a letter. Pointing to her. All in the only language he had left."

I turned to Sonny, whose face had gone pale. The mask of stoicism descended on her.

"The tempo marking was the final piece. *Andante non vivace,*" I said.

Hoagy spoke up. "Walking not alive."

"Right," I said. "Or walking dead."

Sonny's hands trembled, so she clasped them behind her. Her posture went more erect, her chest out. "Please. That's ... coincidence. Musical terminology—"

"He was writing your confession," I began, "in the only language he knew. We may never know why. You had music training. Maybe he hoped you would figure out the code. Maybe he wanted you to know that he knew but didn't want to turn you in. Seems like him. But he knew you were killing him, and he left us a musical message saying exactly who and how."

Wonderly shook her head. "But Felix was poisoning himself with thallium."

"Arsenic," Dash said.

"Both," I said. They looked at me as if I were an alien. "Felix was poisoning himself with thallium just as his confession stated. Sonny started making regular visits to him and added the arsenic. She didn't know. He figured it out and left the coded composition."

Dash looked between the music and Sonny. "Which, as I said before, would be pretty clever. However, Dekker, you're suggesting Felix Cantabile was documenting this all along?"

"The manuscript was just sitting on his piano. One composition among dozens. But he knew I'd recognize the contradictions—the key signature that doesn't match the title, the impossible time signature. He was leaving bread crumbs only I could follow. Or something Sonny could discover if he was feeling sentimental."

I stepped to Sonny's desk where her phone sat on a wireless charger. "Hoagy, call the number on the music."

My jaw clenched. If I was wrong—if I'd misread the cipher, if this was all coincidence—I'd look like a fool in front of everyone. Worse, I'd have wasted our one shot at justice for Felix.

But the contradictions were too deliberate. The 13/7

pointing to our cipher's birthday. Her full name in the title. Ten notes, ten digits. Coded message on the Billie Holiday record. Felix knew what he was doing.

He trusted me to figure it out.

Hoagy punched the numbers into his phone, and her private phone rang like a funeral bell. Sonny's face went the color of old bones.

In my experience, Sonny had the emotional range of a metronome—technically functional, but you wouldn't want to dance to it. Now the springs were popping.

"Show me your hands," I said.

The room went still.

"What?" Sonny's voice was barely a whisper.

"Your hands. Both of them."

She kept them at her sides, fingers curled into fists. "This is ridiculous. I've already—"

"The G string," I interrupted. "Wire that thin, under strangulation tension." I shook my head. "It would have cut through anything. Latex, cotton, even leather. And the gloves in the dumpster. Felix's, I presume." I took a step closer. "I want to see your hands, Sonny. Rather, I want Detective Handler to see them. I finally did when you held up your hand to stop your security from approaching."

For a long moment, she didn't move. Then, slowly, mechanically, she pulled her left hand out first, then her right. Thin scabs ran across both palms, the left worse—deeper, angrier, still healing after five days.

"You've kept that hand in your pocket or behind you since the crime scene," I said. "Every meeting. Even when you were pointing fingers at me. Couldn't risk anyone seeing the cuts and asking questions."

"Not at first." Her voice was hollow. "The rage, the jealousy. It was like a fire in my hands, but I didn't care. By the time I realized I was bleeding, by the time the wire cut through the leather and into my skin—" She stopped. Swallowed hard. "I couldn't stop. Wouldn't stop. Do you understand? I needed him to stop creating. Needed it more than I needed my hands whole."

Dash studied her hands. "You threw the gloves in Jazzy Jacob's dumpster."

Sonny nodded slowly, still staring at her hands. "I forgot I was still wearing them. When I realized, I was already at the Hedgehog. The dumpster was right there. Convenient."

My left hand trembled slightly. The war had taught me to notice hands—who was armed, who was afraid, who was about to do something they couldn't take back. Felix taught me to notice musicians' hands. And Sonny taught me that sometimes the evidence you're looking for is hidden in someone's pocket or folded across their chest for five straight days.

"Where did you get the violin?" I asked quietly.

Her eyes were distant. "His mother's violin. First-chair in the symphony. She wanted him to follow her path. He chose the trumpet instead." A bitter laugh. "He kept it anyway. Guilt, maybe. Sentiment. The G string was already loose, hanging there. I just … reached for it."

"The instrument he rejected," Dash said.

"The instrument that rejected him first," Sonny corrected. "Every time he looked at it, he saw disappointment. His mother's. His own. And mine." She met my eyes. "Seemed fitting."

I glanced at Dash. He was on board now.

"He knew," I said to Sonny. "Felix knew you were killing him, and he left us a musical confession in the only language he trusted—one only I could decode. And he still loved you."

Cree was nodding in agreement with my conclusions. Dash got a step closer when he saw another domino fall. Wonderly and I both tightened our angle to the door. I suspected she might run while Dash was sliding his last piece of resistance into place.

"Felix was telling us who put the final blow on him, and how it felt, walking toward death instead of life," I said.

Sonny's head was shaking, her eyes darting frantically. She fell forward, catching herself on the glass top of her desk. "That's ... that's just standard musical terminology. All of it. Coincidence."

Suspects break in different ways. Some crumble, some explode. The controlled ones are the hardest—their walls built so high that even the truth can't climb over.

Sonny wasn't showing her face to us, but I could see it in the reflection from her desk. She was fighting. Her breathing was irregular. But flashes of fire burst out, trying to plan the next move.

In one of those moments, she stood upright. Her eyes were red. She wiped the rolling tear away with her finger. "How dare you!"

Not the control type, despite previous evidence.

Sonny turned to Dash. "And you won't arrest him?"

"I think I'd like to hear your response to all this, albeit done improperly," Dash said.

I glanced behind me. Wonderly's stare told me she was happy with how it was going. And somewhere beyond this building, the Statics walked the streets in a world of failing Whimsy, indifferent to the drama playing out here. Out there, people went about their lives while I tore apart what was left of Sonny's.

But we hadn't solved the big problem.

The DHR goons, however, shrank back, and they were wrestling with loyalty. But that's the thing. Loyalty without a test is just a promise. These boys were being put to the test.

Dash stepped forward. "Sonny Mordent, you are under arrest." She was shaking, but he continued. "You have the right to an attorney and all that jazz. Then we're going to talk about Felix Cantabile."

Cree stepped forward in defiance. "And Jazzy Jacob."

Every muscle in Sonny's body tightened. Her knuckles went white against the desk edge, and I could hear her breathing from across the room in short, sharp gasps like a cornered animal's. Her eyes were seconds from becoming Niagara Falls, and her lips were as tight as a guitar string tightened to the point of breaking.

Cree guessed, and she guessed wrong. I knew that.

"Riff Parker killed Jacob," Sonny said.

My gaze snapped to Cree. I could feel the anger in her, but she was keeping it in.

"How could he?" Cree said. "When he was with me when Jacob was murdered."

"We could call Riff and get him down here," I said to Sonny, but I knew Riff didn't do it, either.

Phrygian. Cree. Riff. None of them could create irrythmia.

"You should be interviewing them all instead of accusing me," she said. "The musicians."

I nodded. "Who would you like to start with?"

She looked away as she contemplated it. I realized she was looking at a piece of paper on her desk with several names crossed off. She read the only uncrossed one. "Roland Tomasi."

"Who the hell is that?" Dash asked.

"Doesn't exist. I made him up and gave the name to Sonny to add to her hit list."

She glared at me with pure venom. The jig was up. "Fine. I killed him." Sonny's lips tightened, and she seemed uncertain if she wanted to laugh or attack.

Cree bolted forward. Wonderly and I raced to her and held her.

Sonny was cementing her composure. She had found that place in her mind where she was above all this. "Riff had nothing to do with it outside of breaking into Mr. Kohl's place with the key he stole from you." She looked at me, then at Cree with malicious satisfaction. "He really enjoyed that. He did a good job."

Cree's face went white. "He stole my key?"

"What convinced him to do it?" I asked.

"It's amazing what you can dig up about people. Like why they suddenly moved to a new city." Sonny's smile was cruel. "I told him exactly what leverage to use against you, Ms. Morgenstern. And he nicely informed me where you kept the spare key to Dekker's apartment."

I could feel the negative energy coming from Cree. It wasn't just taking the key. The look in her eyes told me they had fought about it. Wonderly and Hoagy stuck to her while I narrowed the distance to Sonny, ready for that final touch.

"So that's why you pushed the surveillance photos," I said, shoving all the pieces into place. "Had someone compile three weeks of footage showing me walking past your building on my normal route. Made it look like stalking. Two rabbits with one shot—discredit me and throw suspicion off yourself. Meanwhile, you had Riff break into my apartment and destroy my ossia, so I couldn't investigate magically." I avoided the obvious jab at Riff's personality, though watching Cree's face, I might not need to. "Why'd you kill Jacob?"

"I had no choice," Sonny spewed between clenched teeth. "He had been interviewing Felix when I showed up. I let myself in. Felix was telling Jacob that I was trying to destroy Whimsy, him." Her gaze met mine with a fire burning inside. "So you don't know everything, Mr. Kohl. You didn't know everything about Felix." She shook her head tightly, more like she was having a tremor. "So I had to speed the whole thing up. They didn't know I had heard. I asked Jacob what he was up to, and he told me he was going to the Hedgehog."

Her whole body quaked, and her eyes were red. The office smelled of fear, sweat, and desperation. Even the air-conditioning couldn't clear the stench of a life coming apart.

"I wanted to use the wire again," she said. "Same as Felix. But I couldn't grip it. My hands were too damaged. The cuts kept reopening every time I tried."

Dash grunted. "But you didn't need wire because you had the spell."

Eyes wide, she shook her head. "No. No. I can't do those things."

It could be denial. Rimsky thought she had latent ability. Given her job, admitting to magical ability would be career suicide at best. "You sure?"

She squeezed her eyes shut. "I had my thumbs and fingertips. I strangled him with my bare hands." Her eyes met mine, defiant. "Your ME said it was strangulation. Not your magical nonsense."

"The ME said there was bruising," Dash corrected. "But not enough to cause death. The heart gave out from irrhythmia—exactly what Dekker said. Someone used magic."

I didn't know if that was true, but I accepted it.

Sonny stared at the floor, voice barely a whisper. "That's why he didn't resist much."

At that moment, I knew that even if she had latent abilities, they had not surfaced yet.

Hoagy's head bounced between all of us. "So, who killed him with magic?"

"An Ombroso," I said.

"A what?" Cree asked.

"Ombroso. Opposite of a Virtuoso."

"Great," she said. "You have a Sith Lord, too."

"But who?" Hoagy asked.

"Rimsky." I looked at Dash. "So-called Internal Affairs Dante Rimsky. He's not just a DHR bureaucrat. He's one of the Ombrosi. That's why he avoided Jacob's crime scene. He didn't want to leave his magical signature where I could detect it. He was safe in Felix's apartment."

Why couldn't I ever get an easy case?

Dash frowned. "But he was at Felix's apartment."

"But he didn't murder Felix, which I was focused on. And he never got close to the body." I thought back. "He didn't go to the second scene at the dumpster because it was unrelated to his investigation, he said. Sonny did the physical work—strangling. Rimsky cast the irrhythmia spell from a distance. No direct contact. No signature in the immediate kill zone."

Sonny closed her eyes and tried to steady herself again. Finally, she gave me a menacing stare. My face gave nothing away.

"Go arrest Rimsky," she said.

"And prosecute him on what? He didn't touch anybody in the mundane world."

"You think you've won, Mr. Kohl?" Sonny's voice was rising, losing the controlled modulation she'd maintained throughout our confrontation. "You think you're some kind of Conservatory genius, but the damage is done no matter what you do to me."

Her hands were shaking now, ten years of suppressed emotion finally cracking through the bureaucratic facade.

"Whimsy is dead. I killed it!" She was shouting now, spittle flying. "It is just the beginning. Breaking up the musicians, isolating them from each other, that's what finished it. You can't sustain a Virtue when its people can't even gather in the same room. And you know what? It felt good! Every day I watched him create effortlessly what I could never achieve. Every night I listened to him compose masterpieces while I could barely manage scales."

Dash took a step forward, but she whirled on him.

"You want to know why I killed Jacob? Because he was going to expose everything before I was finished! Before I could complete what should have been done years ago!"

She turned back to me, her face contorted with rage and

grief. Not considering that we had just told her she wanted to kill Jacob—and tried—but didn't.

"The Conservatory creates monsters, Mr. Kohl. People who can manipulate reality with a song while the rest of us struggle for every note. Well, now you know how it feels to lose your gift. How it feels to be ordinary."

Her breathing was becoming erratic, her chest heaving. "But I won. Even if you arrest me, even if you execute me, Whimsy is gone. And without it, your precious Conservatory will crumble. Things will be as they should be—equal. Silent. Fair."

"That's enough," Dash cut in, stepping closer.

For a moment, she almost had it back—that bureaucratic mask, that professional distance. Then I saw the exact second it cracked. The dam had burst. "To wake up every morning next to proof of your own inadequacy? I studied piano for fifteen years. Fifteen years of lessons, practice, and competitions. I was good, technically perfect." She clenched her jaw so hard she might shatter teeth. "But Felix could sit down and compose a melody that would make people weep, and he'd do it while eating breakfast. The Conservatory rejected my application twice." Sonny glared at me. "They said I had 'insufficient emotional resonance.' But they worked overtime to pull him from Juilliard."

Her voice broke completely then. "I loved him. God help me, I loved him so much it was killing me. So I made sure it killed him first."

Then, as if she was seeing herself clearly for the first time, her face went pale. "Oh God. What have I done? What have I become?"

Her voice was barely a whisper. "I used to love music. I used to … before the jealousy ate everything else." She looked at her hands as if they belonged to someone else. "Felix never knew. He never knew how much I hated him for being everything I couldn't be. And he loved me anyway."

When she collapsed, it wasn't just surrender; it was the

weight of finally understanding the magnitude of what she'd destroyed.

She swayed on her feet, the confession having drained the last of her strength. When she collapsed, it wasn't just surrender or theatrics. It was the weight of finally understanding what she'd destroyed. Not with a scream or a sob. Just a long, empty exhale, like air leaving a punctured tire. She folded in on herself, all sharp angles and broken edges, a marionette with cut strings. The weight she'd been carrying for years—the jealousy, the rage, the desperate love—finally won.

As Dash led Sonny away, Rimsky stepped into the doorway, pale eyes calculating. Our gazes met for one long moment.

"Inspector," Dash called. "Need your statement."

But Rimsky was already backing into the hallway. He knew how to read a room. "Of course. I'll gather the relevant files from my office."

He turned and walked away with military precision. Something in his posture made my stomach drop.

"Dash—" I started.

But Rimsky had already disappeared around the corner.

I ran into the hallway. Empty. No footsteps. No elevator ding. Nothing.

"Where'd he go?" Hoagy asked, breathless beside me.

Wonderly joined us, frowning. "That's not possible. There's only one way out of this floor."

Dash emerged, hand on his gun. "Where's Rimsky?"

We searched the entire floor. His office was empty. Not just empty of Rimsky, but empty. No desk. No files. Just bare walls and that institutional carpet.

"His name was on the directory," Dash insisted, pulling out his phone. He dialed DHR security. The conversation lasted thirty seconds. His face went white.

"They're claiming there's no Inspector Rimsky. Says the office has been under renovation for six months."

I stared at the empty office. "Claiming? You mean lying."

"They say he was never officially employed by DHR. No personnel file. No ID number in their system."

"Bullshit," I said. "He led a raid at the Cinnamon Hedgehog with a half dozen agents. He was at Felix's crime scene."

Dash was already flipping through his notebook. "I've got reports with his name. Witness statements. Hell, he interrogated Cree Morgenstern and Riff Parker in front of twenty people." He looked up, jaw tight. "This isn't him not existing. This is them claiming he doesn't exist. There's a difference."

"The twelve conspirators," Wonderly whispered. "A network. Rimsky wasn't here to observe her. He was here to make sure she succeeded. And when she failed—"

"They're burning him," I said. "Making him disappear on paper so they can deny involvement. Classic intelligence agency move."

Dash's jaw set. "Then we document everything. Every time any of us saw Rimsky. Every word he said. Every place where he appeared." He glared at the empty office. "DHR can deny he exists all they want. I've got a file folder full of evidence that says otherwise. This is conspiracy to obstruct justice, and somebody's going to answer for it."

"But he's gone," Hoagy said quietly. "Physically gone. How did he just vanish?"

"Because whoever's running Project Silence has resources we don't understand yet. And they want us to know they're still watching."

Dash nodded. "Then we'd better start watching back."

CHAPTER 31
ISOLA SONORA

Friday, May 29—Day 7

TWO DAYS.

That's how long it took for the magical world to assemble at Isola Sonora. Delegates from every continent. The Aboriginal Keepers of Earth Songs. The African Keepers of Crossed Rhythms. Delegations from China, Japan, the Slavic countries, Indigenous nations across the Americas.

Armando had invited me against his better judgment. Or at least he wanted me to feel that way.

In a demonstration of its power, the Conservatory convinced the prosecutor to keep it out of the papers. DHR didn't fight it. It wasn't a good look for them, either. The whole fiasco was buttoned up by the next morning in terms of the public. But with Whimsy hanging by a thread, no one cared.

Dash and his men had brought Sonny to the Conservatory. They probably didn't appreciate the honor they were given to go this deep into the Conservatory. Cops don't like places where the walls have more history than their case files. But to be fair, once they handed her over, they were escorted out before they saw the good stuff.

The detective had protested that he wanted to talk to me but they were not permitted. The last person to speak to me before we were sequestered was Dr. Melodius.

The man screamed mad professor, which was how we treated him. He knew it. "Virtuoso Kohl," he began, "I didn't know who to give this to. The Council seems preoccupied. But someone should see it." He shoved a piece of paper folded in half into my hands.

Reading medical reports on a magical island in the Mediterranean wasn't how I'd planned to spend my afternoon, but here we were. "What is it?"

"The musicology report on Ms. Mordent."

"Anything important?" I asked, flipping it open.

Like any medical report, it was loaded with numbers and text blurbs saying things with many abbreviations. But the musicology report was akin to a toxicology report except that it was related to magic latent in humans, Statics generally.

"Read it when you have time."

I agreed, refolded it, and shoved it into my inner jacket pocket.

With Guardianship issues, that meant we needed the full Harmonic Council—not just Columbus, but representatives from every tradition worldwide. Which meant traveling to Isola Sonora, the hidden seat of magical music, hidden somewhere in the Mediterranean.

We gathered in Transposition Hall, another underground vaulted room with Renaissance-style art of angelic people with lyres reaching for the colorful center wheel of the Circle of Fifths, zodiac, solfège, and so much more. What looked like an oculus inside a seven-pointed star glowed blue and cast light around the sanctuary like light coming from a swimming pool. Warm LED firelight glowed from sconces around the room. A matching marble mosaic was on the floor.

Hoagy stood next to me, shaking.

I put my arm around him. "It's okay. You'll feel good. Like you're soaking in a sensory-deprivation tank, then a beautiful world of color and amazing weather."

"I've never been in a sensory-deprivation tank."

I squeezed him tighter. "You'll have to go through by yourself. Do you want me to go first, or would you rather I follow you?"

"Will I still be me after Transposition?"

"One hundred percent."

Ahead of us, Armando and the Council members had already gone through. Two of the Custode had gone ahead and the bound Sonny was placed on the matching seven-pointed star on the floor. She either didn't fear the process or was so lost in her own thoughts that she didn't notice.

Hoagy watched intently as the room filled with a swelling string ostinato punctuated by a mark tree at the moment of Transposition. Then she was gone.

"She's alive?"

"Yes. She waits for us in Isola Sonora."

"The notes matter or they're decoration?"

I squeezed the kid's shoulder again. "You hear the brass quietly in the background, which is fire. The clarinets and flutes float around like water, flowing and expressive."

Hoagy's eyes lit up. "The strings are foundational. So Earth?"

"Right. And the airy mark tree is the final piece that lifts you up."

He looked at me as the Custode followed Sonny in order to keep her under guard. "So we could do this anywhere?"

"No. Each Conservatory has this sanctuary. It only goes to Isola Sonora. And there are some other sounds going on in there that you haven't learned yet. Eventually."

He inhaled sharply. "I'll go first."

With that, the kid stepped into the light of the oculus and held his breath. I gave him a thumbs-up and a wink as the music swelled. And he was gone.

I turned to face Wonderly, who stoically seemed unbothered by this process. Cree, on the other hand, looked nervous. Fear screamed inside her head, but experience taught her how to mask it. Wonderly's hand held Cree's, grounding her while they waited. The line was another thirty behind, so I stepped into the oculus to Transpose.

It is like a sensory-deprivation tank. No kidding. You feel yourself floating. It's dark, soundless, and warm. You can't hear your breath or feel your heartbeat. The first time it is scary. You wonder if you're dead. I've only done it a few times myself for special occasions. After the first trip, you wish it'd last a little longer. As Maestro Park paraphrased Aristotelian physics to me, it's the spaces between that measure. The silence that resets.

I opened my eyes to see Hoagy. He beamed at me. Okay, maybe not scary for everyone. Or he was just glad to be alive.

Three Custode Prima in gold-brocaded purple robes greeted me and presented a golden chalice with an aromatic, earthy, spicy wine. I took a sip. The Custode with the cup said, "*Vis Naturalis.*"

"*Vita nostra,*" I responded, returning the cup.

With that, we waited for the others, and then the Custodi guided us from the chamber into a long hall. At the end, an archway led into the light. As we walked, the narrow slits in the wall slowly let in more light so that when we reached the exit the light was not blinding.

Hoagy's mouth hung open. I glanced back at Cree and Wonderly, both equally amazed.

"What is this place?" Cree asked.

"Isola Sonora, the home of the Virtuosi, the real Conservatory and seat of all magic."

"The Vatican of Magic," Wonderly said.

The island sat in the middle of the Tyrrhenian Sea in a location that Statics would never find. Near the Aeolian Islands, and, perhaps, the mythical island of Aeolia itself. The centerpiece was a massive cathedral with a giant dome. At the top of the main dome, a giant golden lyre reflected the Mediterranean sun.

"What is the sound?" Hoagy asked.

I pointed to the craggy rocks making a *U* shape around the building, with cypress trees lining paths and statues similar to the one outside Sanctuarium Re back home.

"See the holes in the rock?" The kid nodded. "Natural formations from the volcanic foundation of this island, like mini lava tubes. The air flows through them, creating the island's own music."

"It's amazing," Cree said.

There wasn't much opportunity to look. Outsiders were rarely let in, and they had to swear magical oaths that would create an uncomfortable sensation if they tried to speak about what they saw. Regardless, the Virtuosi didn't want them lingering or seeing more of the island.

We were led into the Cathedral of the Vis Naturalis and into the main room under the large dome.

Sonny was on her knees on the mosaic floor of Guardian Hall, which had a domed ceiling painted with more Renaissance painting depicting classical images of the greater Virtues. The room had a balcony level with a stone balustrade that surrounded the dome. The kind of architecture that made you whisper even when you had nothing to hide.

The Four Cardinals and all the Guardians lined the balcony, robed, faces obscured from view by elaborate masks. You could not detect age, gender, or anything else. All of them were there except Whimsy, of course. In Felix's place stood a tall candlestick with a fat candle burning.

At the top of the dome, stained-glass windows allowed late-afternoon sun to stream through, creating a focal point a couple dozen feet above us. That point of light spread out and created a spotlight on the bound Sonny Mordent. They had put her in a white dress devoid of distinguishing style. She was barefoot, makeup free, and her hair pulled back. Her shoulders slumped forward, but she stared ahead.

The Harmonic Council sat in purple-cushioned chairs fit for kings on a dais with three wide steps to it. Armando was at the center, as usual. He sat on the edge of his seat with a staff in his right hand, with a crystal treble clef mounted to it.

Harmonic Councils from the other regional conservatories lined the wall, prominent but not the main focal point today. They were a splash of colors with delegations representing each of the traditions: the aboriginal Keepers of the Earth Songs, the African Keepers of the Crossed Rhythms, and representatives from the music traditions of China, Japan, the Slavic peoples, the Native Americans, and many more that I didn't know.

"Sonata Allegra Mordent," Armando began, knowing how to use the acoustics of the room to his favor, "you have been remanded to the Harmonic Council for judgment. The DHR has agreed to this. Your crimes will not be known to the world, but you will now hear our judgment and be charged."

Armando looked around the room, including the balcony. "Are there any who would say a word to support the defendant?"

Dr. Phrygian stood from the bench where the spectators sat. He was also permitted to see Guardian Hall at my insistence. I fully intended to show him that there was Hope and to help him find the Joy in himself to celebrate his daughter's life.

Armando gestured to Phrygian.

"I feel that Jazzy Jacob's life was as much my fault as hers."

Armando nodded. "I understand. And Virtuoso Kohl has

volunteered to resolve your part in this with you." He looked around the room again. Seeing no response, he continued. "Seeing no other supporters and given that there are no family members or friends present to make a request on the defendant's sentence, we will proceed."

Sonny collapsed to her knees, shoulders shaking with silent sobs.

Dr. Phrygian spoke quietly from his seat next to Cree. "When my daughter was small, she couldn't keep a plant alive. Too impatient, too focused on the end result. But after she started painting, after she learned to see beauty in the process rather than just the product, her garden became magnificent."

Sonny looked around the chamber at the masked Guardians, at the Four Cardinals, at all of us who had every reason to hate her. "I destroyed so much. How does it get fixed?"

"The same way a broken bone heals stronger," Wonderly said, winking at me. "Because it has to."

To my left, Cree smiled and squeezed my hand. We'd made up. I'd even told Riff I forgave him for being an idiot, though I'd also threatened him if he hurt her. Seemed like a stable foundation for a working relationship.

Wonderly caught my eye and nodded. Time to make my move. Both women tried to pull me back to the bench as I stood.

Armando's eyebrows rose; then his brow furrowed. I wasn't the one he wanted to see standing on her behalf. Why would I? I suspected he hoped I was so broken up I'd have to leave, or that I needed to take a Beethoven-worthy, post-coffee movement. Instead, I broke free of the women and stepped forward.

"Virtuoso Kohl, this is irregular."

I stopped beside Sonny. "I think this entire case is irregular."

My eyes went down to Sonny. She looked up, eyes red, pleading with me that I not make it worse. I wasn't sure if I was making it better or worse, but I was sure she would think it was worse. At least today.

"I would like to make a suggestion," I said.

"Virtuoso Kohl, this proceeding isn't a suggestion box."

"No, but I think you should hear me out."

The Council members murmured among themselves. Armando was going to reject me, and then I saw him look up over my head to the balcony. I turned and saw the Four Cardinals with their arms out toward me.

Armando sighed loud enough that I could hear. "Let's keep this to a minuet, not a symphony."

I nodded. "*Allegro con brio.* Sonny Mordent murdered Felix Cantabile, Guardian of Whimsy. She didn't need to. He was already dying to get your attention. But her rage made her complete a pointless task, forcing this esteemed body to solve something you didn't plan for. Although the Council should have if they'd just listened."

"Virtuoso Kohl," Armando said with a deep rumble.

I knew not to push it. "And she attempted to murder another in her path. She destroyed a Virtue itself, slowly draining the very essence of Whimsy from our world. Perhaps we could have gotten Felix's message and saved him. We'll never know." I turned and pointed to Dr. Phrygian, who was almost in tears. "She manipulated a genuinely good and inspiring man to do her bidding."

I returned my gaze forward. "Prison won't bring back Whimsy. Hard labor won't restore what she's drained from the world. Death won't undo the damage." Feeling the weight of the room's attention, I paused. "But there is a way to make her repair what she's broken."

Sonny's head shot up, confusion and fear warring across her face.

"The Virtue of Whimsy is dying, dead, because she severed its connection to its Guardian. She knows how she did it. She understands the magical pathways better than anyone alive." I looked directly at the Four Cardinals. "Make her rebuild what she destroyed. Make Sonata Allegra Mordent the Guardian of Whimsy."

The gasp that echoed through the chamber was deafening. Sonny scrambled backward on her knees. "No. No, I can't. I don't want—"

"It's not about what you want," I said, my voice cutting through her protests. "It's about what you owe."

Armando looked like I'd suggested making a tornado the Guardian of Calm Weather. "Virtuoso Kohl, you cannot be serious. She murdered—" He glanced up at the Cardinals and the Guardians as they talked to each other. "Virtuoso Kohl is on administrative leave because he—"

"The Virtue of Whimsy is dying because she severed its connection to its Guardian," I shouted to the Council. "The same pathways she used to drain creativity can be used to restore it. But only by someone who understands both the theory and the emotional cost."

Armando frowned. "Explain."

"Sonny isn't just magically connected to Whimsy's destruction. She's emotionally connected. She knows what it feels like to lack it, to want it desperately, to watch others have it effortlessly." I gestured to where she knelt. "Every moment of joy she creates as Guardian will cost her, because she'll remember being the person who tried to destroy it. That emotional resonance, that guilt, that understanding of loss is what will make her connection to Whimsy genuine."

One of the Cardinals leaned forward. "And if she simply refuses to restore it?"

"Then the binding will show her every creative soul she's damaged, every moment of wonder she's stolen, until the weight of it destroys her," Wonderly said, stepping forward. "Magical justice isn't about punishment; it's about balance. She unbalanced the world by destroying Whimsy. Now she has to rebalance it by becoming its perfect protector.

"She murdered Whimsy," I continued. "Now she has to bring it back. Not as a reward. As punishment." I turned to face the balcony. "Bind her to it. Make her feel every lost song, every silenced laugh, every dream she helped crush. Force her to rebuild Whimsy, knowing that every moment of Joy she restores is Joy she tried to steal."

One Cardinal leaned forward. When they spoke, I couldn't tell if the voice was male or female, young or old. It was muffled through the cherublike mask. "And who would guard the Guardian? Who would ensure that she doesn't simply complete her destructive work? It is supposed to be the Guardian training the replacement? Now who? There is no living memory of the last time a Guardian was lost without a replacement."

Wonderly caught my eye and nodded almost imperceptibly.

"Eliza Wonderly," I said. "Leader of the Improvisationists. She'll monitor Sonny's progress and ensure that she follows through. The resistance she built to protect creativity will become the network that spreads Whimsy back into the world. Non magical but supporting the needs of the Vis Naturalis and the mundane world."

Wonderly smiled. "The Improvisationists will accept this responsibility."

Since I had put her on the spot without warning, I was thankful that she followed me.

She continued. "We've proven that Whimsy requires more than magic. It thrives on genuine human connection. We'll tend to the human side while she"—she looked at Sonny with barely controlled anger—"tends to the magical essence she nearly destroyed."

"The defendent is also nonmagical," Armando said. "Illogical to have her as a Guardian."

"I don't believe that's true," I said. "She has latent signatures of magic. The musicology report states that there are traces of Vis Naturalis in her. Not from residuals, but her." I looked down at Sonny. "She doesn't know it—didn't know it—and can't use it yet."

Rimsky had been right about one thing, but she didn't know how to use it like he did.

It took the better part of three hours for the Council to reach its verdict. The Cardinals and remaining Guardians retreated into private conference twice. When they finally returned, Armando's face was grim.

"The Council has reached a decision." His voice echoed through the chamber. "Sonata Allegra Mordent, you have committed crimes against the very soul of human creativity. You have killed Felix Cantabile, the physical embodiment of Whimsy itself."

Sonny was shaking so hard I thought she might collapse.

"Therefore," Armando continued, "you will become the Guardian of Whimsy. Not as an honor, but as a burden. You will carry the weight of every creative soul you've damaged. You shall feel their pain as your own. The rest of your life will be spent rebuilding what you destroyed, knowing that every moment of Whimsy you restore is a moment you tried to steal from the world. We need a world with Whimsy. We require it."

A binding circle glowed around Sonny on the mosaic floor. She tried to crawl away from it, but invisible forces held her in place. I stepped back. My part was done.

"Furthermore," one Cardinal called from the balcony, "you will be bound to Ms. Eliza Wonderly, who will serve as your guide and warden. Should you fail in your duties, should you attempt to harm Whimsy again, the magical backlash will destroy you utterly."

The hall echoed with the word.

"I can't," Sonny gasped. "I don't know how to be a Guardian. I don't know how to protect anything."

"You will learn," Wonderly said, stepping into the binding circle. The magical energies swirled around both women now like a thousand fireflies with blue and purple tails dancing in teal as wondrous as the Mediterranean coast.

Wonderly absorbed it with her eyes closed for a long moment before addressing Sonny again. "The Improvisationists will teach you what it means to value creativity. What it costs to lose it. What it takes to nurture it."

The light from the dome windows intensified, pouring down like liquid gold. Sonny screamed as the magical bonds settled around her, but it wasn't just pain. I could see understanding dawning in her eyes. She was feeling it. Every musician she'd dampened. Every artist she'd broken. Every dream she'd helped crush.

"This is what Ruby Blue felt," Wonderly said quietly. "And Slide Donovan. And Reed Holloway. And your husband. Feel it all, Sonny. Feel what you did to them."

Tears were streaming down Sonny's face, but for the first time since I'd known her, they seemed real. Raw. Human.

When the light faded, both women remained in the circle, but something had changed. Sonny was still bound, but Wonderly … there was something different about her aura. Something that suggested this arrangement might serve more purposes than anyone realized.

"It is done," Armando declared. "Guardian and Warden are bound. May this arrangement serve Justice and restore what was lost."

As we filed out of Guardian Hall, Cree grabbed my arm. "You think this will actually work?"

I watched Wonderly help Sonny to her feet and saw the complex mix of anger and pity on Wonderly's face. "I think it's the only chance we have. Sonny knows how to kill Whimsy. Now she has to learn how to heal it."

"And if she can't?"

"Then the magical binding will destroy her, and we'll find another way." I looked back at the two women. "But I think she'll surprise us. Feeling other people's pain has a way of changing you."

Sonny broke free of Wonderly and charged at me. She looked mad. A Custode Prima stepped in to defend me, but I waved him back.

"You must listen," she said, looking at everyone watching her. Sonny seized my hands and squeezed them so hard she might break bones. Her voice lowered. "Felix tried to warn them, and they didn't listen. You did. You heard Felix. Now hear me."

"I'm listening."

"The dampening chambers created something."

"Yes. That energy has to go somewhere. It can't disappear."

"That energy is alive," she said. "And it makes music and the environment go wrong. I don't know all your music terminology."

"Dissonant."

She nodded furiously. "Yes. Dissonants. They are free."

I nodded. "I'm on it."

As I joined the rest of the guests, I wasn't sure if I believed her, or if the transition had given her a touch of whimsical madness. But I'd seen the energy. Felt it. She wasn't wrong that something was there.

Dr. Phrygian approached me in the corridor. "Mr. Kohl, what you did in there ... giving her a chance at redemption instead of simple punishment ..."

"Everyone deserves a chance to make things right," I said. "Even if they take the rest of their lives to do it."

He gave the first genuine smile I'd seen from him since we'd reconnected. "Samantha would have liked that." He straightened, some of his old teacher authority returning. "The Improvisationists will need guidance. I'd like to help, if you'll have me."

"We'll need all the help we can get," I said. "Whimsy won't restore itself overnight."

As we walked through the Conservatory's halls, I could already feel it beginning. Subtle at first. A musician humming in one of the practice rooms, a student laughing at something in the library. But it was there. A tentative, fragile return of wonder to the world.

It would take time. Sonny would have to learn to nurture what she'd tried to destroy. Wonderly would have to balance justice with mercy. The Improvisationists would have to prove that human creativity could flourish alongside magical protection.

But for the first time in weeks, I felt Hope stirring. Not just for Whimsy, but for all of us. Sometimes the best way to heal the world isn't to punish those who break it, but to make them part of fixing it.

Even if they spend the rest of their lives trying to atone.

The story wasn't over. In many ways, it was just beginning. But as I stepped out into the late-afternoon sunlight and heard the distant sound of children playing in the park—really playing, with laughter and imagination instead of sitting silent on benches—I knew we'd made the right choice.

Whimsy would return. It might take months or years, but it would return. And this time, it would be protected not just by one Guardian, but by an entire network of people who understood what the world lost when Whimsy died.

The real test would be whether that network could hold.

Before we had returned to the Transposition Portal, Dr. Ama Osei, a polyrhythm specialist and one of the Keepers of Crossed Rhythms, pulled me aside. She seemed to move even when she wasn't. Her powerful physique was evident under her colorful robes.

"Knowledge that Virtues can be killed and restored is not proven," Dr. Osei said. "Guard that knowledge carefully. It is dangerous and could inspire copycats. I hope that you will come to Ghana and deliberate with me on this, as I think you, Virtuoso Kohl, will be one of our greatest warriors for Truth."

"I am many things; truthful isn't the top of the list."

"You will visit me?"

"After some silence, yes."

CHAPTER 32

INTERMEZZO

Saturday, June 20

THREE WEEKS after returning from Isola Sonora, on a Saturday that felt like the first real morning in months, I stood at the window in my apartment drinking coffee. The sky was bright. Mixolydian sat atop the piano, asleep on her back with her legs sprawled.

Cree, Riff, and the other musicians were back to their normal musician behavior. They were creating and working. Doing their part to spread Whimsy even without knowing what they were doing. Riff was doing community service, teaching kids music. DHR had stepped back for damage control, but it wouldn't last.

Project Silence and these new creatures—Dissonants—were waiting for me, but not today.

There was a knock at the door. "Enter."

Dash walked in. "Back to being magical again?"

"I was always magical. But back in the good graces of the Council. Mostly. Hoagy's back with me. They have an eye on me, but I can still be me."

"Good." The detective came closer. "I have a feeling I'm going to need you again."

I put my hand on his shoulder. "Dash, you can use me even if the Council disagrees."

"Sure, Dekk. Works just like that. The Conservatory and DHR are very accommodating."

I shrugged. "Do you have a case for me now?"

"No." He swallowed hard. "With all that weird stuff going on with Ms. Mordent, I didn't want to bring it up, but we have a problem. Remember Rimsky?"

"Yeah."

He pulled out a file. "Three other DHR cases over the past five years. Different investigators. Different departments. But in each case, right before the investigation closed, someone reported seeing a 'tall man in a gray suit, pale eyes, slight accent.' Each time, DHR claimed no one matching that description worked for them."

I flipped through the file. Seattle. New Orleans. Vienna. All cities with active Conservatories. All cases involving mysterious deaths of creative individuals. Nothing as dramatic as Whimsy. "We think he's running Project Silence."

"Or he's one of twelve," Dash said grimly. "Sonny mentioned a network."

"And now they know we know."

Dash nodded. "Which is why we're documenting everything. Every sighting. Every witness. They can erase Rimsky from DHR's files, but they can't erase him from mine."

He shifted uncomfortably. "There's something else. Last night, Maestra Flanconade called it in. Someone broke into the Fencing Academy."

My stomach dropped. "The basement?"

Dash's expression was grim. "I see you knew about the hidden basement. The fencing coach heard sounds late at night and thought it was plumbing. By morning, the entire basement was burned out. Nothing left but ash and scorched support poles."

I closed my eyes.

"The fire marshal said it was electrical, but I know better." Dash pulled out his notebook. "Found this in the ashes." He showed me a photo—a partially melted business card with a blackened name and number no longer legible.

"They tried to breach it. Triggered a firetrap."

"Whole Academy's gone?"

"Nah. Just the basement."

"Anyone injured?"

He shook his head.

Maybe they didn't need that space anymore. I hoped so.

He handed me a card. A business card, blank white except for a musical note in the center—cleanly crossed out with a single diagonal slash.

"That was slipped under my office door last night. No cameras caught who left it."

I studied the card. "They're escalating from 'we're watching' to 'stop investigating.'" I pocketed the card. "So we watch. Document. Wait for them to surface."

"And hope we're ready when they do."

"Not good." I stared out the window for a moment. "The to-do list of tomorrow's problems keeps growing." With a smile, I glanced back at Dash. "But they put Dr. Phrygian as the head of DHR."

"Uh. No. Vetoed. Too many Conservatory connections."

"Who's in charge?"

"They won't tell us yet."

The detective picked up a stack of papers on my piano. He skimmed the first page of my entry for the Archives on Felix and the whole case.

"Sonny took his life; I had to preserve its meaning," I said.

Dash nodded at me. "Posterity or ordered?"

"That's what Trovatore do, Dash. Tell the Truth even when killers try to hide it."

Wonderly stepped through the front door with a case in her hand. My worst fear was that Wonderly was leaving town because Sonny had failed. She stopped in front of me.

Dash greeted her with his usual suspicious nod, shot me a look that said we'd talk later, and left. He'd done his job—planting doubt in my head just when I was starting to feel resolved. Couldn't have that. So he put a little tension in there.

My eyes went to her case.

Wonderly smiled broadly. "I'm not moving away. I have an organization to run. And a Guardian to watch."

I nodded. She set the case on the kitchen table. "Something for you."

I followed her and opened the case. It was a brand-new ossia, beautifully made. I could sense the power in it. The art on the face of it was elaborate. It would take me a while to decode it.

"Does it mean something?" I asked.

"Of course," she said. "You'll figure it out. Look at it as a puzzle. But only when you're not working."

"Yes, boss."

I lifted the ossia from its case, feeling the magical resonance thrumming through the wood. It was the fretless neck leading into the bulk of the instrument. But no normal ossia body. Two black ebony curves that could be removed shaped what would have been the body. I could take the arms and make the instrument compact. The arms mounted at the bottom of the ossia and curved up halfway like a lyre. Wonderly liked the symbolism.

It was perfectly balanced, waiting for music to bring it to life. I walked back into the living room strumming it. I may have been in a minor mode, but Wonderly was pure, unadulterated major.

After inspecting the instrument more closely, I noted there was no pegboard. Instead, the tuning pegs were tucked under the body.

Wonderly laughed. "In case someone else has any ideas."

I laughed, too.

Through the window, something caught my eye.

A blue butterfly danced past, but this time it wasn't flying in a desperate straight line. It wandered aimlessly, stopping to investigate a flower box, spiraling up toward the sun, then drifting back down on a whim. Behind it came another, then three more, all following their own chaotic, beautiful paths.

I smiled, plucking the ossia's strings. Each one sang true and clear.

Sometimes the world breaks in ways that seem impossible to fix. Sometimes the people who break it are the only ones who understand it well enough to put it back together. And some-times—if you're very lucky—you get to watch Whimsy return to the world one butterfly at a time.

I played a simple melody, nothing fancy, just the tune I'd written for Wonderly in the basement. The notes drifted out the open window, joining the symphony of returning life that was slowly, carefully, rebuilding itself.

"Does it have a name yet?" Wonderly asked.

"No," I said. Naming it felt too personal, too much like admitting what the melody meant. "Not yet."

The world wasn't right yet. But it had started to be. It had Hope to be. And if the bright sunny June day outside and the summer breeze blowing through my window weren't enough, the blue butterflies wandering aimlessly past—stopping periodi-cally for who knows what, then moving on—cemented it.

Whimsy might disappear, but it finds its way back to those who leave the window open.

I - ♭VII - IV - ?

CODA

ACKNOWLEDGMENTS

Tempo: *Espressivo*

Books are funny things. Sometimes you aren't planning one and something hits you out of left field. During a drills session at the fencing salle, a student commented that I had no whimsy. I riposted, "Whimsy died." The drills continued, whimsy-free, but the idea stuck. The title arrived in that same breath, and the investigation began. This book is the result. I suspect I personally remain no more than 17.1% whimsy.

No book is the work of a lone blade. My deepest gratitude goes to **Jacob McConnell**, my developmental editor and primary investigator into all things Urban Fantasy. His keen eye for the genre and relentless critique kept the magic system—and my wandering ideas—on track. Every story needs a lead detective; he was mine.

Dan Larsen was equally instrumental, providing meticulous line editing and a sharp eye for detail. Editors are hard to find and harder to vet; I found a gem in Dan who made this manuscript far better than the one I handed him. Any remaining mistakes are entirely my own, likely born of obstinance or the 2:00 a.m. witching hour.

In this day and age, you can't write a book and not have an audiobook. I'd like to thank **Jay Myers** for his excellent work on the audio version and for breathing life into the characters and finding the rhythm of the story.

I must thank my wife, **Julia**, who supports this craziness with a patience I don't deserve. I am lucky to have her to love and cherish (even when she hides the chocolate).

Finally, I refuse to thank my cat, **Persia**. Despite having only four legs, she insists on interfering with the writing process. I can only assume it is professional jealousy toward the six-legged variety found in these pages.

To hear the next movement, join the Conservatory mailing list at **swordistry.com**.

May your blade be true with a little swing,

Tim A. Mills

Columbus, Ohio, May 2026

ABOUT THE AUTHOR

Tim A. Mills spent his childhood dreaming of writing and the blade, captivated by the heroics of *Scaramouche, Captain Blood, The Three Musketeers,* and the Jedi Knights. While it took him until adulthood to finally pick up a sword, he hasn't put it down since.

Based in Columbus, Ohio, Tim now spends his days orchestrating urban fantasy and his evenings teaching Olympic fencing with his beautiful wife. When asked whether the pen or the sword is mightier, he refuses to choose. He simply uses both.